I0613401

Anonymous

Captain Herbert

A Sea Story: Vol. I.

Anonymous

Captain Herbert
A Sea Story: Vol. I.

ISBN/EAN: 9783337083175

Printed in Europe, USA, Canada, Australia, Japan

Cover: Foto ©Andreas Hilbeck / pixelio.de

More available books at **www.hansebooks.com**

CAPTAIN HERBERT

A Sea Story.

IN THREE VOLUMES.

VOL. I.

LONDON:

CHAPMAN AND HALL, 193, PICCADILLY.

1864.

TO

Dr. DOUGLAS MACLAGAN, F.R.S.E.,

PROFESSOR OF MEDICAL JURISPRUDENCE IN THE

UNIVERSITY OF EDINBURGH,

THIS TALE,

IN SLIGHT TOKEN OF GRATITUDE FOR THE GREAT KINDNESS

OF A " GOOD PHYSICIAN,"

IS AFFECTIONATELY INSCRIBED

BY THE AUTHOR.

CONTENTS OF VOL. I.

CHAPTER VIII.

CHAPTER IX.

CHAPTER X.

CHAPTER XI.

CHAPTER XII.

CAPTAIN HERBERT.

CHAPTER I.

HOW BROADBY AND CO. SPECULATED.

No English seaport appears better situated by
nature, for all the various objects of such a resort,
than the large city of Bristol. There the great
estuary of the Severn brings the sea into England's
very bosom, tempering the unbroken roll of the
Atlantic from Newfoundland; while from within,
the current of the Avon and of the smaller Froom,
after having watered many a rural mile in the rich
southern counties, wind into each other amidst the
town, so as to spread wet docks and floating harbours in its very heart, beyond sight or hearing of
the sea. Up to the date of our tale, accordingly, its
practical success had verified these presumed advantages; the crowd of warehouses and masts, no-

where far apart from hospital-roof and almshouse, and elaborate church-tower or spire, testifying to a race of merchants who had been as stately in their expiatory charities as they had been bold, nay, sometimes unscrupulous, in their enterprises. Many historical events of importance had been immediately connected with Bristol; but none so momentous, so varied, as those involved with the present narrative. Great Britain, even in the earlier years of George the Third's reign, was beginning to revive from the Dutch-set primness of her habits, her high German formalities, and French tastes, and all the fancied cosmopolitanism of an empty time. The occasion of her awakening was rude: it was the obstinate and growing resistance of her disaffected American colonies to the very mildest system of law under which a community could well exist, and to the natural indignation by which the law had been vindicated.

There were sundry reasons, some of them a little odd, why Bristol was far less likely to suffer by consequent changes in the colonial trade than most other seaports. Her dealings were rather of a grand kind, or partook of the mysterious and picturesque. As long as Spanish wool and wine lasted, with fruit from up the Mediterranean, and spices from farther East, she was half secure; she did much in African timber, palm-oil, gold-dust, ivory; there was a sort of monopoly of the West

Indies in her favour, that had by this time made
her sugar-bakers proverbial for purse-proud feeling,
and for those manners which are characteristic of a
sudden rise in the world. Lying out apart, too,
with as it were a "channel" of its own, the city had
a corresponding tendency to separate itself, making
up for great risk or slow return by large transactions, and by heavy profits: a thing wonderfully
entwined, no doubt, with the early odium against
the place, of having had more than a due benefit by Cromwell's freights to "the plantations,"
and in the more iniquitous deeds of the later
crimps and kidnappers, who procured what they
called "apprentices" for South American mines,
or for Puritan settlers farther north. Such delicate expressions had, in fact, lingered about Bristol,
giving an apparent propriety to certain lines of
business which still enriched it, though carried on
at a distance. The armed Bristol merchantman
was often years away, lawfully engaged in the
"ebony trade" between the Guinea coast and somewhere about the opposite Caribbees; and on her
return the keen supercargo and the bold captain
looked brown, but honest; the respectable owner,
having seen nothing save various bills of lading
and exchange, went in the more thankful mood
with his family to church; while the good craft
herself, repainted, as the fashion is ere coming into
port, and with rigging all repaired, would through-

out the rest of that Sunday seem to survey herself
in the still water of the dock with a considerably
more conscious air than any of them—since her
well-moulded bows would contrast with many a
clumsy neighbour, and she would have a black
cook on board—looking idly over, wooden-legged,
or ignorant of English, or with no human meaning
in his visage, so that the freedom conferred by
British soil would have been of no use to him—
nor could he tell any tale. In conformity with all
this was the very mixture of attractive and repul-
sive, bustling and tranquil, manifested in those
prosperous days throughout the city at large:
where the foreign and the homely mingled, the
drays jarred and groaned beside the slow plash of
the unloading ships ; while through the cathedral
trees came the chime of its clock-bells above the
noon-day roar of the town. And catching sight,
some summer's day, of all that tropical effect shed
through the dull-red warehouses with the shining
of the smoke,—scenting those far-brought smells
of timber, and West India matting, and tar, and
sugar, with the sudden sense of a half-Venetian
grandeur amongst dingy English common-place,—
many a lively young spirit had there projected its
first venture in life. It needed an old head, and
that a wise one, for the period, to discern the
hardest realities of the scene ; few as yet saw in
those days the mean foreheads and the brute faces

which were there, or shrank from the thought of
misery, ignorance, ruffianism, and vice, or remembered then, with any sort of applicable force, the
belief that was said in churches.   At night, no
doubt, when all the hatches of vessels were pad-
locked down, and the last ship-keeper, custom-house
officer, stevedore, or apprentice, left the floating
avenues by himself, he might happen to feel an
undefinable discomfort at the sounds beginning to
be made by the night tide about the bottoms of the
craft behind him, or at sight of the sky's chill re-
flexion over the dark images of warehouse tops,
with, perhaps, a dead dog slightly dipping in it,
calmly distinct and black.   For a moment it would
make him look up, troubled by thoughts of he
knew not what; till with the greater relish he
would light his tobacco-pipe, and hurry into some
city lane, towards the nearest noise of joviality.
He, of course, could not dream that the eighteenth
century, which was within him and without him—
even *him*—had been hitherto a reckless, heartless,
insipid age, and must leap into sudden strife and
fierceness ere it ended—nay, that throwing off the
cover of its liberality, its philanthropy, its politeness, and its elegance, like some man about town
whose vice has been half *ennui*, it would die a
naked maniac, raving for savage virtues and para-
disiacal innocence.

Amongst more opulent, or longer established,

houses at that time in Bristol, there was one which
bade fair, in the natural course of things, soon to
rival the very highest; the stage of prosperity it
had yet reached being only not complete enough
to disdain competition, or to rest satisfied with the
mere holding of its place. Merchant shipowners
on a large scale, " Broadby and Company" had
from the outset borne a commercial designation
more proportioned to the large outward tokens of
their success, than to the slight substructure of its
private agency. Under the ample mercantile designation, and behind all these activities which were
made more imposing by it to the uninitiated, there
really existed then but two persons constituting
the entire firm, with that kind of filmy difference
from the outward show, which in such establish-
ments would seem preferable : but it was a fiction,
if fiction it must be called, that extended even to
the inner penetralia of the counting-house, so seldom discovered by an ordinary foot; it reached
from the dray-sledge bearing that inscription along
the street, to all the work performed, however re-
motely or subordinately, for the unseen power in
question, and from the indentures binding the apprentice body and soul under a penalty, to the
mystic signature, which it would have been death to
counterfeit. Their warehouses formed the entire
corner of a huge brick range upon the river-side,
near the harbour's centre, divided from neighbour-

ing ship-yards by a creek, which seemed to float
boat and barge into the very thick of the town;
nor was a busier scene to be found in busy Bristol
than that, which, originating from this particular
centre, abutted there on the general complexity.
Yet was neither of the two partners really even
named Broadby; a patronymic which only represented a still more singular inconsistency in the
previous existence of the firm. The actual founder
had, indeed, been a certain John Broadby, of obscure derivation, who had doggedly worked his way
to wealth from the very humblest position, somewhere, as was said, in the coasting colliery line of
business; a person on that account highly admired
during his lifetime by all who knew about him, and
although of rough and uningratiating manners to
an extreme, yet, by many, almost beloved; so that
a handsome marble tablet to his memory had been
placed, after his death, within the parish church—a
place where no former habit was likely to take his
ghost to see it, if old John should then actually
discover he had had such a thing as a ghost at all.
He had, however, been uncommonly shrewd while
alive. At first with regard to those other persons
whom he had joined in partnership, they had been
generally understood to exist solely in his own
brain, till the consistent use of the title had its
gradual effect, and people had found themselves
believing it: it was perhaps a coarse whim he had

indulged, the more to gratify his chief boast, that he had risen from nothing, and never owed a guinea in his life. He himself, in his dotage, was ultimately known to have believed in this old association with other partners, sometimes fearing, sometimes wishing for, even talking to them; while he had latterly refused taking any important step without their advice, had excused himself on that ground from some troublesome expectations, charities, or public offices, and had thus been justified in rigours or hard measures from which it was thought his own disposition would have relented. Still, curiously enough, he had often seemed so much superior to himself in wisdom or calculative foresight when so doing, that the confidential clerk, who had grown old and dry in the business, on a pittance which sufficed at least for his few wants, continued to the last to attribute the prosperity in which John Broadby left all at death—to his latterly "giving in more to the firm." Nay, not even when the whole of it came over by legal inheritance—stock, good will, with all dues, assets, plant, credit, and connexion, and floating capital, to a single individual—in the person of old Broadby's nephew, who had latterly married his only daughter, and done much in the way of active management —not even then did this faithful dependant resign his superstitious sort of respect.

He believed in old Broadby and his words, not

only against ledgers which he had himself kept and balanced, but despite legal definitions to him unintelligible; for it had been the sole reason which John Broadby had always given for not taking this very nephew into partnership, that he could not do so unless all the partners agreed on it, and that he rather thought they considered the company large enough without Matthew Ffloyd.

Now, however large the sum of money which old Broadby had made in all his various modes beyond what the firm required, he had expressly bequeathed it all to the building and endowment of a grand range of almshouses in the town for poor people of certain names, or on sundry quaint conditions. If Ffloyd could have been then well excluded from the business, probably he would have been; since the old man's prejudice against him seemed to have strengthened with age. He had been long abroad about the West Indies, where he was supposed, in fact, to have commanded more than one vessel employed for old Broadby; though after his return he had set up a sugar-bakery on his own account, and had grown elderly, and heavy, and a family man, and even devoutly connected with the new Wesleyan meeting-house, toward which, above all, the disgust of the old man—a Churchman and Tory—had been conspicuous. But Ffloyd had seen a good deal of the business; his wife was Broadby's own child; and it might be that

Broadby's shrewdness had grown so eccentric as to fancy that *it* would survive himself, or might in some unintelligible way fulfil his own desires. Mr. Ffloyd became sole successor, therefore, with the firm conviction that his uncle and father-in-law had been, strictly speaking, no better than a sharp old cunning hunks, mean-minded, and bearing him a grudge; which same qualities he, in his turn, at once applied to the work with a hearty zest, and thoroughly repaid all the hatred with compound interest. Such, up to well-nigh the period now concerned, had been the precise key-note of all his transactions. The capacity which was adequate to make mere manufacturing gain, however, had soon found itself bewildered in the centre of a scheme like old Broadby's—one which had ever involved its past results in new and wider measures, with a promptitude resembling instinct, and a caution that gradually rose into quick sagacity. With Ffloyd, to stand still or to venture was almost alike detrimental; he had in his hands little more, as yet, than the machinery of a vast fortune, if rightly used—or even, if prudently wound up, the materials for a safe competency. To the first originator, doubtless, acquainted with every spring and wheel, its guidance had become an easy task, and the speculative pleasure had very nearly absorbed the more sordid appropriative feeling; but in his successor's fingers it grew matter of chance, the avidity

of the gambler joined to more than the gambler's
dependence on luck. He had even begun to see
the separate sugar-baking business, which he had
been too covetous to relinquish, sucked into the
whirlpool; while it had become too plain that
Broadby and Co., with Ffloyd to boot, were going
down—clerk, counting-house, warehouse, drays,
ships, and cargoes—all sinking hourly nearer to
their original source in nothingness, where they
had no relation to each other. It was this undeniable fact, shown by figures, and backed by the
old head-clerk's solemn faith in the virtue of plu-
rality, that had made Ffloyd accept the real partner
whom circumstances led to offer himself. Mr.
Spencer, a gentleman of good family, of well-
known abilities, and some private fortune, had of
his own accord come forward at that crisis, to give
the benefit of these to the firm in which he agreed
to become an equal sharer. Enhanced as it was
by much knowledge of foreign countries and their
political aspects, as well as by considerable previous
attention to commercial matters, his accession in-
fused new blood into the business; departing confidence was almost at once restored, without as
within; the house of Broadby and Co. revived and
flourished, as if a lost amulet had been found
again; the old clerk, perched at his high desk,
with his brown wig, snuff-coloured garments, and
drab gaiters, no longer wandered as through a

hopeless labyrinth when he posted the ledger or surveyed the bill-book, but jogged on more cheerfully than ever under the influence of a mastermind.

A stronger contrast could not have been seen, certainly, in all Bristol, than that between the two partners: they were incongruous alike in intellectual capacity and in personal habits; so as to be only capable of drawing well together, because Mr. Ffloÿd once more betook himself chiefly to the sugar-baking concern, in which he was quite at home. He still inhabited a mere portion of old Broadby's dull house at the corner of a street near the quays, where improvements in the town had latterly made it profitable to turn the lower part of the abode into a shop; and it was thought Ffloyd must be making money fast on his own account, and hoarding it; at all events, he did not spend it in show, or encourage luxurious and expensive habits in his family. Mr. Spencer was essentially of that class, on the other hand, which had ever had an intimate connexion with the spread of intelligence in communities, and the introduction of the liberal arts: it was as much the turn of his mind—a habit that grew indispensable—to do things on a large scale and in an ample way, and to surround himself and his family with agreeable or refined appurtenances, as it was any deliberate principle for the result's sake. And while the firm already supplied the means of what was called, in those days, a genteel establishment—a carriage, governess, and servants, for his wife and daughters; an Oxford education for his eldest son; for himself, horses, library, and pictures—Mr. Spencer was not devoid of further views—nay, of a kind of vague ambition. Beyond even his definite aim of possessing, at no very remote period, an estate in the county, there had floated up somewhat less distinctly in his mind the prospect of yet applying talents which had found commerce easy, to the acquisition of influence. Still remoter—and he thought it a weakness himself—was his notion of eventually obtaining, it might be, the revival of an obsolete family title. Politics were in those days as necessary—as essential to a gentleman—as a memory of Horace, or port wine after dinner; and Mr. Spencer was a decided Whig; the more decided, because such views had then fallen into the Opposition, while they allowed of most constitutional grumbling against the course of Government towards the colonies, with whose disaffected acts he had thus caught himself almost sympathising, like many other good folks, till their open rebellion restored him to the true English cause. In fact, he had sometimes suspected that when he should have more time for attention to State affairs, possibly he might be led to modify his views still further.

Mr. Spencer's house was high on the Redcliffe

side of Bristol, not far from where the river begins
to open out below the city, betwixt the steep Leigh
woods and the lofty Clifton Downs; it was one of
a style of dwellings which that reign has handed
down, in all their native indifference to the picturesque, as being thoroughly English, or rather
John Bull-like; though the absence of any positive false taste, combined with the mellowness of
age, has now endeared them. Sober, solid, and
substantial, with cramped windows glittering, dark
and heavy-framed, out of the rough-coated wall;
it had a porch-disguised entrance, one tent-like
expanse of blue slate for roof, two most mathema-
tically correct gable-ends, and as many low top-
walls of formal chimney, to all of which a great
jargonelle pear-tree or two, regularly pruned and
trained, gave little relief: the still more prim-
looking kitchen-wing behind was a remnant of the
Hanoverian tastes of Mr. Spencer's grandfather.
Neither quaint with Elizabethan instinct, nor elegant in the French fashion, it could only boast an
air of inward comfort; the sloping lawn and large
old trees close at hand were almost merged in contiguous lanes and suburban fields; but there was
the high-hedged garden near by, overflowing with
a bowery greenness, which would have redeemed
even duller mansions; nor least prized, the rising
ground on which all must have been expressly set
for the sake of the glorious "view," hanging or

widening to each several window.   The truth was,
however, that there were marks of a tendency to
innovation in the presiding hand; a new coach-
house at one end; in front, a modern gateway with
two globe-topped pillars; the greenhouse erecting
in the garden for fine foreign plants, where an
old sun-dial and arbour had stood; the glass-
doors thrown out to the lawn, too, and the projected French folding-casements for the sunny
breakfast-parlour.   Alterations still more effective
would have taken place long ere then, but for a
milder influence which was near, to check or
soften the other.

Mrs. Spencer, being the daughter of a Somersetshire squire not far remote, and brought up in the
country, had a natural clinging to the old-fashioned.
Whatever the suitableness with which she now sustained her more conspicuous station in the world,
even to a degree of rather elaborate dignity, it was
she who had had ivy planted to overgrow the new
coach-house, had saved the wooden pigeon-cote
beside it, and preserved more than one incommo-
dious tree; besides her rescue of the high garden-
hedges and warm brick walls, when they were
doomed to sink before a more open style on the
planning of the greenhouse.   As for the house
itself, too, though built by his father according to
the newest method then in vogue, which packed as
many closets and cupboards as possible in the odd

places, taking advantages of nooks neglected by its
predecessors, and thinking nothing of a step up or
down into an older room ; yet Mr. Spencer had come
to think the old gentleman had left rather much
to the architect. And if the merchant stumbled in
a passage, or found a room too dark for his newspaper, it suggested some fresh change to him, such
as a bay-window, the removal of a step or corner,
perhaps the throwing down of a whole partition.

"It is so comfortable as it is, Henry!" his wife
would mildly say, "compared, too, with the misery
of having workmen about!"

"It may be comfortable," would be the answer,
"but, I assure you, 'tis by no means convenient."

"Then, the window-tax, think of that!" she
would respond, concealing a glance of triumph.

"Pooh! the late window-tax, my dear? You
might as well say, the fresh tax on hair-powder—
which I wear simply because I can afford it. Nay,
more, it is contributing to the revenue of——However, Mary, you can't be expected to understand
politics."

"I suspect, though, Henry, you will never get
the poor old house perfect," Mrs. Spencer would
persist, "unless you rebuild it altogether;" while
some slight trace of an unconscious smile would
pass from her lip, as she simply proposed by way of
cure for the obscurity of the apartment, that the
candles should be brought in. And the sole re-

joinder, without the slightest perception on the
husband's part that such a proposal was at all rele-
vant to the discussion, would be a gracious " Do,
Mary—yes, ring for them."

For he would smile too, with far milder complacency than she, at the twofold unction he
could lay to his partly-ruffled temper. He recol-
lected female inconsecutiveness, and at the same
time recalled his own private intention of having a
new mansion altogether; till at length it sometimes
surprised Mrs. Spencer, in her unsuspiciousness,
that these changes almost altogether ceased to be
set astir.   He, perhaps, avoided doing what might
make the place pleasanter to him, or more difficult
to leave ; it might be that he was only busier than
usual, after all : while a thing most characteristic
of him was, that his having suffered the oldest portion at the back of the house to remain intact, appeared to him rather in the light of a meritorious
sacrifice to filial remembrance, which compounded
for other alterations, than as a sign of any newer
project still.

CHAPTER II.

OF SOME NOBLE CAPTAINS.

Mr. Spencer had experienced but little trouble
with any of his rising family, except one. This
was the youngest, Henry, whose singular dulness in
the acquirement of ordinary knowledge, was combined with no slight wilfulness of disposition, pro-
ducing, about the age of fourteen, as was natural in
the kind of place which Bristol has been shown to
be, a strong dislike on the boy's part towards all
schools, tutors, or books of any kind, and a pro-
portionate inclination for what is called "the sea."
His expressed wishes at length induced a seeming
compliance from his father; though if the merchant had been a man with less knowledge of the
world, and one who ever readily yielded, or gave
up his own purpose, he would probably have mentioned the king's service as the most appropriate
sphere for a branch of his family; a little patience,

with a preparatory course of spherical trigonometry for the young aspirant in the mean time, might have enabled one of Mr. Spencer's fortune and standing, though a Whig, to bring the requisite amount of ministerial interest to bear circuitously. He intended Henry, however, in his own private thoughts, for a merchant, to be trained in the counting-house, and to take his own place when he should eventually retire; he saw no objection to the boy's seeing something of the world, though it might be in a rougher way than either of them had calculated; and he acted with the judicious firmness and forethought of a man of the world. Henry had, indeed, been despatched on his favourite tropical voyage, and that quite as promptly as he himself could wish; but not in one of the vessels belonging to the firm, which, as Mr. Spencer did not disdain to show the boy himself with great candour, would have been at once to defeat his ardour for maritime experience, by the consideration paid to an owner's son. The anxieties of the mother were consoled, on the other hand, by most assiduous information with regard to the solidity, size, and classification of the West Indiaman, which was A 1 at Lloyd's, joined to frequent statements of the great value of her cargo, the various insurances on it, and, above all, the character of the master, who was steady, practical, and careful; so careful, as to be entitled, among those who best knew him, Careful White.

Nevertheless, so protracted was the absence of the
Dorothy, and so tempestuously did the equinox
come in at Bristol, while the colonial struggle had
risen to a crisis, with rumours, too, of privateers and
pirates who assumed the new American flag—that
at Beech Grove, as the substantial old house was
called—there began to be a great deal of irrepres-
sible uneasiness.   Even Mr. Spencer's well-judged
measures, and his far-stretching design in the
matter, ceased to convey any further solace; he
himself evidently failed to derive confidence from
them, as he argued the case each time at greater
length, and each time was more apt to lose temper;
the silent manner of his wife at these moments,
and her averted face, were becoming the more
painful, in that she had not said a word the least
like reproach.

As it turned out, neither the barque *Dorothy*
nor her careful master had been heard of abroad
for some months; at Bristol they were virtually
given up.   But one afternoon Henry Spencer himself arrived, quite quietly and in an ordinary way
from London, completely unaware that the West
Indiaman had not returned as usual, and perfectly
well and cheerful, though in rough sea-clothes.
All his father had purposed was apparently gained;
for he at once professed himself thoroughly sick of
the sea, as well as impatient to begin attending
warehouse and counting-house; and Mr. Spencer,

whom the vast confusion of the arrival had interrupted in his after-dinner wine, at length re-seated
himself, re-stretched his legs upon the rug, and
viewed Henry's increased stature and changed
looks with a complacency he had never shown the
boy before; while he pushed the decanter to him for
the first time in his life, and could scarce conceal
an excessive pleasure as he asked him to pour himself out a glass of port, and sit down, and at least
let him hear *something* out of that Babel of voices.

As for the *Dorothy*, commanded by Captain
White, Harry knew nothing of her, he uncon-
cernedly said, after they had reached Kingston in
Jamaica, where he had been led to take a further
trip with an abler commander. On the subject of
this last he avoided to particularise, having, it
appeared, paid a similar compliment to *him* in
turn, by making the best of his way home with a
third navigator, who seemed to have been at least
morally preferable. But he now declared his firm
belief, uttered with an indifference to recent associations which horrified the entire domestic group,
that "old White must probably have been drunk
in his state-room, and the barque have foundered
with all hands aboard." The sudden gravity of
the father's look soon relaxed; it was pleasing to
observe, as he acutely did, how little of a dolt the
boy really was after all, and what an amount of
practical quickness he had acquired; indeed, how

oddly he had chanced to escape a fate by this
time almost indubitable. So that, far from blaming
the step taken by Henry, it was now impossible to
refrain from a smile. Good Mrs. Spencer, for her
part, scarce knew as yet whether to cry or laugh
at his appearance; nor was the amusement of his
sisters at all equal to their annoyance, especially
that of the elegant Jane—who was considered a
beauty—at the very idea of his arrival having
been seen, or of how the servants were to understand it. So brown was Harry's face, his hands
were so hard, and he had grown so vigorously
stout and tall, with a loud voice and an awkward
roll in his walk; while, as to dress, he had gone
away a delicately formal young gentleman of the
eighteenth century, in coatee and knee-breeches
and silk stockings, with a great deal of luggage;
and had come back in a short jacket, with huge
trousers, apparently made from some old ship's
sail, and a painted straw hat; all he carried
besides was a small bundle in a pocket-handker-
chief. It seemed still doubtful whether there were
not some strange whim mixed up with his mode of
reappearance, especially as he appeared now and
then a little anxious about something, to judge by
looks toward the window, or attentive notice of
sounds at the gate—naturally enough attributed to
expectation of the trunks he had taken away, with
that additional burden of foreign rarities which he

had always used to dilate upon to his sisters. The indisposition to dwell upon his history at sea, or the inability to relate it, surprised no one, from Henry, since he had never been addicted to talkativeness.

"By the way, Harry, my boy," suddenly inquired his father, looking up from a brief reverie, amidst the renewed medley of conversation round the hearth, "when you were at Jamaica did you happen to hear anything of one of his Majesty's ships which I understand was thereabouts at the time, a frigate, if I mistake not; the—the—one of those grotesque Admiralty names which seem invented to escape one's memory?"

Henry looked up promptly from the family circle, with an eye that all at once sparkled. "Perhaps you mean the *Diana?*" he said. "O— yes, sir, a new ship, thirty-eight guns, with a bright figure-head? They say she's the first ever sent out to try the new plan of copper sheathing; why, yes—when we went into Kingston harbour she laid at anchor outside, at Port Royal. You'd have thought all the boats in the country were paddling about to see her, as near as they could go, both whites and blacks; and the midshipmen went swaggering about like so many lords, though most of 'em weren't half my own size. All because she was a crack ship, built on the model of one we took from the French, they say, last war.

However, the captain was an earl's son, and that was why everything about her was so tip-top and different from the common."

Mr. Spencer had eyed his young hopeful during the animated statement with a rather more inquisitive and critical glance than before. " Hoity-toity! whither is the boy running to?" said he, abruptly. " And pray, Master Hal, since you appear to have paid such very particular attention to this vessel, can you inform me as to the names of any of the officers? "

" Only the captain's, sir," replied Henry, more deliberately; " he was a post-captain—Lord something De Vere."

" Ah, Lord Edward de Vere, no doubt!" said his father, with respectful interest, and looking to his wife, while he dwelt a little on the aristocratic thought. "Lord Brookford's brother, you know, Mary—second son of the Earl of Deepmere—a Gloucestershire family, my dear! Hum! rather inclining to proper liberal views, too, though as haughty a set as possible. Lord Edward was becoming so popular in the county there, a year or two ago, that the Tories have, of course, thought best to flatter his family and him with hopes of a different nature. Very neat and convenient indeed; but really, really, in the present petty contest, so far as the navy is concerned, all ideas of martial fame are, of course, preposterous in the

extreme—every leaf of laurel must be cut up into
particles—and even the prize-money, pooh! it
would not, I fancy, keep a post-captain in shoe-
buckles! Then some of Lord Edward's officers
also," he concluded, turning again to Henry, "are
probably from this neighbourhood?"

"Well," was the answer, "I know the first-lieutenant was a little, sharp-faced, cross-grained, old
fellow, and our men fancied he was there for no
end but to keep the captain right, putting the
orders into his mouth, as it were, and doing the
rough work!"

"Very likely," Mr. Spencer remarked. "As his
youthful lordship must, for the last two or three
seasons previously, have made more improvement
in political than in professional knowledge."

"At any rate," added his son, "when the other
frigate came in, that relieved her on the station,
the two somehow or another exchanged first-lieu-
tenants. If you'd just seen how the *Diana's* men
stood looking out to see the two boats pass each
other half way, as if they'd fain have given three
cheers at getting rid of that old file of theirs;
while the other frigate felt as black, everybody
said, as thunder—her first-lieutenant was such a
favourite aboard! But the captain of the *Diana*,
you see," paused Harry, sententiously, "could do
pretty much as he liked with the admiral, whereas
the commander of the *Spitfire* was but a——"

" *Spitfire!* " repeated his father ; " why, my boy, that is exactly the name of the ship in question, I think ! "

" Dutch built ? " suggested Henry, with eagerness, in an interrogative manner of entire sincerity. " And deep-waisted, with a stump billet-head and a terrible heavy quarter-gallery—quite the old style—besides having ugly black yards and mastheads aloft ? "

" Very possibly," was the somewhat dry rejoinder ; though the dignified merchant was constrained, apparently against his will, to indulge a smile. In the boy's mother and sisters his animation merely excited a vague interest, as if events of mysterious importance were involved in the account. " Not having had the pleasure of ever seeing this fine vessel, though," continued the father, good humouredly, " what I simply want to know is, whether there was a Mr. Herbert among the officers—a Lieutenant Herbert ? "

Mrs. Spencer turned towards him, and from him to Henry, who opened his eyes wide, in obvious surprise. " Why, it was Lieutenant Herbert joined the *Diana*," he at length said, " from the *Spitfire!* Everybody knew about him, there-away—you've no notion what the men would have done for him —regular rough bears of fellows, even, sir, that kept deserting at every chance from the *Spitfire*, especially after he left her."

"Do you mean one of *our* Herberts?" asked Mrs. Spencer, still looking at her husband with new attention, in which a degree of curiosity mixed.

"My dear, what I may have meant was of little consequence," ran the rather grave answer, with a momentary biting of the lip. "But it so happens that I did mean *the* Mr. Herbert—your brother's absentee neighbour — Herbert of old Herbert Court itself! No matter: then he exchanged to the—the *Diana*, you say, Henry? Ah! and when was that vessel likely, do you know, to return to England? But stop—let's see! Why, boy, it must have returned already! I surely saw Lord Edward de Vere's name mentioned lately in the paper, on some account or other."

"Yes, papa," suggested the fair Miss Jane from the sofa, where her returning fashionable languor was for the instant stirred by the fresh allusion, "in the list at the Hot Wells, and the—ah! the patronage to the race ball!"

"Why, child, his lordship is to stand for the county," said her mother, "in place of poor old Sir Thomas Cliffe. But you do not seem aware, Dudley," she quietly added to her husband, "that Mr. Herbert himself is at home at Herbert Court just now. True, none of our letters from Wrixworth took the trouble to mention his return, nor does Kate say a word about it, or their first meeting with him—just taking it all for granted, by the way, in one of her gay, thoughtless billets, as if 'twere a mere trifle in the village. 'Twas otherwise in *my* day, certainly. I, for my part, would have dwelt on it finely, you know, papa, in writing from Wrixworth to Bristol."

Mr. Spencer had raised his eyebrows as if totally unprepared for the intelligence, and really placing some private importance of his own upon it. Yet it was evidently no unpleasing surprise. He laughed freely, and said, " Assuredly, Mary—I agree with you—however dilapidated the place, or necessarily secluded the owner, that so long as Mr. Herbert retains Herbert Court in his possession, his arrivals and departures are things of moment about Wrixworth, and ought to be faithfully recorded."

"The poor Herberts!" said the matron again, with a slight sigh, which pensive recollections of her own early days in the country might have helped to produce. " I well remember the time when their fortunes looked fairer, surely. The other boy—the eldest—seemed like to live and do them credit; this one—the younger—had just entered the navy with excellent prospects. That fatal accident to the first of them, it was, you know, that led to their mother's death in childbed; and no wonder old Mr. Herbert never got the better of the terrible stroke ! "

"Very sad, indeed," agreed Mr. Spencer, re-
fraining from any further use of his wine-glass
on account of it—"very sad! Some of these old
families appear to be doomed to extinction! A
fine old place the Court, too—really worthy of a
more suitable fortune to keep it up—in new hands,
better fitted to the times, I mean. For the present, unluckily——" But here he stopped, looked
somewhat grave, and almost sighed too.

Young Henry Spencer had turned an ear of
unwonted notice to the episode; and he proceeded,
when again made principal speaker, to convey in
forcible terms the disastrous condition of the ship
left by Lieutenant Herbert; how her old bull-dog
of a commander grew twice as bad after receiving
a Tartar in place of such a man for his second in
authority, till neither sentries' muskets nor sharks
alongside could retain her crew at nights; and
every boat that went ashore had armed marines,
and the yellow fever got on board; and after pick-
ing up recruits of every kind or colour, how she
had had at last to sail in a hurry, on her way south
to look after Captain Cook the voyager's return
home; while the *Diana* had become a happy craft
—so full of hands, that they would not even take
in a powder-boy more. Meantime, by the inherent
vividness of such facts, glowing even through so
unadorned a recital, and betraying all the greater
personal interest in the matter, the less the narrator

seemed inclined to show it—the various members
of the household were characteristically moved.
The graceful Jane, when at home, was wont to sit
luxuriously doing nothing, with an air of inanimate
satisfaction inscrutable to the rest, save on the
supposition that soft cushions, with the gloss of
silk and touch of velvet, basking in the firelight
or enjoying the shade, enabled her to bear up till
the next party; yet, even *she* had at least vouchsafed so far, once or twice, as to open her sleepy
eyelids, and survey her brother in a kind of slow
wonder, as if she for the first time noticed him
particularly, or with sufficient fortitude.   The
plainer Mary, ever busy at some small piece of
feminine work in the elegantly useful way, had
more than once let it gradually drop in her hands,
her eyes fixed on Henry, and her lips wider parting, till she could only wish Kate were there to
hear.   But Catherine was at Wrixworth, at her
uncle's, where her grandmother oftener and oftener
would have her to stay; nor had Harry seemed as
yet to observe this absence, or take any heed of
the slight references to her; though Kate was the
youngest but himself, and he had quarrelled with
her worse, and teased and made it all up with her
far more frequently than with any one else.   As
for Mrs. Spencer, who, good lady, had hitherto
possessed no more conception of the seafaring life
than a very vague fancy on such matters supplied

—she had, in her horror at the thought of having ever permitted her boy to undertake it, allowed the tea-urn to flood the tray, over which her preparatory evening offices were being discharged, until diminutive cups and saucers of that day began absolutely to float about. Then did the management of the stiff fashion of her dress—aggravated as it was by the dinner-table hoop of the period, however tucked up and abridged by means of a spring—alone prevent her, perhaps, from at once folding Henry in the maternal arms; for the very apparel of that odd age, strictly speaking, was somewhat unfavourable to the active promptings of emotion. "My dearest boy!" she could but exclaim ere the sight of the tea-tray checked her agitation, "my dear, dear Harry, is it possible? What must you have gone through! A—a powder-boy?"

"So then," his father observed, as he turned a scrutinising glance, though kindly, on Henry's face after his last disappointed allusion to the favourite frigate—"so then, Hal—*you* actually applied to be taken in, did you? On board this same popular *Diana?*"

The boy reddened, and was silent.

"To go and look out for Captain Cook *too*, no doubt? Really, my dear boy, I can scarce regret having committed you to the charge of one whose capability for the trust turns out to have been

over-estimated—if 'twere only that you might learn
for yourself, mark, so early a lesson! Just observe, pray, that the most apparently agreeable
posts in life are invariably just those the most
likely to be preoccupied. Had you rather tried
the dreadful *Spitfire*, now, Harry," he continued,
with less of the severe didactic pomp; "where there
was room, it seems, to spare, and had you stuck to
it, then you might possibly have *got on* in life.
Who knows, my lad, but that we might yet have
welcomed you as a cabin-steward or quartermaster!"
And the merchant, indulging in a cultivated vein
of satire, smiled a good deal at the thought.

"The *Spitfire!*" repeated the boy, bluntly;
"why bless you, father, the *Spitfire* was nothing to
the Boston schooner *Dove*, where I landed myself
instead! I just wish you'd known *her* skipper, sir;
he'd have astonished you! 'Twas he gave me the
thorough sickening of it all: in fact, if I hadn't
fallen in with him on the quay, and been such a
fool as to take his word for it—that New York
was the finest city going—I shouldn't consider I'd
seen the world at all, to speak of. But, my stars!"
added Harry, with emphasis; "I wasn't long of
finding out what was the queerest thing of all, from
here to there and back again!"

"Indeed," was the paternal inquiry, "and what
may that have been, pray?"

"Just the skipper of the schooner himself, sir,"

nodded the boy very sagaciously indeed, " and a piece of his mind. A change *he* was, and no doubt about it."

" Good gracious, my dear love!" exclaimed his mother, much excited, " who *was* he?" To which Harry shrugged his shoulders, and shook his head.

" Well, mother," he said, holding out his cup for more sugar, with an attempt at extreme indifference, " unless you knew him, of course 'twould be of no use to say. He *called* himself Captain Itefell Dodge—though it's not likely any man could have been christened so—but of course that's neither here nor there. At any rate, he hadn't as much conscience as this spoon here; and as for a fellow's *life*, why he'd care no more for it than— than——" in vain he looked round the room for a simile, " than the main-boom. What do you think now," pursued the boy, in a more confidential tone, " he had *been* all his days, till a year or two before?"

There was a hopeless unanswerableness in the question, which was so depicted on the countenances of the ladies, and afforded such evident gratification to the propounder, as to extract another smile perforce from the paternal features; although the latter were betraying some degree of grave annoyance.

" Why," continued Harry, contemptuously, "nothing but a hay-farmer—and pretty like it he

walked the deck, too. He couldn't have found the
longitude to save his life—he couldn't have fairly
spliced a rope, I *do* think—and when once he'd
got the schooner hove-to in a gale of wind, he
didn't know how to let her fall off safely again.
Then, sometimes she'd run clean away with us, as
she hadn't hands enough for her size—and there
would be the skipper, holding on by the tiller with
half the crew, and his legs astride, looking out like
grim death, till the fore-topmast would go, sail and
all. He called it trust in Providence. But somehow we were sure to turn up in the end, you know;
and the captain, for one, always fell on his feet
—all his fingers were fish-hooks—and if he couldn't
tack her properly, he'd wear right round, and go
off before it for the next port. There never was
anything too hard for old Dodge to try, though he
hadn't so much as seen it before in his life—he'd
be sure to contrive some new way to come round
upon it, at any rate—and he didn't mind grinning
and saying he wanted to learn for himself. His
own men used to swear his face was as much brass
as the top knob of the binnacle!"

"And did you really leave Captain White for
this ignorant idiot?" said Mr. Spencer, in astonishment.

"Why," said Harry, frankly, "I knew you
wished me to learn the profession, sir,—and there
had been Captain White never done taking care

of me. He wanted me to be always looking over
the side, when he was sober—or dining with him
in the cabin, like a passenger, till he got screwed;
then he'd tell the steward to lock me up in a
state-room. I wasn't to go near the men for fear
of low manners; and if I went aloft I was to be
made fast in the rigging; till at last he kept himself so regularly slued when we got into blue
water, that he knew nothing of what went on.
So, all of a sudden—— !"

He hesitated, coloured, and was evidently indis-
posed to proceed. " Go on, love," said his mother,
leaning forward with her hand on his shoulder,
and her eyes fixed on his face; " however dreadful,
do let us know the whole! You are quite safe
now, you know."

Henry only laughed, however; seeming inclined
only to wriggle from under the affectionate weight,
as if it were too heavy. " Pooh, my dear!" Mr.
Spencer interposed, apparently wincing with an air
of some confusion from further particulars; " never
mind. The detail must be painful, I think."

" Oh," rejoined the boy, for the first time eyeing
his father with a sidelong and peculiar air of curiosity,—" not so bad as that comes to, either. I
dare say they meant no harm, now I think of it;
but the mate seemed to take it in his head he ought
to see I worked my passage—out of spite to the
captain, I fancy; and the two passengers mistook

me for a footboy, no doubt out of spite at the mate; as for the men, they had a notion I ought to be kept always a lubber, out of spite at the whole of us. So between 'em, they all took such precious good care of me, that I was hardly ever on deck till we got into harbour, and there I wasn't to be let ashore. Now, you know, sir, nobody could stand that sort of life—and one night I just slipped out of a stern-window, and made free with the boat astern, to take what they call French leave. As for Captain Dodge, again—though he *offered* everything that was fine—neither he nor his crew took any care of me at all. He didn't care, when I was sent up to stow the gaff-topsail in a squall, if he never saw me again, so the sail was safe."

"Well, well," said Mr. Spencer, hastily, and he rose to take a library candlestick from the buffet, " as was remarked before, my dear boy, you have acquired some valuable experience, though at a rather painful cost; and I dare say you have profited by it."

"That I have, father," said the youth, with animation. " And what's more, sir, I shan't be inclined to try it again."

"No, certainly not," was the rejoinder, in an indulgent tone. "You are scarcely fifteen, I believe, Harry, and after all there is not much time lost yet. So take a few days' rest and leisure to yourself. Meantime, for Heaven's sake get some new clothes, after which you may either go back to school, if you choose, or——"

"If you please, sir," abruptly ejaculated his son, "I've no wish to be idle—I'd rather go into the counting-house at once. I don't need any rest at all, for that matter—and I should like to be a merchant."

"Well, we'll think of it. I cannot exactly say, without consulting 'Broadby and Company,' you see." And Mr. Spencer smiled, well pleased again. "'Tis evident you *are* of an active turn of mind, Harry; so at first, I think 'twill be as well to confine you to a sort of superintendence in the warehouse department, where your peculiar experience may be turned to account—eh, Hal?"

Henry signified complete acquiescence. The door closed, and Mr. Spencer retreated to the seclusion of his library; where, however, lively conceptions of Herbert of Herbert Court, Captain Dodge, Captain White, Lord Edward de Vere, and his own restored son, continued ever and anon to recur to him with annoying pertinacity; not so much from the fact that if the worthy ship-master, to whom Harry had been committed, were indeed lost, the firm would lose by him, as because the entire series of these people and their actions had

suddenly assumed a kind of shape which far
transcended the power of arithmetical calculation.
Meanwhile, the evening darkened to the parlour
windows; and Harry, amidst the circle there, still
sat as if something practical were occupying his
mind.

CHAPTER III.

A STRANGE FRIEND.

"WELL now, mother," ejaculated Henry Spencer, drawing a long breath of extreme satisfaction, as he put his hands in his pockets, and stretched his feet towards the first fire of the season, lighted in honour of his return, "after all, this is what I call snug." He looked out of the nearest window at the garden trees, that were scarce visible in the dusk; then approvingly round the room, where the hearth-light alternated with fits of shade on the panelled wainscot, and about the open corner - cupboard with its china, on the carved buffet in the recess, and the well-known portraits on the walls; while, in a whimsical variety, like one that dallied with familiar matter which it loved, or a grand artist sketching from unconscious sitters, the fire now glowed low down, and threw the shadows of chairs and figures hugely up, with heads bent flat upon the ceiling, now left a half-transparent gloom, where the eye, in its escape to the soft blue of outer twilight, was lured among exquisite gradations, and sly interchanges, and fine blendings; till again a flame flapped out high above the coals, casting everything in its way against the remote end, on which the dwindled distinctness fluctuated as if it were tapestry shaken by a wind. But Mrs. Spencer poked the fire into an open blaze; for she saw even less of such mute by-play than the half-whistling Harry, to whom it conveyed a mere momentary notion of intense comfort: she only liked them to see each other's faces as they talked, by that old-fashioned sort of country light to which she was still partial, not-withstanding all her mature consciousness of a position to maintain in the world. "By-the-by, though," added Harry, quickly, with another glance about him, and he sat up erect to put the inquiry, "where's Kitty? I didn't miss her out of the house before, I declare!—thinking every now and then, you know, she'd turn up. I hope there's nothing wrong with Kitty, mother?"

It was spoken in a rough tone, with an off-hand manner, and was almost a solitary proof of feeling on the boy's part; yet the slightest tokens of such a thing from him had always been so hoarded by Mrs. Spencer since it first was called in question,

that she was now much delighted, and threw a
look of mingled confidence and triumph at Mary,
her second, but gravest, daughter, ere she said
calmly, though with a beaming face, "Kate is
down in the country at uncle Charles's. She is a
great deal there lately, you know, Harry, since
your poor dear grandmother began to fail so; and
this evening we have all been too much flurried, of
course, to write to them at Wrixworth. But
to-morrow, your papa wishes the coach sent off
for her direct."

Harry glanced intelligently across at his eldest
sister, Jane, whose lady-like equanimity had really
shown no sign of being much ruffled by the afternoon's event; as if it occurred to him that she, at
least, might have had presence of mind enough to
write a note sufficiently early for the purpose,
instead of smiling languidly from the sofa, or
looking so serenely gracious and beautifully tranquil, with her hair turned high up from her ivory
forehead into a kind of crown, and drawn away
from the temples, and all its darkness softened
out by the white powder, while a rich hassock
before her seemed to court the pearly pressure of
one satin-shoed foot.

"But, ma'am," said she, immediately, appearing
to be roused by the last announcement, though the
same listless style of refinement was carried out by
her voice, "perhaps you forget that to-morrow

evening Lady Die Fanshaw comes to take my sister and me to the rout at the Assembly Rooms —so good of her to be at the pains, you know; and her ladyship can scarce carry us there in her own chair, I think."

"Dear me!" said Mrs. Spencer, distressed: "yes. We had forgot that; then Kate must wait till the day after, I fear."

"And to disappoint Lady Diana would be excessively unkind, considering all her attention to us," added Jane, with more animation. "Besides, since Henry has been so long absent, surely another *day* can make very little difference."

"Mother!" said Henry himself, abruptly sitting up again, "I don't mind starting off for Wrixworth to-morrow morning, a-foot, do you see; so never trouble your head about the coach. When it is sent, Kitty and I can come back in it together."

"What, on foot, my dearest child?" exclaimed his mother, aghast at the supposition.

"To be sure—we didn't have coaches from London to this, I warrant you. Both of us trudged every step of it, though Dick, poor fellow, was worse at it, somehow, than me."

The surprise produced in Mrs. Spencer by this information was too great for her to express by words: the thoughtful Mary, however, soon found composure enough to inquire if he had had a companion, then? " Why, yes," was the reply, " a friend of mine. If it hadn't been for *him*, in fact, I dare say I shouldn't have been sitting here this moment—nor, very likely, anywhere at all." His expressive nod, more than his words, conveyed to the listeners a dark import in that alternative from which the said friend had saved him. " Oh, where is he?" was the mother's eager ejaculation, as she looked round—" my dear boy, why did you not bring him along with you—we must—*must* see this preserve——"

" Oh, never fear, mother," interrupted the boy in haste, with a somewhat embarrassed air. " Dick's sure to turn up—indeed, I shouldn't wonder if he were here pretty soon *now*. I left him to take a rest in the turnpike down yonder, not half a mile off, and he wasn't to come over this way till dark. You see, mother—Dick is not just so well off for clothes at present, like myself—for of course, leaving the schooner in such a hurry, you hadn't time to think of dunnage, and so—so—why, I'd like if you'd just bid the servants let me know as soon as he calls; but for goodness' sake, not to show him right in, you know, not on *any* account."

" Who is he, then, Harry?" asked his sister Mary, glancing up from the piece of embroidery she had resumed: for, having but small pretensions to beauty, she excelled in the useful arts. Mary, though as yet scarcely twenty-one, was already virtually engaged to a clergyman of very good position and no slight learning, whose mature age had not outweighed these recommendations to her good sense; in consequence of which, a continual series of flowery toilet-covers, cushion-pieces, or chair-patterns, mysteriously succeeding each other in growth and disappearance, were now the result of her sedulous forethought.

"Well," her brother responded, "I call him Dick Diamond, myself—but that's not his real name—his real name was one-half too fine, to my notion. He's a sort of foreigner, as it were, in difficulties—for all I know, he may be a prince in disguise, as there's lots of 'em where he came from; but that's nothing to me, you know—he's as true a fellow as ever breathed, and if it hadn't been for Dick, I can tell you 'twould have been pretty well up with me. We never could have slipped the old skipper's clutches, save for Dick's judgment—so don't you be going and being prejudiced, Polly, because he's a—I mean his face." Henry still hesitated, and caught Jane's dark eyes opened upon him with more interest than they had as yet deigned to show.

"For my part," said Jane, as if expected to speak, "I think being prejudiced against foreigners is vastly foolish."

"Of course," said the younger sister, whose British antipathies might perhaps have been enhanced by religious sentiments and ecclesiastical associations : "oh, of course;" while she stitched again more busily than ever by the firelight, and hid from all but Harry the arch-twinkle in the corners of her eyes, as she appended a qualification to her assent. "At least when they are handsome, rich, and titled—like the French Count whom Lady Die says we are to meet to-morrow night—hey, Jane?"

Jane coloured, relapsing into extremer superiority than before, while her mother hinted strong doubts against the principles as well as the wealth of foreigners in general; not excepting even their titles, which might have been thought, from her impression, almost as much a purely British product as the two other commodities in question.

"It is really a pity, though, besides," resumed Mary, "that Kate cannot be home in time for this Assembly. Lady Diana seemed so taken with her last Christmas, you know, mamma, and wished then to bring her out. Don't you think it likely, if a note were still writ off to-night—my uncle might send old Roger and the chaise with her to-morrow, quite early enough in the day for her to go with us after all?"

Mrs. Spencer, however, expressed serious misgivings about the condition of the ancient vehicle, the state of the country roads, and the almost superannuated faculties of Roger, careful and trusty as he had long been known. Miss Spencer, too, again vouchsafed to unclose her lips, with a cold remark as to Catherine being still a mere child, who had time enough to think of such things—possibly next season ; and the rare opinions of the eldest daughter had none the less weight with the maternal mind, nor had her style of character the less influence there, because of her extreme unlikeness to her mother, or indeed to that side of the house in general.

"Why, Jane," warmly exclaimed her sister, notwithstanding, "you forget she is almost seventeen. And I am sure, after being so long at Wrixworth, where my grandmother needs so much attendance, she would more than either of us enjoy it. As for Lady Diana, too, recollect Kitty will some day or other be a sort of little heiress, as everybody knows by this time, and I fancy these things have rather more than enough importance in her ladyship's eyes, for all her high blood. So don't be too sure, Jane, that Kitty, with grand'ma's fortune behind her, mayn't outshine even *you* in the end!"

The belle of the family made no answer, save by a composure more ineffably placid than before, lowering her soft eyelids with an air of beautiful resignation ; she never could bear, at all events, to quarrel. So that, as Mrs. Spencer became domestically busy between the other end of the room

and the adjoining closet, while Mary bent quietly
again over her embroidery-frame in a fit of thought,
there was a silence; amidst which Harry, who had
merely looked from one to the other as they spoke,
seemed to try to fall asleep.

"Harry," at last said the homelier of his two
sisters, after she had more than once glanced
up at him half abstractedly, "I do wish you
would begin and tell me your adventures to the
end."

The boy opened his eyes wide at once. "Adventures, Molly! I haven't *had* any adventures.
There wasn't a single thing out of the way, all the
voyage—or else I shouldn't be quite so sick of it,
perhaps, and going to turn clerk! Nothing but
what was as tiresome as old Captain White himself, unless, to be sure, it was Captain Dodge. I
must say he *was* what you may call new, but if
that's what you mean, you must ask Dick Diamond when he comes. He's the man that knew
old Dodge best; in fact, he's always coming out
with something fresh about the skipper. Only I
don't suppose you'd understand at first what he
says, and as for telling it right straight along,
it's what Dick, for the life of him, can't do, I'm
afraid."

"Oh no!" said Mary, laughing, "I cannot say
I have any wish to hear more about Captain Dodds,
if he was such a man—— "

" Dodge!" interrupted her brother, correcting her with grave emphasis.

" Well, then—if Captain Dodge was so dis-agreeable a person as you described him. I only hope, as he was so bad, you are wrong in sup-posing him drowned, and the rest of the poor sailors with him."

" Drowned!" exclaimed Henry: " pooh! You're thinking of stupid old White, Mary! No, no: I'm just as sure the captain is lively at this moment, and doing something wide-awake, though he's thousands of miles off, of course—or else think-ing of something he's to do, or looking at some-thing with that gimlet eye of his like a thing screwing right into it—I'm as sure as if I saw it in the red of that fire there. He's a man, I can tell you, that never *will* be drowned."

"Dear me, what a hateful wretch!" instinctively ejaculated his sister; and Henry rather stared at her.

" No," said he, in a meditative way—"no: you're wrong now, Polly. Not exactly to say—hateful. It's rather a hard word, you see. After all, there was something about him you couldn't help admiring, as 'twere. Captain Dodge 'll be heard of yet. Do you know, I can't keep from feeling disagreeable at the thought he's at war with this country—though it's ridiculous, no doubt."

" At war ! " repeated Mary, mechanically.

" Yes : he's a colonial, as they call 'em over the water; and there's some rebellion or other going on there just now, you know. But the skipper didn't join it at all, they said; in fact, if he hadn't stuck to the British ensign at first, he'd have had precious little chance of keeping the schooner. The schooner was getting old and leaky, though; and as for trade, things didn't seem to look well. So what did he do one fine afternoon, off the Bermudas, but order all hands aft, pull out a letter of marque, as he said, from some council, or something—talking a great lot about a fellow he called the great Doctor Franklyne—and then said he meant to go right down to war against Great Britain. If any hand aboard wanted to say nay— why, he was to say it then and there. Not a man stirred, though there weren't three out of the crew but what belonged somewhere about home here; and of course it wasn't *me*, you know, Mary, that was going to walk out first to the old scoundrel— especially as I'd made up my mind to run for it. So he hauled down the ensign directly after, and hoisted one that none of us had seen before, like a piece of a barber's striped jacket, or a butcher's apron, with a lot of spots in one corner; and then ran the schooner fair before the wind, to go a-privateering. Dick and I bolted before he got any prizes; but I know he meant to have a new schooner under him pretty soon, without paying for her—and he'll *do it*. He'll just get alongside on the sly, with his old colours flying till the other craft's his own, however big she may be; then he'll run up the stripes again. I say, Mary, by-the-by, I suppose you don't know whether Broadby and Co. have any particularly fine brigs at sea just now, in that quarter?"

Mary shook her head: she was not aware. As for the force of the question, she had no earthly idea of it; and her brother alone meditated for a minute or two, with his chin rested on one palm, and his elbow on the elbow of the chair.

"Well, it's curious," he ultimately added. "I've somehow or other a notion I shall come across him somehow or other, some time. There's Diamond, now, that's to be here to-night—a sensible enough man on other points; but he won't get rid, all I can say, of the thought that he still belongs somehow to the skipper—at least until the skipper's fairly dead."

"*Belongs!*" repeated both sisters at the same moment.

"Ay—that he's *his* body and soul—if Dick ever made so bold, in fact, as to fancy he's got a soul. And for that matter, Captain Dodge wanted *me* to belong to him too, if I'd been such a fool, you know! By-the-by, though, Mary," he continued, with a laugh, "there was the best joke you

ever heard with Diamond, as we came along from
London. We travelled most of nights, you see—
owing to the suspicious looks we got after us at
first; sticking about woods, and so on, in the day-
time, making the best of it we could, for fear of
the parish stocks. So one night after dusk, coming
down a by-lane, just at a sign-post where I tried
to make out the road to Reading—who steps out
but a footpad, with a pistol as long as my arm,
and claps it to Diamond's head, bidding both of
us stand and deliver. For Dick's part, he didn't
know the fellow's meaning a bit; but he just
looked round at him over his shoulder, out of the
dark of the lane, and grinned at him without so
much as ever turning or saying a word. My stars,
Moll! I wish you'd just seen how the fellow
dropped his pistol and ran, at the mere sight of
Diamond Dick's face!"

Much as Henry seemed to enjoy this recollection, it only made his sisters exchange glances of
surprise, in which a little misgiving mixed. Mary
endeavoured to lead him gently off, rather, to some
account of tropical scenes and foreign manners.

"Well," was the rather careless response, "at
first, you know, one has too much to do to pay
much heed to that sort of thing; and after that,
why, you're too much used to it. There's no
doubt, · of course, it's tremendously hot about
Jamaica; and, now I think of it, the leaves of the

trees *are* a good deal bigger, not to say queerer
and greener. Then there's the Blue Mountains,
with heaps of wood betwixt them and Kingston,
and the rocks, every here and there, as clear as
possible, miles off, and a sky you can't look up at.
There's the green verandahs of the white houses,
and the blacks, with nothing but straw hats and
white breeches, looking quite cool and at home;
and a few sour-faced planters, smoking, and looking as if they'd had the jaundice. Besides, no
end of drunk sailors riding, making a noise like
mad. No doubt there's something different about
the West Indies from ordinary: whether it's the
queer yellow sort of ground and white stones, with
the big ground-leaves creeping full of red ants
and centipedes, and the blue water outside, with
ships looking half the size they ought—or what it
is; but you're disappointed, in fact. And the
whole while it's getting hotter and hotter, till you
can't stand it even under a tree with leaves like a
whole stack of umbrellas; when, at last, down goes
the sun in a blaze to seaward, with everything
bloody-black and big against it like beetles and
crab's-claws, as if the shadows came jumping out
of the port-holes and the windows; and you hear
gun-fire precious delighted, I can tell you. Why,
I see it all clear enough at this moment!"—he had
his eyes half shut as he spoke—" to my very self
on the wharf, and Captain Dodge in that bottle-

green shore-going coat of his, taking the cigar out
of his cheek, and looking down at me out of one
eye, as he spit on the stones, and asked me if I
didn't want to see New York City next."

His eldest sister put up her fair, jewelled hand
to cover a yawn. "La, my dear!" she said,
addressing Mary with redoubled listlessness of
manner, "I really wonder you can find any entertainment in such things. If one actually has such
a low taste, why not stay in such places, or at sea,
altogether?"

"But Harry is thoroughly tired of it," Mary
rejoined. "You are going to stay at home now,
are you not, Harry, and be steady?"

Henry made no answer, but surveyed Jane in
silence from his chair, with a glance which more
and more and more resembled a wink; till she
turned her head away at last, in some irritation.
The feeling was not strong enough, however, to do
more than shape itself on her tongue in the words,
"Shocking boy!" Once or twice, too, she had
raised her silver vinaigrette to smell, with an
expression of vague discomfort in her features;
the truth being, that something like the effect of
harbour-docks at the end of a street had diffused
itself more and more through the room, as Harry
sat before the fire in his canvas trousers.

"Well, I don't exactly know," he at length
deliberately said; "but I dare say, after all, I

want a little polishing up. So you know, Molly, if you were just to take me about to one or two of these routs of yours, or assemblies, or whatever you call 'em, perhaps I might pick up manners."

Mary laughed, and nodded a gleeful assent; insisting, however, on vast improvements in style of dress.

"Of course," continued the boy, merrily; "and who knows but Lady Sally what's-her-name may take a fancy to *me*—eh? Not to say my foreign friend Diamond, too, mind you; for I shouldn't wonder if Jane, there, were to take him in hand herself."

Jane turned her head to him again, and said, with a degree of emphasis which, for her, was surprising, "You are fit for nothing but the cabins of ships, Henry; and I am sure, for my part, I am very much surprised you do not intend going back again, where, I dare say, you might become as famous as an admiral, instead of becoming disagreeable at home!"

This speech drew immoderate laughter from her brother.

"Now, Jane," he next minute retorted, seriously and scornfully, "what do *you* know about the sea, I'd like to hear? *Why* d'ye think, in particular, I left that old sugar-ship my father sent me out in —eh?"

His graceful sister deigned no consciousness of the inquiry, much less did she attempt answering it.

"Just because," continued Henry, raising his voice indignantly—"just because I rather tired of cleaning candlesticks and the binnacle-lamp—ay, and the two passengers' boots, and the pigsties! And why d'ye suppose — ay, what would you fancy, now, was the reason—that I gave Captain Dodge the slip *too?*"

The sole answer vouchsafed by Jane, neverthe-less, was to rise up on the sudden from her cushions, to gather up her train elegantly in one hand, and with a stately disdain, and an endeavour at supreme serenity, to swim rustling out of the apartment.

Henry laughed boisterously, and leant back with an air of self-satisfaction in his chair.

"My dear Harry," said his other sister, in mild reproof, "why do you seem to delight in vexing Jane? You really must not! Now, when you were away, Jane used to talk about you almost as often as any of us—at least to listen to all the rest were saying, and—and, you know, she is so accustomed to be admired; besides being, of course, the eldest."

" Well, but ain't it provoking," was the reply, though in an apologetic tone, " to be twitted with giving up, by a girl that don't know the main-tack, neither, from the captain's spy-glass? I tell you

what it is, Mary, if I'd got to see Jane always opposite me on that sofa, in that high-and-mighty style
of hers, why, I'd soon begin to weary for another
sight of the skipper himself, with his everlasting
old eye. He was a man, at any rate, that always
kept you astir."

Yet, when Mrs. Spencer next returned to her
seat, Henry had fallen asleep, through sheer
fatigue, in the elbow-chair. At intervals, looking
up from her quiet work, Mary noticed his face.
To her mother, a soothing influence seemed for
the first time diffused by the sight of it—reclined
peacefully as it was on one arm, and sliding gradually down — the lips opening and breathing
gently—while the light of the fire reddened the
brown cheek, darkening the shadows or magnify-
ing them upon the farther wall. None had particularly considered the boy before, or attended to
his disposition; and to no other of the family now,
equally with Mrs. Spencer, had there been this
painful bewilderment at that apparently frightful
knowledge of an evil world, that altered and
abrupt style of phraseology, that too emphatic
manner, and that insensibility to the most hair-
breadth escapes. In this forcible impression, the
very dangers themselves had been lost sight of :
till now, she had scarce ventured to be sure she
recognised him. Yet, in truth, of what a rising
band of fresh spirits, about to incorporate them-

selves with the might of England in her hour of
deadliest need, was young Harry Spencer the
representative. The school of Benbow and Anson,
which Smollett or Defoe had painted, had soon to
die out in victory, like those elder sea-soldiers with
Blake, whom Pepys chronicled: it was the well-
nurtured youth at sea—the "young gentleman"—
the boy-midshipman of the great French war—
that had now to begin adding the charm of his
mingled mischief, breeding, and generous courage,
to the romance of sea-history. It was the very
opposite of those subtile schemes, mean jealousies,
and low-sprung instincts for change or profit,
which it had to oppose; and it did but need a
noble captain to gather it together, and lead on.

The rising moon from afar beyond the garden
trees had begun to brighten the panels of the inner
wainscot, making fresh but fainter shadows of its
own beside the others, and throwing a moist light
over outer things, as the boy turned apparently to
deeper sleep than before. Mary smiled, and Mrs.
Spencer bent nearer.

"How like he is to Catherine!" she whispered,
still surveying him; till Harry murmured something that still sounded unmistakably of the most
remarkable among his various commanders. "Poor
dear! what he must have gone through!" broke
from her lips, and she stooped from behind to press
a kiss on his forehead. He was broad awake on

the instant, and sprang up so suddenly, with an ejaculation so resembling a shout, as to startle both his companions almost equally with himself.

"Well, if I didn't think I was gone at last!" said he, rubbing his eyes and looking round; "I thought he fairly had me! Captain Dodge was just putting his thumb softly on me between two water-casks, I fancied, mother! It's curious, I never dreamt of him before, though—or, in fact, about being at sea at all. 'Twas always about home, you know, when one wasn't *there*. One time I actually put my arms about the black cook's neck, when he woke me quietly under the long-boat because the skipper was on the look-out for me in one of his black moods, and a squall coming on to windward. Before I knew where I was, you see, I'm much mistaken if I didn't nearly take the old nigger round the neck, and give him a hearty——"

His laughing and rather shame-faced confession was, however, quite smothered up in the long, intense, repeated embrace it drew forth to him; his sister adding her half-laughing share before he was released. And the first thorough acknowledgment of gladness to be at home again had been given, of the boy's own accord, to their perfect satisfaction, when the footman opened the dining-room door to inform Master Henry, with rather a doubtful air, that some one was at the back-gate of the house,

wishing to see him; one who would not come in
out of the dark, but was most likely the foreign—
and here the servant hemmed and paused—the
foreign gentleman that had been expected, in fact;
since it was thought he mentioned Master Henry's
name.

"Yes, mother," said the lad, rising in a hurry,
"it's no one else; of course, it's Jupiter, at last."

"Jupiter?" inquired both Mrs. Spencer and her
daughter in one breath.

"Tut! Macombo—Dick Diamond, I mean; so
—so I'll just step out, myself, and have him put to
rights, you know, for the night."

"But are we not to see him now?" exclaimed
his mother, in surprise. "My dear boy, your father
will, of course, be delighted to receive him per-
sonally. Mary will inform your papa, while I see
that the sheets in the green-room are aired. We
can excuse a great deal in such a friend! And
you will have no objection to give up the green
room to your friend Mr. Diamond, Harry, I dare
say, and put up with your old bed-chamber in the
mean while?"

"Why," said Harry, confusedly, "I don't think
poor Dick ever slept in sheets or a bedroom, all his
life; I'm sure he'll be quite glad of one of the
garrets; but just you leave him to me, mother.
Only mind you, ma'am," and Henry returned a
step or two from the doorway, in obvious anxiety,

" mind you, Dick's none the less a good fellow, that will stand by you when you need him ; in fact, it's not his own fault at all, you see, if—if he's a—a— well——"

He still hesitated in great unwillingness to mention something.

" What—what, my *dearest* child," was the agitated inquiry, " for goodness' sake, what *has* he done ?"

The look of Mary, too, showed equal eagerness and suspense.

" Then, I suppose, you really don't know it ?" said Harry, with a sudden air of surprise. " I thought, perhaps, I'd mentioned it already ; but, having been a slave, of course it's not so unnatural after all ; in fact, for a negro, Dick is wonderful ; but the truth is, I'm afraid, he's a—*a bit of a heathen.*"

Scarcely venturing to cast a glance at their mute dismay, the boy vanished to attend to the wants of his late companion. On his return, too, he declared himself so wearied, that, as he expressed it, he must go and " turn in" at once ; only hinting, that if the matter were carefully " broken" overnight to his father, the latter might not be " so much taken aback next morning, if he chanced to catch sight of Dick."

So, while Harry slept sound and dreamlessly, his

friend being privately consigned to repose also, the family were troubled all that night by strange visions of waves, masts, the yellow fever, or dead seamen floating to a lonely beach; of sharks more hideous even than the reality; of Captain White all dripping, and Captain Dodge all life-like. To Mrs. Spencer, above all, there was the constantly recurring sense throughout, of a black guest somewhere, who, however mysterious, left his print most indubitably on all the linen!

CHAPTER IV.

TURNING OVER A NEW LEAF.

A HASTY letter came from Catherine Spencer at Wrixworth, to say how glad she was to hear of Harry's safe return, and to send him a whole string of loving messages; but neither her grandmother nor aunt were very well, so that, as there were guests in the Hall, and the county election came on that week, she could not well get home before the next. Henry would fain, indeed, have caught at this, to set off straight to the old country place: and he made more than one attempt to do it plausibly, which could scarce have been grudged him by anybody, especially after the late turbulent passages in his youthful career. But the circumstances just mentioned by his sister were against him; while out of mere consistency towards his father, whose indulgent view had been all along so

manifest through his firmness, the least he could
do was to begin in earnest. It was Mr. Spencer's
decided opinion that if Henry really intended becoming a merchant at all, he ought rather to put
off visiting Wrixworth till near the next Christmas
holidays, and in the mean time set himself with
resolution to his purpose. He would not conceal
from him that it was at the outset a task—nay,
there was a degree of drudgery, of tediousness,
and perhaps, to an impatient temper, of rather
humiliating subordination in it; for the same authority which he himself exercised in the counting-
house, did he fully depute to the manager and
senior clerks over those, whosoever or whatsoever
they might be, who entered under their respective
departments. But postponement would only make
the effort more disagreeable. Indeed, it would be
unavoidable for Henry now to decide. It was time
his wild oats should have been sown. He would
not constrain him in the least; further, at all
events, than to say, that otherwise he must prepare
to return to school.

With which, and several wise sayings and acknowledged truths besides, did the excellent merchant despatch the subject with his younger son;
while, at the same time, in a kind of half-friendly
and confidential way, making a companion of him
on the other side of the table after dinner; when
the ladies had gone up-stairs, leaving the nuts and

wine. In addition to it all, there was the consideration of the black dependant who had run off
with him from the colonial schooner, and who was
now provisionally established in Beech Grove,
wearing a cast-off suit, and showing every readiness to make himself useful, despite his strange
look and obscure language. Yet Diamond—or
Jupiter, as he had been colonially designated—had
been chiefly used to assist in sea cookery, varied by
the greasing of masts, or the heaving down on
handspikes and pulling along of ropes; all of
which rendered him worse than inconvenient in
the establishment, to its mistress's thoughts. And
how to turn his idleness to use, or leave him for
any time without a guide, patron, or interpreter,
had begun more and more to occupy the boy's
mind, till there had actually been something like
parental care in it. So, as he meditatively
cracked another nut, it occurred to him how well
Diamond could do all day about the warehouses,
or by the quay, in the active service of Broadby
and Co.; returning at nights, of course, to his old
garret at the lodge. So he plucked up a firm
determination, notwithstanding the doubts he had
been having within the last twenty-four hours, or
the sort of unsettled disposition he had felt to visit
Wrixworth, and said he had made up his mind.
His father nodded a benign approval.

Then, clearing his throat, the boy entered on

the matter of his *protégé*, adding boldly that there was that between him and Dick—as he phrased it—that so long as Dick stuck by him as he had done, why—in fact, he was resolved never to forsake him. Mr. Spencer glanced at him in a little surprise; then something like an easy smile passed about his lips, and he laughed, and said Henry might manage it as he pleased. Whereupon, the decanter being passed to him, the youth poured himself out a second glass of port, leant himself back more in his chair, and—though in a very mature way surveying the purity of his wine between him and the windows ere he sipped it—passed the remainder of the hour chiefly in respectful attention. It was as well, he said, now he had clothes, to commence next day, for he meant to turn over quite a new leaf.

A very dusky and dull interior was that of Broadby and Co.'s counting-house, shaded by the height of the red brick warehouses in the close lane, past whose nearest corner went on the bustle of the quays, while the whole crash and roar and clash of Bristol was around, with her sugar-sledges, iron drays, and gayer carriages, passing by. Lamps were early lighted in the outer office, and in some parts of the place they sometimes winked feebly all day. No cloister-cell could well have been drearier, more cut off from life, or more like a region for the human spirit to sicken of its own faculties in; yet admirable was the unconsciousness of any such possibility on the part of the old head-clerk, who, with his periwigged head leant to one side, and the queue-tail of it hanging over one shoulder, while his undisguised spindle-shanks were twined round the legs of his high stool, sat posting the great ledger from hour to hour—without the slightest shadow of expression on his shrivelled face, not even when, at long intervals, he sat up to take a pinch of snuff, screwing all his features towards it, as if it had been a portion of life, or a magnetic thing, or a share of the sun; looking round ere he continued his work again, to see if every pen moved regularly. To him the entire system of things had no existence save from that centre, nor had any disturbing considerations from without possessed the least force for him these forty years, since he had been first taken like a tool into the vigorous grasp of old John Broadby. So, whatever his respect for the firm, it was to him much the same in the case of the loutish apprentice from the country, or of Master Henry Spencer, if he detected wrong arithmetic or dulness to the modes of commercial entry; he took out his immense old watch with an equal air of astonishment, to either of them, when a failure in regard to punctuality was concerned. But to have seen the real stir and practice of the wide world as it goes, particularly in the way Harry had caught sight of it, has, after all, a wonderful effect on the intelligence, with respect even to such dry abstractions. In fact, within a day or two, he grew quickly into the good graces of the ancient manager, and could soon put down statements concerning timber and sugar inwards, and iron or assorted goods outwards, by certain vessels, to such and such ports, with all the more accuracy from having known a little of the things themselves; not excluding the further step, to which the very recollection almost helped him, of combination into a grand total with the nice questions of demurrage, bottomry, or salvage, jetsam and flotsam, and the final and supreme metamorphosis of all into sterling gain.

Whereas, it was pitiable, at times, how the older lad from the country would sink down near him into a dull sort of lethargy, or yawn and cut out his initials on the desk under his work, making odd idiotic scrawls upon the blotting-paper; and, perhaps, he had some dim, stupid hankering after the farmer life again, with the trudgings to school, which he had very likely used to hate. For when it was hot in the afternoon between the brick sides of the lane, when a blaze of sun came down above the warehouses and glared right over the blind part of the dusty counting-house window, through a sudden swarm of busy motes to the desk corner, till it spread upon a piece of the wall,

making very plain the cracks in the plaster, with
the idlest thing or mark thereto belonging—then
would the rustic apprentice look up, eyeing it with
an utter vacancy and despondency that were mise-
rable to see, as if the sense of his irreparable
indentures weighed upon him so that no imagina-
tion of the wealth of Broadby and Co. could rouse
him to ambition more. Yet at that very time,
probably, would the mechanical old worthy from
the head of affairs chance to take his round of the
place, or some officious subordinate of his would
cross the floor, so as to make the defaulter's heart
jump at the abrupt sourness of the voice close
behind, and at the experience of those small,
fretting, spirit-breaking consequences which would
ensue, every day multiplying.

Hence, while the apprentice was treated scurvily,
without any chance in the end of escaping the
usual mill-round of his class, and was sure to make
at best, some forty years after, but an additional
copy of the sapless head-clerk himself; it was on
the other hand quite natural that Harry Spencer,
without any influence from his father, whose private rooms were far remote from him, should
almost immediately fall into the very opportunities
by which the other lad might have profited. What
the stripling from the country liked, was just to be
sent out on messages to the dock-gates and attend
the custom-house, to see freights delivered or stand

by with a note-book, stepping upon the gang-plank or leaping from bale to bale, amidst the stir and liveliness of unloading all day long; but he had been too simple to hide that he *liked it*, and the under clerks knew this, so ever after Henry came to the establishment they used to send *him*. For it is odd, that although clerks may have no care for what is going on without, no turn for open air work in all weathers, and indeed may be glad to have got rid of it—yet no class of persons have a nicer instinct, of the repugnant kind, against the little likings of their inferiors; they having suffered from all generations the same themselves.

The boy's negro follower had at once risen into high use in the sheds, or wherever a cargo was under hands; so Harry was very willing to see how Diamond had got on, or to exchange a word with him, and see him grin merrily as he pulled, rolling the great whites of his eyes about to look, and even leading wild choruses among the stevedores. There, if a face of his own colour appeared near, from some ship's cook-house or cabin-pantry, Diamond regarded it with the most obvious scorn, even to opprobrious word or gesture; he was a model African of some unusual tribe, jet black and ruggedly brawny, and dreadfully hideous at first sight, yet shining with a glossy polish and a good humour which greatly redeemed his looks. It was not that Harry cared much for

all this going about. There was doubtless a vast
advantage to him, so far as his getting on thus
easily was concerned, in the fact of his being a
partner's son; but he had a fund of spirits that
stood him in good stead, at any rate; and throwing himself fully into the matter in hand, as characters of real energy do, he bade fair to turn out
a merchant after all.

No doubt, from the high stool on which he was
perched when within doors, he could constantly
see over the obscured lower panes of a window, if
he sat erect, into the purlieus of the harbour,
where it was singular to notice what went on, if
one only looked. A creek dividing the warehouse
from a building-yard, seemed there to run into the
very thick of the town, between the bottoms of
barges and the rigging of vessels, to the dusty
back-windows of a street; and from damp sails
loosed to dry, to the clothes-lines hung out by
housewives, which often gave the parti-coloured
air of flags making unknown signals, or celebrating
a holiday. A sort of sewer it seemed to become,
at low water; while the heat of the noon drew
smells from it, compared to which pitch and tar
were delicate; as kitchen rubbish, blended with
the refuse from cabins, and dead cats, amid a re-
sinous-looking scum, floated to meet mildewed
oranges: then would the ugliest sloops, that had
slowly been leaning down in the mud, appear im-

minently to threaten contiguous casements, or to
set up for the use of collier-looking sailors—half
that night it might be—ready scaling-ladders near
the garrets of servant-maids, to the pious horror
of rueful spinster-mistresses in spectacles below.
In that stagnant surface, at its stillest and warmest
tedium, with what nicety of repetition were the
most trivial things reflected! The water *would*
have one take notice, whether he wished or no.
As when some boy, astride across the beam he was
besmearing, took such pride in his work that he
kept time involuntarily to the brush with his
tongue, holding his head away to mark the effect
like a painter—or if he only pushed himself lazily
round in a boat with one hand, while with the
other he mopped the side, listening idly to the
noises of the town, till somebody with a rough
voice looked over. Again, it might be, a servant-
girl sitting half out of a high window to clean it,
a good way off altogether from the creek, would
be brought upside down in it for behoof of that
counting-house pane. And in the midst of a sum
of dry figures, or while carefully endeavouring to
fill up duplicates of bills-of-lading in the finest style
of his penmanship, such things annoyed Henry
Spencer not a little. He felt then a strange dulness stealing over him, against his will; if he did not
rather catch himself thinking most inappropriately,
almost with a sigh of regret, about Captain Dodge.

It was one day as he sat thus in his place, which was near the railing by the counting-house door, that a carriage was heard to draw up in the lane outside. Directly afterwards, the rather peremptory voice of some one who entered and addressed Harry, probably as being first at hand, made the boy raise his head in surprise. The visitor was young, elegant, and gracefully easy; he had fine high features, of the kind which English people call foreign, and think strikingly handsome; with that peculiar olive shade under the bloom of his complexion, and that pitch-dark eye, which (though the hair-powder could in those days disguise another of the distinguishing marks) no one ever exactly possesses but the tropical creole. He threw an embossed card upon the desk, with the name on it, "Etienne Etherege, Comte titulaire de St. Amand"—then, even more emphatically than before, though without any foreign accent, repeated the same question, as to whether the boy's masters, as he phrased them, were at home. To which, turning sideways in a haughty style, as if to wait a mere messenger's return, he added the emphatic desire that his card should be at once taken in.

Now, the Count was richly dressed in a dark suit, without any finery to distinguish him from an English gentleman; a costly diamond sparkled in the ring on his hand, his lace was of the most exquisite fabric, and he had quite the air of one entitled

to command; but as Henry Spencer's eye met the
jet-dark intensity of the stranger's, he seemed un-
accountably from that moment to dislike the man
—even to foresee that he could hate him, if often
seen, from the very bottom of his soul. He
thought, indeed, he had heard of him before as
some splendid friend of that Lady Diana Fanshaw's,
whom his sister Jane so wonderfully adored, as if
she were fond of no other person. Yet with a self-
controlled coolness he had begun to learn from his
late experience, Harry no sooner felt this deep
personal aversion to the Count, than he all the
more promptly and civilly stated his belief that
Mr. Spencer, at any rate, was most likely in his
private room; and taking the card, he walked
straight along the passage to his father's door,
where he knocked to ask about it.

He had scarcely knocked, however, ere, somewhat to his astonishment, the door opened with a
sudden vehemence, and he was almost knocked
over by the bulky form of Mr. Ffloyd, the elder
partner, and sugar-baker on his own account; who,
with his square features very much puffed and
flushed, and his smooth, light-coloured wig rather
awry on his large head, was coming hastily out,
not looking where he went, in the heat of a discussion which he still kept up as he departed. All the
more in contrast to him was the firm quietness
of Mr. Spencer, tall and gentlemanly and well

dressed, with his hair all carefully powdered white, and yet the prime of life on his refined aspect, as he stood erect in the middle of the room.

"I don't care who knows it, Mr. Spencer!" called out Mr. Ffloyd, blusteringly, as he turned again towards his partner. "No, not I—I'll retire, Mr. Spencer, I'll retire, I say, sir! I'll—I'll not ha' no more o' this—I'll go out into the sugar-bakin' altogether!"

"So you have said, I think, sir, for the last year or two," was the reply of Mr. Spencer. "With the six months' preparatory notice which our deed of partnership stipulates, I shall not, I assure you, sir, have the slightest objection—rather the reverse."

Mr. Ffloyd seemed ready to foam at the mouth. "These here spec'latin' notions 'll smash the business, sir!" he said. "It's no more like the way John Broadby went to work—no more like his cautious line, as a egg is like bricks! And here am I, only wantin' you to invest a thousand or two out of the business—a mere thousand or two—my own money, I might say—at any rate what my uncle John Broadby *made* — and I—I—I can't have it, sir! A perfectly safe thing, too—why, the market's up—rising every blessed moment! Su—sug—*sugar's* a drug this moment—but I tell ye, sir, to-morrow 't'll be at a 'igh prem'um!"

"The simple truth is, Mr. Ffloyd," said Mr. Spencer, coldly, "you wish me to agree to mix up the commercial affairs of the firm with your distinct and separate trade or business of manufacture, purely on account of this opportunity, which, however lucrative, has no earthly connexion with the foreign commerce of this house. Reap it, sir, reap as much of it as you can yourself manage; but do not ask *me* to clutch, or assist in clutching— what might chance to pass between your fingers!"

The look of Mr. Ffloyd, Wesleyan although he was, had been already choleric, but it became still more so, with a dash of malignant cunning. "Hollo?" said he, stooping down and peering askance towards Mr. Spencer's face. "What do I know about the books, here—eh? They're got beyond me! I shouldn't wonder but there's a screw loose some'ere! Ay, ay, I'll have a overhaul, I say, sir! There ought to be more money to——"

"A truce to this, sir!" said Mr. Spencer, sternly, as he advanced; and the sugar-baker, despite his quondam active habits of rough life abroad, receded before the dignified eye and step. "What is this, Henry?" added the merchant, turning to the boy without further notice of his coarse partner.

It was now against the Count de St. Amand, leisurely advancing under guidance of a clerk, that Mr. Ffloyd well-nigh rushed in his egress toward the outer door. The Count, with a scrutinising glance, stepped aside and looked at him with surprise; he in

his turn, rolling back in haste, and making some
awkward excuses, gazed a moment with a bleary
eye at the foreign Count. It might have been that
the latter's survey was not complimentary, or that
his evident West Indian birth recalled disagreeable
associations, if Mr. Ffloyd's late perturbation did
not sufficiently account for all; but it seemed to
Harry Spencer that the sugar-baker actually gaped
at the sight, looking particularly old, toothless, and
ugly at that moment; though the truth was, that
Ffloyd in his earlier days had been reckoned a
handsome man. An odd coincidence, probably
one of Harry's mere quick fancies, struck him at
that moment; for, however young and handsome
the Count might be, and however elderly and ugly
Mr. Ffloyd perhaps was—did not the former show
some glorified kind of resemblance, as it were, to
the latter in his passing excitement? It was gone,
at all events, whenever the sugar-baker's angry
energy ceased; he stood stock-still, smoothing himself into propriety, and staring over one shoulder
along the passage after the visitor; till that gentleman had been shown in with all form to Mr.
Spencer, who received him most politely. Mr.
Ffloyd, indeed, during the whole time of the
private interview which followed, did not leave off
poking about, in the uncomfortable, inquisitive
manner so despised by clerks, through the counting-
house and offices, as if he could not rest in igno-

rance of who the stranger was. It was soon easy
enough to know his name at least; there was
nothing of secresy in the open tones of that voice,
and he had in his behaviour more of a traveller's
easy habit than of the continental demonstrative-
ness; he came out pleasantly from Mr. Spencer's
door, still talking and smiling with the latter as he
went. In the hearing of the clerk who showed
him out, he had readily accepted an invitation to
dine at Beech Grove on a certain early day, which
had been given with more than common cordiality
on the merchant's part; so that the two were
already on agreeable terms. Mr. Ffloyd not being
in the habit of dining at the Lodge, except in
the most formal way, was likely to be little the
wiser for this prospect; neither had Mr. Spencer
shown the least disposition to introduce his new
acquaintance to his own partner, to one of the
best known sugar-bakers in town, if not the very
wealthiest. Had aught been wanted to make the
thing more glaring, it was palpable in the fact,
that in Mr. Ffloyd's actual hearing they had mentioned sundry mercantile foreign houses which he
knew; nay, by various tokens, the Count himself
had commercial interests abroad—in the West
India Islands particularly, it seemed, which were
alike so important and well known to Ffloyd, since
he had once resided there. But the truth was, as
soon as the interesting visitor had reappeared on

his way out, it might have been thought the elder partner's own fault if he missed notice on the occasion; awkwardly shuffling aside as he did, with no little appearance of shyness from the casual observation in that keen dark eye, and making pretence to search a ledger till the Count was past. Mr. Ffloyd, indeed, was never understood to be fond of the very company that might have been expected to please him, considering his earlier career; such as travelled or colonial folks, free-mannered planters on their visit "home," or roystering ship-masters returned from distant parts. He had even inclined to look askance at black Dick Diamond himself, when so unusual a figure had struck him in the warehouses or counting-house, as if suspicious of its appearance through Harry's means. His very garb proved that the sugar-baker had long thrown off "the world," though he must needs still deal with it; but Methodist as he was, he had plainly taken up the devout creed with all sincerity, founding no credit on its mere externals; and on 'change, as at chapel, he was known for a certain rugged, straightforward candour, altogether the reverse of sanctimonious.

He had composed himself before the visitor was gone, and now went back with a somewhat softened step to the private rooms, where he offered his blunt excuses the more freely on the ground of having shown so much heat before a

stranger—a man of such evident quality. "All
rough and sudden with me, you see, Mr. Spencer,"
said he—"might be better for me if I was smoother
a bit; but if there's aught I hate, it's trying to come
the hypocrite! Never could—no, sir; Matthew
Ffloyd never got *that* to his charge—not even
when goin' all lengths among the plantations; and
there an't any cause for it now-a-days. No harm
done, I hope, though, in that quarter." Here he
indicated the direction of the Count's carriage, just
then heard to roll away. But his partner's tempo-
rary annoyance had been almost effaced, it seemed,
by the visit thus referred to, with its agreeable,
though brief conference. Mr. Spencer stood at
the moment—as great English merchants have
characteristically been apt to plant themselves—
erect before the fireplace, prepared to dictate some
of the more important portion of the house's
extensive correspondence to a couple of junior
clerks who had been called in—one of them his
son Henry. He paused in the act, bowed slightly,
and treated the circumstance in question with
elaborate lightness. "Pooh! my good sir," was
his half-smiling rejoinder, "let not that cost you a
thought; 'tis a gentleman who has seen too much
of the world, I assure you—from Turks and
North Americans upward—to be scared at our
homely Bristol manners."

"Nothing to do, I hope to—to goodness, Mr.

Spencer," persisted Ffloyd, hurriedly, " with any of the firm's reg'lar old connexions out west—Jamaikey or 'Badoes? Thought I remembered some name o' the sort, sir, among our correspondents there-away, or the first-rate known planters on our list, or somewhere."

" A mistake, I think, Mr. Ffloyd," said the statelier merchant, inclined to cut discussion short. " 'Tis, in fact, no commercial or mercantile affair at all—nothing, so far as I yet am aware, that concerns us jointly."

" Oh, if it's private, of course," was the huffy retort, " that's enough. On'y it struck me, as you came out together, you was directing him to some'ere else about town, in the way of business. Might ha' been in *my* way, I thought, if he'd aught ado with the raw produce himself, or even acted for other parties ; and for that matter, it's done in these troublesome times by the best in Kingston. But no matter—not at all : I see I'm to be thrown over. Only, you know," added he, falling back to his coarse manner, " so long as I *am* in the firm—— "

Mr. Spencer signed to the embarrassed clerks to withdraw, and moving a chair towards his dissatisfied partner, seated himself calmly. " Perhaps it may save trouble, Mr. Ffloyd," said he, still smiling superior, " if I at once state what I know of Monsieur le Comte de St. Amand—or, rather, as

he modestly prefers to be styled, Mr. Etherege.
In short, then, I very recently had letters to
announce his visit, both from my own London
bankers, and from a friend abroad. It appears
his French title is only one of courtesy, through
the mother's right; he is, by the other side, of the
very best Spanish blood, on which he naturally
seems to pique himself more. Be that as it may,
however, it is with regard to a connexion of his
house, in the maternal line, with an old English
family in this neighbourhood, that he has visited
Bristol. A purely personal matter, you observe;
Mr. Etherege, or the Count, is even so far re-
moved above commercial or pecuniary questions as
to have no other interest but a genealogical one in
the matter. It so chances, that from my own
slight knowledge of the Continent, acquired in
travel—from my having once visited the West
India Islands, and from connexion through my
wife with the county and neighbourhood where
Herbert Court is situated, he could not well have
been directed to a more suitable source of information. He is a grand-nephew of old Sir Ralph
Herbert of Kingswood, whom I have met—although the baronet, I believe, resides in the prin-
cipality; and he is a cousin of the proprietor of
Herbert Court—a place I well know. I was able
at least to tell him something of both—among
other things, the trifle which you, sir, have over-

heard and construed so oddly; to wit, the fact accidentally known to me of his cousin Lieutenant Herbert's present residence at the old family mansion, after a long term of naval service abroad —spent, by the way, latterly on the West India station. I mentioned the nearest road down to Somersetshire from this part of the town, and, I believe, pointed towards the bridge there, which directly leads to it. Here, then, you have it all, Mr. Ffloyd—the entire mystery—with the exception of some little discourse on affairs at large. Is there anything else, pray, relating to the slight occurrence, on which I can satisfy your mind?"

The mind of the elder member of the firm of Broadby and Co. was manifestly, in some way, relieved, though he made clumsy endeavours to disguise the feeling. "Um!—well," he returned, "the fact is, we're in ticklish times just now; folks are got timorous; the least thing sets 'em up, you'll allow—when it's quite touch-and-go with credit, unless you're well prepared to meet a run, Mr. Spencer. Wouldn't do for you and I to appear any way divided, it struck me, before strangers. Then again these fine foreigners—they're apt to come over with their credentials and what not; but I'd always be cautious, sir—blessed cautious (you'll excuse me)—against honourin' any draft without seein' my way clear. Not to speak of the villanous colonial agents that's afloat at the present time, sir, in all sort of treasonous errands amongst us!"

"I repeat," answered his partner, with a smile more than ever reassuring, "we may be perfectly at ease as to Monsieur de St. Amand on all these points. To politics, without affecting the least ignorance, he is indifferent ; money, in any shape, he does not want or need. No better proof of that fact is requisite than the circumstance of his omitting to cultivate his opportunities with the rich old Catholic baronet, Sir Ralph Herbert—by whom he has already been seen and acknowledged in London—apparently for the mere sake of finding out his other relatives here. These are now solely represented, as I said, by his surviving cousin—a needy sea-lieutenant—the wreck of whose decayed property is scarce clung to by himself; who has, probably, too, by giving up the old family creed, thrown away his sole chance of the Welsh baronet's inheritance. You know his Kingswood coal-estate, Ffloyd ? it alone will make the fortunate successor what you would call rather a warm man—hey ? "

"No mistake about that!" was the ready response. "A man must be a fool not to know it— unless, to be sure, he's been led to take up desperate serious convictions indeed. *They* an't likely to suit, either, if he sticks to the navy; it's all churchmanship there, Mr. Spencer—nothing to

take hold o' for the soul, mind ye, when it's any
way in need to—a—a—that's to say, in earnest!"
Here the sugar-baker, embarrassed for a moment
by somewhat too confidential expressions, coughed,
and drew in; but did not altogether hide an
upward motion of the eye, twinkling fervently, as
if thankful that his case was different. Mr.
Spencer continued to lead the strain of conversation agreeably away. "On the other hand, though,
'tis impossible to be many minutes in Monsieur St.
Amand's company without perceiving his cultivated mind, liberality of sentiment, and utter
freedom from superstitious ideas—on the Continent, I can assure you, they have now become
very liberal in this respect—still his creed is
avowedly that of his French and Spanish parent-
age. We have only to consider the old baronet's
notorious zeal for Pope and pretender, in drawing
an inference from the fact that he is past eighty;
that he has had a recent warning, in the form of
a paralytic stroke, to make his will; and, that little
of his property is entailed. The title must, of
course, fall to the elder branch, and St. Amand
descends from the younger. But as regards the
estates, however careless his own ample fortune
may render him on the matter—why, in my
opinion, Sir Ralph's briefest glimpse of so eligible
a grand-nephew was enough to decide the point.
The young Count's manners, Mr. Ffloyd, are quite

as ingratiating, as you must have seen that his personal appearance is attractive. He stands the nearest conceivable chance of being yet a mil-. lionnaire."

"Gold always *does* draw gold, somehow," nodded Mr. Ffloyd, with thorough sympathy. "As to good looks, well, you're right. Ay, if so, all I know is, I'd just like his name, here, at a good sound check— if it was only but his acceptance at a long date, I'd undertake to discount it. Money's so scarce," added he, suddenly coming round to the old subject, "as I was a-sayin' a little back, with raw produce up most terribly, that here is a good sound going business like my own, even—all right yet as to credit—would be much the better of the use of some, though ever so short a time."

"I am far from wishing to deny it," was the reply, in a tone of considerateness; "nay, as things go at present, my good friend, I can quite enter into the position you describe. But none knows better than yourself, how in proportion arduous is the management of a House like this. To avoid the least entanglement of its concerns with our own individual and private affairs is essential, Mr. Ffloyd. It is, however, possible——" Mr. Ffloyd, with a renewed attempt at amiability of look, once more attended. "It is, I say, possible that the case might at once alter, in certain supposable circumstances. Taking care, I mean, of aught like involvement out of doors, we *might* see our way to moderate cash-advances of the nature you individually require, were our capital by any possibility so augmented—its basis, I should say, widened by the infusion of new strength."

"Just speak plain English again, Mr. Spencer," interrupted the other, rudely, "and say if the Avon runs up Brandon-street. Them fine phrases don't mend the matter a whit to me, you know."

"A moment's patience, Mr. Ffloyd, pray. You can surely understand the supposition," persevered Mr. Spencer, "of an extended partnership strengthening the firm at this troubled period? Were a fresh support to be gained for its unquestionable stability—not, observe, without some degree of tact in the process—and that in the shape of an acute, spirited, wealthy coadjutor with the most brilliant prospects—then, I presume, you would throw no obstacle in the way. It would certainly be opposed to your own interest, to the object you mention—to do so."

"That alters the case," said the sugar-baker, returning an inquisitive leer; "not a doubt of it, Mr. S., but what d'ye drive at? who the goodness d'ye mean—not the—no—not possible you've this same Count what's his-name in yer eye!"

"Mr. St. Amand—ah, no other—the Comte de St. Amand," smilingly assented the merchant.

" There was one singular thing about the impression he gave me, Ffloyd, I confess—and it was this. Disguise it as he might, or however the interest in his Herbert Court relatives was put forward, he certainly had some more direct motive for the visit to me. I have come too much in contact with men at large—men of different countries—not to have this instinctive kind of feeling on occasion. Something in the first penetrating light of his remarkably deep, dark eye, told it to me—there was a keen expectation of personal interest in myself, which I have reason to think was not disappointed. Nay, more—he had the acuteness to perceive at once that I was aware of it, and with a delicate *finesse* of courtesy to be found in travelled men or foreigners alone, instead of continuing to hide the inclination, he virtually avowed it thenceforth. He gave it the polite turn of a general wish to know more of our great English mercantile houses—the nature of our co-partneries, the kind of preliminary experience required to fit one for entering them— in particular, he appeared struck by the curious fact of Broadby and Co. being singly represented in the person of—that is to—well, I mean its whole burden being sustained on one poor pair of shoulders."

" Oho, he did, did he ?" was Ffloyd's impatient remark, partly sullen, but more in suspicion. " Indeed, I'd be inclined to call it infernally prying of him; besides, I an't just shoved aside yet, altogether. Whatever I *may* be!"

"My dear sir!" returned Mr. Spencer, " *I*, at all events, am the last to wish it; on the contrary, I had far rather you dropped every other view, and concentrated our whole strength here. Come, come, Ffloyd, if I did not mention that I had a partner out of doors, you can infer my reason. I did not even see, till the Count had left, that you were still at hand; and as to *his* motives, as I tell you, you utterly misconceive them. I had a pretty shrewd notion that the absence of all ambition in so young a man, the total want of aim, the complete indifference to action, however sincerely professed, were open to argument. No sooner had I touched, with this view, on my own similar feelings before I travelled—on the change produced after a single voyage across the Atlantic, with the consequent sickening at all idle romance or wayward adventures—passing to a brief statement of the full satisfaction to every energy, every mental impulse, which commercial enterprise affords along with domestic happiness—no sooner, I say, had I so begun to speak, than the flash of Monsieur de St. Amand's eye lit up again. Of excitement in some shape he is undoubtedly capable—and there

is excitement enough and to spare, as you and I
could have told him, hey, Ffloyd!"—wherewith the
merchant looked half-jocosely to his out-partner—
"to be found in the said track. But I did not
in the least press the topic; in fact, the glance of
the young West Indian has all the strange, indo-
lent way of meeting yours on a sudden, which you
must have observed in these creoles; he had lost
the thread ere I was done, and still more confused me by venturing to ask, as he said, after the
health of Mrs. Spencer and my family. Of course,
Ffloyd, as you may suppose, before parting I could
not do less than invite him to dine at the Lodge.
In an easy, quiet way. On Thursday next, at
six."

"I know," said Ffloyd, bluntly. "Heard as
much already among the clerks—and he was ready
enough, I hear. So he's West India bred, is he?
Well, if he *do* want to invest, I s'pose his money's
as good as another's, after all. An' if talkin' over's
what he needs, why I fancy he'll have it."

Mr. Spencer's features winced a little, but they
were set on soothing measures. "What I really
wish, Ffloyd, is that you should meet the Count
and judge for yourself. Join us at dinner on the
occasion, my good sir—a quiet evening, with one
or two other friends, including our worthy bankers
here. As for the conversation, certainly nothing

more than the plain, pleasant, straightforward talk on things in general, which an Englishman's table allows."

The sugar-baker had looked up, rather startled; he considered doubtfully within himself, and seemed more embarrassed by the compliment and the prospect than otherwise. "I don't much care about fine company, and that's the fact," mumbled he. "As to your counts and foreigners, or—or your West India creoles, they're all very well—don't think I'm afraid to face 'em—not I!"

"You have seen a great deal more of the colonies than I have, Ffloyd; you were there vastly longer, and know something, I think, if not of French, at least of Spanish or Portuguese, I forget which. This might come well in, you know—St. Amand is half a Spaniard. Remember that even putting aside the partnership notion, at any rate such an influential, intelligent corresponding connexion in the islands would be of vast service in these precarious times of ours." Mr. Spencer added to this complimentary pressure of invitation by suggesting a more practicable motive. "Besides, in any view, 'tis as well to avoid all show of division between us at present. I think you must feel that instead of hinting at such a thing as a dissolution of our co-partnery at any near date—if, indeed, at all; we ought rather, as you yourself justly remarked, to keep up appear-

ances which I do wish were consistent with the
fact. 'Tis the interest of neither to do otherwise."

"I don't know that, Mr. S.," was the annoying
answer, uttered with a dogged and quarrelsome
obstinacy by which Mr. Ffloyd had succeeded in
covering an increased distaste to the social offer.
He thrust both hands deeper in his pockets, and
looked uneasily round, settling to an air of dull,
stolid anxiety. "I'd on'y spoil yer meetin', and
be coming out with somethink unpleasant to the
fashions, as it's a while since I knew 'em, and
don't want to be led into 'em again. What's
more, I an't got time to wait on for your chances,
Mr. Spencer; fact is, sir, I'm not the man for
you—no, sir, nor I don't pretend feelin' like your
kind of high views, and I'm resolved against spe-
culatin'—safe and slow's my maxim! All I want
is a small advance at fair interest, out of the main
concern; it ought to be able to afford it, and—
and—anyhow you'll think over it? P'raps you're
busy—I'll look in by the afternoon and see, Mr.
Spencer." Wherewith Mr. Ffloyd, glad to go till
then if his point were gained, took his hat and
shuffled to leave the private offices.

"For the third or fourth time I repeat," said
Mr. Spencer, rising too, "that much as I regret
denying you, Mr. Ffloyd, I cannot and will *not* do
what is an impossibility for the present."

" 'Twouldn't help the main firm, then, would
it," replied the sugar-baker, looking sideways up,
" if I was to put down the hod, as it's called, *to-
morrow?* Eh—tell me that! Broadby and Co.'s
credit would shake for't, that's all! We're too
closely connected, sir, to risk it; but support I
must have, or *smash* it is before a week's over,
willy, nilly! Look here, if we *can't* draw together,
why just let's cut it, and part friends as aforesaid.
I allow there's six months' notice provided by the
deed. Well—I'll make a handsome offer—come—
only put down a little cash, let's draw on you for
the rest at three, six, nine, and a year's time; both
our credits is solid at the bank yet—it'll help *me*
all to rights, and—why, there's this Count as good
as ever for *you.* On them conditions I'll sink a
good round per-centage of my fair share in the
business for the sake of the meantime. I'm
anxious to give every one his honest due, Mr.
Spencer, on'y keepin' a little peace o' mind to
myself, you know, till the finish. The way it's
like to be just now," added he, vehemently,
putting his hands to his head with a troubled
gleam of the eye, bloodshot and feverish, " it's
more than can be stood long—it's dreadful to look
at. I've a name to keep up as well as Broadby
and Co.; I've the whole chapel-meetin' to watch
me, look. More than that, sir, a great deal more,
I've to try and hold firm by—no matter—ye

couldn't be expected to understand it, Mr.
Spencer. But I just tell ye that's what it is."

Mr. Spencer had been pacing the room to and
fro in no slight disturbance, and now stood reflect-
ing with concern for Mr. Ffloyd. "My good sir,"
returned he, at length, "pray be calm; give me,
then, as you said, till the afternoon. I will really
give the proposal you make my best consideration.
On such terms as you suggest, for the sake of
bringing matters to a close between us, 'tis, in fact,
probable I may agree. But my legal agent, of
course, must be consulted first."

"They're terms which I'm ready to stick by,"
repeated the sugar-baker, as he departed in a more
cheerful mood. "As soon as you say we're to be
quits upon 'em, why, it's a bargain!"

In spite of various perplexities which this occurrence tended to enhance, the merchant found the
temptation of being freed from an unsuitable yoke
with the coarse sugar-baker too strong to resist.
He decided on stretching a point for this desirable
result; and on that same afternoon, accordingly,
by all the requisite formal steps, the inharmonious
partnership was to all intents and purposes at a
close. The house of Broadby and Co. at last
rested its Atlantean weight upon Mr. Spencer's
resolute shoulders alone.

CHAPTER V.

FAMILY MATTERS AT BEECH GROVE.

THE juvenile clerk, Master Henry Spencer, was far less interested in the separation of the firm from all connexion with the sugar-bakery, or the consequent disappearance of Mr. Ffloyd from the premises, than in the young West India gentleman whose visit seemed to have had a part in precipitating the event ; enhanced as his curiosity was, by the additional circumstance of a relationship being whispered about the desks, between this attractive stranger and the wealthy Sir Ralph Herbert of Kingswood. By a duller youth than he, the further fact could soon have been scented out, that the said rich old baronet was indeed an uncle of the *Diana's* late popular lieutenant, Mr. Herbert. That the latter belonged to Somersetshire, he had already found; moreover, he had not failed to take note of the connected piece of information,

that the lieutenant, like himself, was once more at
home. However, he was not at all inclined to
babble office business, and had obvious reasons, on
this point, for avoiding its hasty identification with
his own. His youngest sister was down in Somersetshire besides, and at her return might chance to
have some suitable news to give; for Kate and he
had always been most together, and Wrixworth
village, if not Wrixworth Hall, was rather a gossip-
ing place. Moreover, before then, unless Kate
came home pretty quickly, there was this dinner-
party next week, at which the French-looking visitor
might possibly drop some words that had to do
with the relative most important to Harry. So he
kept his counsel quite shrewdly during the interval,
adding nothing whatever in the family to what was
mentioned through his father, which seemed little
enough. To have seen Harry diligently and
punctually plodding to the counting-house in
Froom-lane, each morning, might have satisfied
the most anxious friend; his homeward walk, a
little brisker, could scarce have detracted from the
impression, save from one slight circumstance, not
at first perceptible, but apt to surprise the Bristol
people of that day. Since along the swarming
street, across the bridge, out of the suburb, and up
the road towards Beech Grove, the negro Diamond
might have been as regularly observed to follow,
precede, or keep parallel with him, at some cal-

culable distance, as planetary satellites do in the orbits they perform. British soil might have given liberty to Dick, but he either did not know, or could not profit by it. He took an uncouth, heathen interest, but very vivid, in all the family concerns; and, as it happened, the afternoon on which Miss Catherine returned earlier than expected from the country, he had reached the house before his young patron. He came cautiously hurrying back through the shrubbery with the news for Harry, as if it had been a secret of the utmost moment to all; while scarce controllable joy radiated from the blackness of his visage, and glistened in the whiteness of his teeth and eyes. Even Harry, who had desired gradually to establish a proper interval between himself and his late fellow-fugitive, yielded to the impulse at once, and made but one spring up the door-steps, from which his uncle's chesnut hunter was being led to the stable, with the pony on which Kate had ridden beside the squire all the way from Wrixworth; while trusty old Roger, leading his seviceable brown cob, followed behind.

The hale, hearty Squire Duttridge, Mrs. Spencer's brother Charles, needed no one to tell his whereabouts as he trod about the parlour; drinking his glass of ale before dinner, and talking, after his long ride, with his loud and rather boisterous voice, his weight of person, and his well-known top-boots.

As for Kate, being a half a dozen times stopped to talk with some one on her way up-stairs, she still had not reached farther than the first landing-place, when Harry caught her as she stood—in her dark-green riding-habit and dark beaver hat with a black ostrich feather—looking very fresh, bright, happy, and excited by a whole day's journey on horseback. So, having already heard something of black Diamond, she fairly screamed at Harry's sudden way of coming upon her. Then there was a long business of the eagerest, most confused kind; making the landing-place a perfect parlour of itself, and even the bedroom another,—sitting about on trunks and bags that had come by coach, till undefinable sounds and scents of coming dinner from below turned the party into a scramble.

The spirits of Kate absolutely overflowed that evening; in her glee she did what she liked with her father's dessert-plate, tasted her uncle's wine, and almost seemed inclined to take a little too much herself: for, being but a year and a half older than Harry, and the youngest of the girls, she had been less rigidly managed by the governess they had had; while having of late been more in the country, and, in fact, turning out one of those general favourites who seem likely to be spoiled, the truth was that Catherine had something of a sly little consciousness of her power, and *did* use small winning ways to come at a thing. Her

father said she must have got her head out sadly
during this last visit at Wrixworth; but her uncle
denied the accusation. "Here was Harry come
home safe," the squire said; "and happily, her
fond grandmother had got fairly set up again; and
as for the election, why, nothing could have come
off more completely to their hearts' content—since
Lord Edward de Vere had gained the day so
gloriously on the good old side, although before
these colonial disturbances began, he was known
to be Whiggishly inclined; no wonder the girl was
in good spirits." Now, the political point was a
delicate one, as Mr. Spencer had been thus inclined
himself; but his characteristic moderation was such
in all things, that his wife could safely rise up, and
carry Kate off among the rest, at the height of her
liveliness.

Up-stairs, while the gentlemen sat at their wine
below, the girls gossiped about the whole village
of Wrixworth, its church, its country people, the
very cows and poultry at the hall, till even Harry
almost wearied.

"Were you not at Herbert Court, Kitty?" he
asked abruptly, at last.

"No," Kate said, briefly. "That is, not *in* it,
you know."

"Of course," was his rather impatient answer.
"You don't know the Herberts, and neither does
my uncle, I suppose?"

Catherine Spencer said nothing; the twilight did not so much make it dusk in the apartment, as that where she sat, near a window, nothing but the shadowy shape of her head and neck could be seen, with her hand supporting her chin, and the elbow on the window-sill. She seemed to have been getting sleepy, or tired of talking, or dull, with her face turned to look out; for now that the skirt of trees by the garden had begun to lose their leaves, the windows of the withdrawing-room kept the light pretty long from the distant western sky, and even showed far off where the Avon and Severn joined, with the silver lustre of the great Bristol Channel lying vivid between blue Somersetshire and faintly-azure Wales, while a moist yellow light in a lighthouse began to burn on a point of coast, and a spectral sail or two was seen.

" What did you say, Kate ?" asked her mother, who sat apart on the sofa. " I thought your uncle said something before dinner of Mr. Herbert? He praised him for some opinion, or some trouble he took, or something before the election; so I thought they must really have got acquainted ?"

" Oh, yes," said Kate, " he knows him. They fell in somehow, I'm *sure*. I think it was in shooting. Mr. Herbert canvassed a good deal, I believe, for Lord Edward de Vere, who had been his captain, or whatever it was. He actually came and canvassed at the Hall, though he might have known perfectly well, of course, every day in the week, what all of us thought!" And she laughed in the same merry way as before. "But he's a Catholic, you know; at least, from his family, I suppose, Mary, *should* be?"

Of all the family, Mary had the best reasons for knowing the affairs of Wrixworth parish, to whose dignified and personable though middle-aged rector, it was well understood, she had the fairest prospects of being some day auspiciously united. That comfortably-beneficed incumbent of the cure was wont to visit it occasionally, and though but recently bereaved of a wife for whom he mourned, had given unequivocal signs of wishing consolation in the cheerful comeliness and healthy looks of the merchant's second daughter, noticeable as they were in the squire's pew; a certain propriety of delay was now the main obstruction to Mary's filling up the vacancy in the rector's heart, and bringing her placid, motherly manners to the care of his one little girl. To her younger sister's passing question, therefore, Mary returned rather a hurried assent; she "fancied so—yes—most likely," with something more of a blush than might have been thought her right, perhaps, on the ground of so unromantic and sober an arrangement. "A Catholic, I dare say; but as for *should* be, why, you surely forget, Kitty, this is a land of Protestant—I mean a free country!"

"La, I vow! And did your uncle actually invite his acquaintance!" was the exclamation vouchsafed by the eldest sister, Jane.

"True, the Hall was one of the last places you'd think," agreed Mary; still, as in duty bound, with evident demure remembrance of her pledges to the rector. "All the Herberts have been Catholics; old Sir Ralph, the rich baronet of Kingswood, is a thorough bigoted Papist, they say, and Jacobite. 'Tis the politics, however, perhaps that may incline my uncle, in these innovating, Whiggish times of which he speaks so often. And I suppose, Kate, the old priest may be dead, or have left Herbert Court?"

"Why, no," was the rather careless answer. "Left it? oh, no, I fancy not. Nobody comes to church from there, at any rate, except the gentleman himself; and he seldom, but of an afternoon service. To be sure, there's no pew for them of their own; indeed, you'd suppose he was guilty of something or other, when he stole in so, always as near the aisle-door as possible; not much accustomed, either, it would appear, to the liturgy. Do they really use the Prayer Book much in ships, hey, Harry?"

And with this, the boy received an arch glance of inquiry from Kate, which made him colour up; her jesting tone by no means pleased him on a matter of so much interest to his mind.

" Lieutenant Herbert belongs to the Royal Navy, miss," said he, with a becoming gravity, " and every king's ship of any size carries her own chaplain, to have the service regularly read. As for a lieutenant being a Jacobite, or anything of the sort, why——"

" True, quite true, child," Mrs. Spencer interposed, " *that* is above question. And now you talk of it, 'twas but last night your papa chanced to mention this young gentleman, in regard, I think, to his uncle Sir Ralph's property. Your father says that no officer can hold the king's commission without he professes himself a true churchman; so that if Mr. Herbert does so, I am sure, my dears, we might all save our pains. A more honourable family never breathed than the Herberts, and I make no doubt his Protestantism is as good as our own, though mayhap scarce so noisy."

" Besides," coincided Mary, as gently as could be wished, " it must thus be awkward enough, when at home, with the old Abbé Horne ever near. 'Tis long suspected the old chaplain, for all his mildness, is a Jesuit."

" If it really is so, ma'am," returned the fair Miss Spencer, with unusual emphasis, " he will assuredly lose everything from the rich old baronet, save the title; Sir Ralph's sentiments are well known. Is it not all the more surprising, mamma, that these visits should have been encouraged at

Wrixworth? A decayed squire, at the very best, you know; still worse, a penniless sea-lieutenant, or a poor shabby baronet, without a single estate but the old mortgaged place."

The girl looked up at her maturer sister in obvious surprise, till their mother had laughed the hint aside, with a prudent nod which Kate could not have seen. Her bright eye sparkled, though, and the colour rose in her rounded young cheek, as she spoke somewhat spiritedly for herself:

" By *whom* do you mean, Jane? Encouraged!" But then she laughed too, and added, " Pooh! the truth was, we were all too full of politics, you ought to know, for aught else. About Mr. Herbert's poverty, I cannot say, nor his expectations either; at all events, he remains in the navy, I think, and means to go to sea again as soon as possible. You mistake about his present rank being a lieutenant's, too; at his last return he was what is called professionally, I believe, a commander."

" Must have got it through the admiral on the station," explained her brother, very readily; " came back, it's most likely, in acting command of some sloop of war, and they've confirmed it at home, here."

" What is he like, Kitty?" asked Mary, cordially. " Is this young Herbert - Court handsome?"

"Handsome?" she repeated. "Well, no, scarcely; nay, to my taste, not at all. Not young, either— looks much older, I should say, than he is. You would not call one handsome that has been marked by small-pox some time or other, and has had a deep scar on the cheek, over one ear; not to speak of the kind of colour taken from hot climates on a fairish complexion, with eyes of a clear grey, like a falcon's, to be sure, when they happen to turn your way! But *that* is not often—he's very silent, grave, reserved, and, to strangers, shy."

"Vastly odd, indeed, in one canvassing for an election," observed the eldest of the sisters; "though, from this account, my dear, fortunately, not dangerous."

"Whew!" ejaculated Harry, with sudden impatience—"that's as you take it; I warrant ye a rebel colonial wouldn't say so, nor a Cuba buccaneer either. Just please to let's hear all that Kitty knows of him; he's the very officer I heard so much of at Kingston, mind you, and tried to get sight of, understanding he belonged hereabouts. You don't say aught of his build, Kitty—looks the right sort, does he, in that respect?"

Kate seemed rather to see through this equivocal curiosity, and her hazel eye laughed back to his as the firelight was stirred, with a meaning he could not but take. "Aha! Mr. Harry," said she, nodding her capricious tresses at him; "you shall not have any unsettling from me, sir; remember the counting-house! If you had still had aught to do with such affairs—why, Captain Lord Edward de Vere was the true person to talk of; he was staying there — at the old Court I mean — and I flatter myself his lordship really took some little notice of me, as a very likely child of my age. 'Tis always done though, mamma, before elections for the county. That was a fine man, now—if he had been taller!" Harry in vain pricked up his ears; it would not do for him to confirm any imputations of over-anxiety about Lieutenant or Commander Herbert, by asking if *he* were short in stature too. "They say he likes the old mansion-house, though leaving it," pursued Kate, in the same breath, "and means to have it repaired when he can. Lord Edward would do anything for him, it seems, and has interest enough to get him made a post-captain, if war with the French were so lucky as to——"

"Why, child, how you rattle on!" broke in her mother, smiling. "I declare! you mix 'em so together! I thought you spoke last of Lord Edward! Not a word of war, pray!—heaven grant *that!*"

"Strange mad notions to have her head stuffed with, I must say," remarked Miss Spencer, with raised eyebrows. "The French, you saucy young chit, you!—war with the most polished, the most agreeable of nations, forsooth!"

Here did Harry's juvenile experience prompt him again to interpose, though in a manner aiming at politeness. "Begging your pardon, Jane, I wish you had only tried one or two of 'em as ship-mates; they're not always so pleasant, nor, what's more, particular about cleanliness. Our ship's cook in the *Dorothy* used to—well, no matter—no occasion to stop your ears as soon as one speaks. Besides, now I recollect, he was a Genoese. Only they're not all so smooth as you think: there's your fine foreign Count, even, that's coming to dinner on Thursday—you seem only to have *heard* of him."

"Ah! from the best possible source!" the beauty condescended to reply; "from his intimate friend—from Lady Diana Fanshaw herself! And pray, Henry, what of that? That is, I imagine you mean the—that brilliant young Monsieur Etherege."

"Who?" asked Kate, with revived spirits. "A Count—foreign—rich and handsome, no doubt—dining here the day after to-morrow! My stars! you had all forgot to tell me so! Is he French?"

"I understood *not*, my love," answered her mother, quickly. "No—only a travelled gentleman of title, and very good family, nearly connected

with some here; he merely happens to have been
born abroad, I believe."

" 'Tis still one of the lowest vulgar English
ideas," observed Jane, affecting a somewhat foreign
shrug of her fair shoulders, " thus to fix the birth
of every one, however raised above it by the habit
of good society. Even the use of titles becomes, I
think, mamma, rather *mauvais ton* on the Continent, where M. Etherege resided much. Lady Die
herself smiles at her own, and says she will hail
the time, certain to come, when it must become a
provincial *gaucherie* to address her so, as 'tis already
in the best Parisian *salons*." Mrs. Spencer, however, could not see her way to approve such novel-
ties of behaviour. She had always been taught,
she remarked, to give every due respect to station.
"I can only say, ma'am, he is all the rage at
the Hotwells just now," added her eldest daughter,
and, I am told, round the whole of Bath, so that
Catherine might well be surprised. In Bristol,
the few people worth mentioning would give the
world for papa's singular good fortune. The Count
is one of Madame du Deffand's very set, Lady Die
assured me on my carrying your invitation to meet
him—himself among the most enlightened of them.
To report her very words, a philosopher, a true
cosmopolite ! "

The manner of this statement being no less
oracular than elevated, the entire Spencer family

then present were for some moments duly im-
pressed. The feeling might have taken no clearer
shape than was evinced by Mary's renewed anxiety
about dresses for the imminent occasion, or by the
dreary look of disappointment in Kate, as she
sank back again from the firelight, which had
danced in her starry eyes, whispering sleepily to
Harry her distaste for young wiseacres in spectacles. But, owing to maternal care, the topic
caught a last flicker of strange interest. " In
religion that is, I suppose?" inquired Mrs.
Spencer, after a pause. " A—a cosmokopite?
Dear me! Indeed, Jane, I forget what this exactly
means." Mary, too, was undoubtedly thinking
over it in her settled attitude; the growing
shadows of the room rather tended to flutter than
favour the elegant languor courted by Miss Spencer's silence. " Most likely *he*'s a Catholic also,"
doggedly assented Harry, from the obscurest
corner. " And for all we know, it may mean a
chief inquisitor."

The general merriment at such an extravagance
was suited to turn the difficulty aside; and when
candles were brought in, the conversation flagged.
There was something provoking to Harry, too, in
the uselessness of his attempts to renew it in a
corner with Kate; she really appeared to know
nothing of the possibility she had hinted at for a
moment, about a French war; she did not incline

in the least to save him the awkwardness of direct
questions, which he thought it better not to put,
on the matter of Commander Herbert's recent
ship and his expected frigate ; indeed, she betrayed
gross ignorance of the subject altogether.   Being
truly tired with her late journey, short as it had
been, with the addition of so much talking since,
she expressed a decided wish to retire early.   It
was odd of Kate, at all events, to have now got so
decided in her wishes.   It was odd of her to have
grown so much during his single voyage ; and to
have changed, in short, so singularly that he felt
once or twice disposed to call her Catherine.   He
rather attentively got the candlestick for her as
she went up-stairs, and said aside in the gallery,
" I tell you what, Kitty, I was going to have said
before, when I was interrupted—whatever Jane
likes to fancy about him, I've *seen* him, look ! "

" Seen who, Harry ? " was her rather listless
answer, putting up one hand to her mouth in
unmistakable sleepiness. " Oh—the Count ! " It
was difficult to keep from laughing either, at
Harry's earnest gravity on this point.   " And—
yes, is he really so handsome, then ? "

" Oh—you're all of one side with what's to be
told about people's looks, Kate ! " said he, sharply ;
but plainly enough letting out the undeniable fact
as to Mr. Etherege's personal appearance, by a
mingled air of reluctant admission and professed

disgust. "Of course, there's different tastes," he allowed; "and mine's the other way altogether. I like a big, manly - looking figure, for my part—no matter for features. Come—one good turn, you know, deserves another — you understand?"

"I shall go fast asleep on the staircase—that's poz!" she gaily answered. "You want me to dream about a Count without a face, do you? Never mind—'tis not so very long waiting till Thursday evening, when I shall judge for myself."

"Ah! but there's something more I could tell you, miss," he persisted, putting on a sidelong look of excessive knowingness. "As it's leaked out somehow to the clerks, no doubt from old Ffloyd, it can't just be called confidential. None of you all, here, seem to suspect whose relation the Count is, down in Somersetshire; or, what's more, not a hundred miles from Sir Ralph Herbert's Kingswood collieries! It appears to lie between the two of 'em *which* succeeds to the old popish hunks of a baronet's property; and if sticking by the navy's to spoil one's chance, why, Kate, d'ye think, then——"

"Think! and I dying with fatigue and sleep, you heartless boy! I can only think, then," exclaimed his sister, half indignant, "if 'twere only you that had this chance, 'twould be *quite* spoiled! How can *you* know the difficulties, pray—I sup-

pose you've been brought up a Protestant? This
Count of yours is rich enough already, ain't he?
In that case, all I can fancy is, he'd become a
Crœsus—absolutely you make one tremble to meet
him. But, pray, sir—as they say in the romances
—*unhand me!*" Very like a mock heroine, indeed, she stamped her foot from the stairs at him,
as Harry kept hold by the train of her full
dress. "You'll tear it, mind, Harry — 'tis the
newest, too—all I have, indeed, for the unforeseen
occasion."

  "Well, I must say, Kate," came his somewhat
sullen admission, "your fault don't lie in mis-
taking one's drift—you're only a thought too quick
with it. To come out as plain as you like, of
course I meant Mr. Herbert—they're somehow
cousins, it appears, this Count and he. If he goes
to sea again, it's clear there's little chance of old
Sir Moneybags's fortune, as there ain't any Roman
Catholic commissions likely in the fleet. Just
stay, though—there's quick promotion and lots of
prize-money, mind you, in case of war with——"

  "Goodness gracious, Harry," she broke out,
ready to run, "have I not told you my unlucky
tongue made a slip at mere random, when I hit on
the phrase. 'Twas but the idlest word in life—I
had no foundation whatever for such silliness. As to
the French, I tell you I know nothing against the
poor people, not the least reason to dislike 'em.
Nor, for aught I saw, has your hero, Mr. Herbert

—nay, I should rather have said they were favourites of his, at least of the worthy old chaplain, the Abbé Horne."

"Ah! but by way of duty, you see," persisted Harry, "that don't much signify. Suppose it happened, we'll say—and Mr. Herbert gets a frigate through Lord de Vere, and goes. Don't you think now, Kitty, in that case," and with this he edged closer up to her again, in a glaringly wheedling way, "as *you* happen to know Mr. Herbert—besides, you said you met his lordship too, his former captain out West, and that he took notice of you—why—well, you might use the freedom just to say a word in—in my favour?" He was so undoubtedly serious in the matter, as to have sunk his voice to the most cautious whisper at the end, glancing prudently along the drawing-room gallery, lest others might have observed the conference; then did Harry endeavour to assume a preposterously careless air, for Kate's amazement at the proposal somewhat startled him.

"What! to Mr. Herbert did you actually mean?" she cried, flushing up and waking wide enough at the thought. "How could you suppose, Harry," added she, again merrily, "I knew enough of him for *that?* The acquaintance was but very slight—and his is a countenance that could be stern, I warrant me, on occasion—proud, too, very proud under all. As a midshipman, I pre-

sume, Hal, eh? Why, you might not like him
long. Those other captains you mentioned, they
might be nothing to this one, if you found him
harsh. I have heard, yes, they say there's something wrong about the family. Their heads, that
is," she explained.

Evidently her brother scorned to answer such
fancies. "There's the old chaplain you speak of,
then," persevered he. "A note might do, through
the chaplain; or my uncle—when he goes home,
say—might do something if you asked him. You're
such a favourite of Uncle Charles's, you know,
Kitty; but, as to my father, for heaven-sake
not a word as yet—no." As he spoke they could
hear the two gentlemen in question coming up the
lower staircase together from the dining-room,
where they had lingered their full time, the
hearty squire's loud voice contrasting strongly,
though quite amicably, with the firm measured
tones of the merchant, as their closing theme
proved to have been the politics of the crisis.
The latter had manifestly agreed that the young
colonial rebellion was parricidal, and must be
crushed in the bud,—that it ought to rally all true
lovers of the constitution round the church, the
throne, and the vigorous coercive measures of his
most Gracious Majesty George the Third; the
former covered his glee at the admission by hum-

ming the catch of an old loyal tune, which savoured quaintly of the Jacobitism that was ex-
tinct.

The girl nodded full approval of Harry's caution,
as to their father's being told this scheme so soon ;
"For the rest, believe me," she concluded, hastening, "'tis folly—'tis far beyond my power, Henry.
Good night, dear ; don't let your thoughts run that
way—don't dream of it.   Hark to the wind to-
night, how it rises, and 'twill fast be winter on us !
They're dreary enough to think of, surely, without
the sea—without the war—without a silly boy of a
brother to keep awake for, you know, wherever he
may be ! "   Half playfully, blowing a kiss to him
as if she half trifled with his wishes, Kate had disappeared.

Sleep, indeed ! Sleep ? The evening was scarce
gone, the night was early yet.   True, the long
nights were at hand, and a last chilly October
breeze stirred through the unleafing branches that
evening, as Harry, in an ill temper, with his hands
in his pockets, loitered about behind the house.
Partly it was to indulge an uncivilised and sur-
reptitious practice, far from fashionable anywhere
in Europe as yet, at which good Mrs. Spencer
would have been more horrified than even at the
arrival of Dick Diamond—that use of the American weed, not hitherto so far grown on the boy as

to be a habit, but which he rather feared might soon
become necessary if he stayed in Bristol.   In default of better company, he certainly had here one
faithful friend, in the shadowy shape of black
Diamond lurking as near as possible, availing himself of the most convenient shelter, and looking
only like a deeper bit of the obscurity he sat in,
but for the fitful glow of his humbler tobacco-pipe
through the dark.   Whatever tacit communion
might already in those days be felt between mor-
tals so engaged, in spite of social distance, such
must have been open to Harry.   Dick and he had
certainly gone through some odd chances together.
But the negro's silence was extreme; it might
have been the deepest slumber, except for the
said intermittent kindling of the spark amidst it,
like the red hollow of a Cyclops's burnt-out eye
that the wind puffed up—like the far-off view of a
revolving lighthouse from a tossing sea—like a
match in the hand of a ship's gunner waiting
secretly to fire—like anything but good company.
The very contentedness of Diamond provoked
one; he made himself so snug under the kennel
of the surly watch-dog, whose gruff intimacy he
had gained of course, and sat there, it seemed,
quite at home, with his knees drawn up near his
nostrils, one arm about the chained neck of big
Bowser, who most peacefully slept the while.   A

single sign of life only did Diamond make, and
that was worse than his stupidest lethargy. He
picked up the half-used Havannah thrown away in
disgust by his young master, rubbed it in his
hands, pressed it into his pipe, smoked on, and
seemed content to smoke—without so much as
seeing one breath of it—for ever. But what
could Dick know — what could it trouble *him*
how they were to stay or go! He was a dark
heathen, was Dick; for aught that appeared
he might be worshipping one of the stars there,
right above the dark where he sat — the planet
Jupiter, an old namesake of his, by-the-by —
that smouldered away white over the blowing
clouds from the west, where the Bristol Channel
spread.

The autumn breeze alone harmonised with
Harry's mood. Outside the dulness of the house
it kept up a stir, and grew even more restless with
the darkening of the twilight. The quieter all
grew within, it rose and blustered the more discon-
tentedly, till an eddying rush went through the
rusty tops of the clustered beeches that gave the
place its name, sounding like signs before a gale
on the Atlantic. A great pale plane-tree hard by,
with but a scattered foliage left it, creaked sullen
sympathy; one by one its large leaves began to
hover past like sea-gulls, whirling to join the smaller

rout; at times there came a sharp, cracking rattle
of planks from a wood-yard down the lane, that
finished off with a louder clap, and seemed echoed
once from the distance of King's Roads, beyond
the narrow harbour, by the real sound of a great
gun, brought heavily in the wind. A wild red
streak or two in the sky, as if royalty must indeed
at last die in the Far West, had faded underneath
the clouds where the Channel stretched; but the
lights of all Bristol threw a flicker up in the air,
and the long black bristling of the great river-port
was darkly shown between, down through the half-
bared avenue from a turn of the hedge-bank where
Harry loitered. Rather a short turn it was, and
might have been thought of itself the dullest corner
of Beech Grove, being but part of the walk to its
back-offices and kitchen-garden; yet he sauntered
back and forward there mechanically, and still,
with an obstinate preference for the spot, the more
restless his steps, the quicker did he retrace it.
The feet of Harry had, in fact, of late, begun to
tread the said limited portion of ground into an
obviously beaten path, somewhat unaccountable to
mere passers-by. It was solitary of an evening, it
was snug on one side, it looked far the other way
as the leaves fell, and, since it offered a full view
of sundry important windows, also favoured a safe
conformity to the ways of an orderly household.

Ever, therefore, as the breeze grew livelier that night, and took the character of a rousing equinoctial south-wester with fits of rain, he paced it quicker to and fro in the bustle like a sentry, only stopping to peer out more irregularly, and rolling more in his gait.

CHAPTER VI.

THINGS IN THE WIND.

THE breeze still blew next day, but it was
mixed with daily duties, and spent for many an
hour against barriers of solid trade. There was
only another busy day in Bristol port, all the
busier, no doubt, for the windy bustle from the
river. The wide harbour space of the " Grove"
swam full of shipping, divided midway by its
brown canal, where the eddies caught a greener
shade about the bulky pitch-bronzed hulls, and all
shapes of emblematic figures met, with all sorts of
names from earth or heaven ; while bridges were
seen through each other across the vista, and still
more masts upon the other side, as the intricacy of
rigging rose with its white poles into the sky,
stretching airily in the gaps between houses higher

than the loftiest. Cries were above, below, and between, of hoisting and hauling; voices short and authoritative, responded to by voices hoarsely obedient, struck through the varying tumult; the clank and crash of iron, the hollow blows of wood and the clatter of ropes, were near or far off; while huge mechanisms slowly moved, and when the ear might have been thought to have no further room or faculty, then would come the swift creak of a crane-chain running down suddenly, after some great load had been hoisted and swung from wharf or hold to the sharp intermittent rattle of a ship's windlass; yet each noise would still find its proper place in the wild medley. The whole mid-space of Bristol, in fact, groaned, plashed, and creaked, as if struggling to untwist a network that had entangled it overnight in its sleep; and far from the afternoon bringing that day the least cessation, the hour of low water was then past, the slow waxing of flood-tide began to show itself about the dock-gates, and the lighter air that had lately trifled alike with the topmast vanes and steeple-cocks, to set again steadily. The worst of it was, that the wind gave still no signs of being favourable for the many vessels it had kept waiting in the Severn channel; and in those days there was no help against a breeze save tide, oar, sweep, or towing-line; whereas to Broadby and Co., who had one of their largest vessels reported in the river, it

chanced to be of no small consequence that the
freight should forthwith arrive. And it was a
matter very natural for young Harry Spencer
the moment he heard of it, to go straight to his
father with the offer that he would take a boat
down the Avon at once, ere the tide fairly turned,
and get on board the *Mary Jane* in time to let
them understand how she was wanted that night.

Indeed, at flood-tide in the narrow Avon, even
for a burthen of four hundred tons, two or three
horses could do wonders on the towing-path, if a
vessel were but got so far at the right time. So,
no sooner did he get the half-incredulous permis-
sion, than, hurrying down to the shed where black
Diamond was rolling casks, Harry made a most
unceremonious pressure of him into the service;
needing only further to find a boat, with a second
rower in the shape of the cabin-boy who was mop-
ping it out, ere he was steering out of the confusion of the " Grove," to go down river.

Meanwhile, the bustle of the city seemed still to
grow, until the cathedral clock tolled four, and,
hard by, the sunset reflected from glistening black
hulls began to burnish the water under them, as if
in brazen patches it had taken fire; here and there
glowed a half-loose sail like gold against the upper
sky; while he that ascended to wrap it together
for the night, saw range beyond range of windows
flash like amethyst and diamond. But he looked

stolidly over, man or boy, into the changing lights
and shadows that contended for the city among
its smoke; nor was it anything to him if, through
a maze of intersecting cordage, the shady cathedral
precincts of St. Augustin's already reposed about
the solid walls, while the broad battlement of its
tower grew deeper purple before the cool keen
blueness of evening in November, and the figures
of people passing across the open green were
thrown forward by twilight. Alike unheeded, opposite, might shoot up the tall square shaft of St.
Stephen's, its western front all glorious as a vision
of old, with work far rarer than the jeweller's,
gilded over by the sun from the Atlantic ; or the
richly-pointed bell-tower of St. Mary Redcliffe's,
where young Chatterton had moped but eight
years before, might stand in dusky form another
way. What such folks cared for was but the breeze
blowing sharper along the quays as they grew barer,
and coming round the corners in sudden gusts. It
brought up wild clouds in the east, and promised a
wet and windy night, as it drove the smoke clear
of the city away into the transparent sunset.

The coming tide, too, made a living sound into
the town; the buoys and fending-logs dipped, the
quay-sides plashed, and it was odd to see how the
white or yellow masts of the sloops were swaying
with the motion, while the shadows of them moved
upon the wall—and how cheerily the coloured vane-

flags blew out; though all was still bright, and the mellow, honeycombed old forehead of some church rose but the more illuminated above in the moted streams of sunshine between the ridges of the roofs, for all the deep shadows of houses projected from over the way against its front, with the varied outline of their gables and chimneys. Yet wind and tide were nothing to the murmur, ferment, and increasing bustle and excitement of the streets, which floated up the more confused on that particular afternoon as business ceased.

The truth was, although no one could tell which was the most likely out of a hundred rumours, there had been singularly creeping all that day, through the very work and trade of Bristol, an unaccountable disturbance. Some said it was another incendiary in the port, like John the Painter who had just been hanged at Portsmouth; others, that a mob of "Levellers" meant to rise in the city that night; again it was the pirate Paul Jones in Bristol Channel; and now, the failure of a great house, or else a grand disaster to the British army in the American colonies, or a terrible shipwreck. The harbour telegraph had been at work from time to time, answering in its mysterious style to another above Brandon Hill, which Government had lately posted there; and a passenger by the stage from London, three days on the road, had been said to shake his head in a manner that said much, though he was so prudent a man as to avoid explanations.

It was to such an account, from a quick-voiced barber at his door, that courteous attention was paid by one of two gentlemen, evidently from the more fashionable part of the city up-hill, who seemed to have been tempted so far out of their way by curiosity. The erect carriage of the other, with the cockade on his gold-laced hat, marked him military; he was a young man of twenty; his features fine, the freshness of youth not yet effaced from his cheeks by a certain air of dissipated life and late hours; to which the puffed-out and powdered hair, with the triangular upturned brims of the beaver, lent their insipid effect, as of would-be old age. He affected to talk French with his friend, despite the apparent wish of the latter, and his evident familiarity with the native tongue. *Englishman* was stamped, however, on the officer's whole aspect, from his blue eye and common-place good looks, to the haughty glance of supercilious-ness he threw about him in the crowded street, to his easy step, and the fancied grace of that studied negligence in his dress, amidst all its fine extrava-gance of gold button and brocaded flap, embroi-dered waistcoat and lace cravat, or elaborate ruffle; nor the less conspicuously, as his companion seemed a contrast to him in almost every point. A taste too exquisite to display itself was in each item of

the latter's dress, his manner, the very tones of
his subdued voice; he had all the quiet, retiring
air of the civilian; his dark eye glittered with the
keen notice he gave to each thing or person, yet he
looked as young as his military friend—perhaps
even a little younger. He seemed now gay, now indifferent; and though no English sun could ever
have given that tinge to his marked features, still
neither his accent, nor any other circumstance
within the power of human will, could have betrayed the fact.

"What the deuce can the fools mean, St.
Amand?" said the young officer, talking very
loudly. "Why, they seem actually to gape at *us*,
as if we had something to do with it!"

"'Tis possible, my dear Cobham," was the calm
answer. "So we had better, I think, talk a little
lower."

"Pooh!" said Cobham, raising an eye-glass;
"to pass through this vulgar scum of shopkeepers
and porters? Not I! Let's talk French, I say,
Comte—that's the safe thing. A language I prefer,
for my part!"

The Count made a slight, careless shrug of the
shoulders, raising his thick black eyebrows, and
saying in the tongue required, "Well, as you wish
it, my friend. In this free country of ours, we
shall probably get mobbed; but it is indifferent.
My mother, as I think I told you, was of French

origin—yet I speak the language no more than passably."

"Can you imagine any reason for all this?" repeated Cobham.

The young Comte de St. Amand—or, as he had rather preferred to be called in English society, Mr. Etherege—shook his head in reply. "Rumour has a hundred tongues," he said. "To reconcile, to trace them to their source, demands a keener wit than mine. 'Tis true, such a source they must have, probably the merest trifle, some accident, something not worth the pains!"

"Ah!—Ha!—You are right! Nothing is so stupid as human nature!" responded the young Cornet in vociferous French, which sounded but ill after the easy fluency of his companion's. "What a *canaille!* Such inconceivable stenches! Back, fellow!" and he pushed aside a shock-headed mechanic, who reeled sulkily amongst a knot of dock-porters and street-chairmen, whose curses he received and returned.

"Pah! This is insupportable!" ejaculated the officer, as they pursued their steps. "Suppose we return?"

"I am perfectly at your service, my dear friend," was the courteous answer. "Nothing, of course, that excites these good people there, can be of the slightest consequence to either of *us*. Still, perhaps it is equally philosophical to go on a little. The spirit of the age, my dear Cobham—which both of us so admire—is an inquiring one."

"Of course—of course!" the young officer hastened to agree; "admire it, my faith!—so I do. Indeed, when one was in the mood, it used to be excessively amusing—the folly of people, and human nature, and all that manner of affair, see you! But really—really," and the Cornet used an eye-glass in a languid way, eyeing the people, the houses, the very sky, with a supercilious indifference which appeared to find nothing worth attention; nor was it till after the interval of a slight yawn that he finished his remark. "Really, Count, one *does* get over all that, eh? You and I are both about equally *ennuyées*, I fancy, or—or worse than that, what's the exact word?"

"Blasés, perhaps," was the smiling suggestion.

"Ah, ah, perfectly, *blasés*, you're right. We want change, that's to say," nodded the Cornet. There was studied suavity in the other's manner, and in every tone of his voice, yet a delicate irony played through his answer. "True, my dear Monsieur the Cornet—I forgot—in England, it occurs to me, we live so rapidly, our blood is so impetuous—our passions, our pleasures, our apprehensions, so quick and strong—that we become philosophers earlier than elsewhere." The renewed smile might have been owing to Cobham's unscrupulous French; to the further idea, possibly, of so

young a victim to that new malady, which found
the world empty ere it was seen, and stripped existence of its charm before enjoying it ; probably,
too, there was some underrating of the Cornet's
apparent capacity to judge.

" Why, about philosophy," rejoined the latter,
promptly enough, " I don't know, I don't pretend
to have tried it more than yourself, M. de St.
Amand. As to my French—well—it amuses you,
I see, but no matter—I can manage to carry
through with it somehow, as we did on the grand
tour, my old tutor and I, one summer."

" On the contrary, you speak it but too well, M.
Cobham !" laughed St. Amand, openly, as he drew
the Cornet's attention to a whispering knot of on-
lookers while they passed. " We are taken for
foreigners, you perceive ! Perhaps, to judge from
that eagerness, for spies ! Can any plot have been
discovered ?"

" Bah—the city member very likely dead," said
Cobham, with scorn ; " or Government to be turned
out, or a fire in a warehouse or so."

" I think not," was the answer, still suggested
by a steady survey on either side, from the jostling
thoroughfare to its clamorous side-lanes and gos-
siping alleys. Now the ferment seemed increased,
if only by the sudden break of some cross-street
that brought along its gust of wind from the river,
with the gleam of masts through the high gap,

and rigging woven across; where the ropes clat-
tered and the gunwales ground together in growing agitation, while lighter poles swayed to and
fro, and flag and vane streamed out from the cold
blue bareness of the sky. Again, from obscurer
vistas of the port, out amongst the bare spindle-
shanks of the townsfolk and their ample skirts,
came a loose flutter of seamen's dress, as they
rolled in a boisterous group to the door of one
early-lit tavern; hat-ribbons flying, with rough
brown visages, bundles in their hands, and here
and there a great bright shell or curious foreign
leaf to show, or a gorgeous parrot from the West.
" I think not," repeated the Comte de St. Amand,
as if disposed to pause. " A straw, my friend, even
though senseless in itself, may tell to an observer
how the current tends. Towns-people do not inquire of *seamen* about burnt warehouses, or political changes at home."

" Is't true," rose a cry at the noisy tavern-
corner, " there's been a terrible earthquake in
Spain?" " What news, my lads?" called sundry
hurrying voices,—" Did ye see aught of pirates—
was't a hurricane—is the Chiney fleet safe?"
Coupled with surly growls and rude laughter from
the sailors, as well as profane epithets of disdain
for landsmen, came but the doubtful response,
" Safe be blowed! All right, anyhow, with the
Mary Jane." " Well, they *did* say," it was being

added by a younger and more civil comrade, "off Ushant, ye see, my masters, in a French lugger we chanced to speak——" But the rest of his meaning was lost in gruff impatience, and in uncouth huzzahs for the ready house of entertainment. "The *Mary Jane?*" repeated a nearer tongue or two; "that's one o' Broadby and Co's. ships—she's just come into port from the West Indies. What could *they* know, of course!"

The graceful St. Amand returned to the supercilious Cornet's side, took his arm again, and blandly yielded to the fretful movement he made homeward. "After all," assented the former, "'tis but some vessel that has been missing, and has presented itself! The 'grand tour,' you said, my dear Cobham? So you made it—*you*, too, have travelled?"

" O, for that part, not much—to tell the truth, we broke down in it," the young dragoon confessed, "at some town in the Low Countries—never precisely knew the name of it. Why, we wanted change, see you—and the farther we went, by St. Paul, sir! for all we could tell, the less of that! The very same confounded things meeting you—the very same houses, in fact, with shops, churches, and so forth—sky and everything else to match. No such great difference in the people, either, or the language; this Bristol rabble, now, confound them! they may be talking Dutch at present, for all I understand. As usual, too, the fellows' faces were all—a—a—all eyes and nose, by Jove!"

"All travellers, in the end, my dear Cobham," was the composed rejoinder, as if there were nothing whatever absurd in the Cornet's disappointment, "must feel the truth which you so rapidly perceived. You and your friends but anticipated the result, so obvious on the ruins of Carthage, or the Attic shores; in Switzerland, where you would only have seen the Alps; in Italy, mere pictures! Among the Turks, the Chinese, the Arabs, or negroes, you would have despaired all the more hopelessly; you were right in not proceeding; you have brought back at least something of the national expectation. We want change, as you remark. Well, to observe the popular feeling here—the impression, almost amounting to a prophetic instinct—we have but to look round us. Could you not imagine them seeking its import from the sky yonder, like the older plebeians? Ah! see the flight of birds, too—how appropriate—the very cranes of the antique Ibycus; we may hear their pinions creak!"

The Cornet looked up also, in obvious wonder. "Ha, ha!—*cranes*, my good fellow!" he broke out, with a very English horse-laugh, "they're only wild geese cackling away high over the smoke. We're not troubled much in this country, I fancy, with cranes. The deuce is in it, though, they fly right inland—a bad sign of the weather. In spite of the fine sky, it looks rainy; and to-morrow, by George! I've a shooting party to Clevedon Manor!"

St. Amand, slightly biting his steady lip, had for the instant turned on his military friend a glance, in which some little increase of conside-ration seemed discernible. "Yes, you may post-pone it, *mon ami*," agreed he, with suavity all the completer for being now rid of any apparent disposi-tion to smile. "It will rain, and heavily, too. Too many voyages have been forced on me, not to show *that*—passages by sea, I mean, for of course they have merely been such. Probably, these good folks are so interested in this event, simply as being citizens of a great harbour, the partisans of trade and of insurance, alike with those of the pilots, the wreckers, perhaps even of the anxious spouses of the mariners."

This time, indeed, the pointed remark was accompanied by a sneer, just such as to make it clear enough to the Cornet, who relished it with full aristocratic superiority. "Good—very good, Monsieur de St. Amand; upon my honour—good! Ha! ha!—exceedingly likely! A mean *canaille* of traders, with their bourgeois ideas. Bristol is not the least to my taste, I can assure you, Count.

We had not been quartered here three months, till, upon my honour—— "

"Excuse me, but there seems some danger of this mob," interrupted his companion, pressing his arm and speaking low. "They are excited—riotous. They scowl at us ominously! This way—let us avoid them, *mon cher* Cobham."

It seemed too late, however; the very uniform of Cobham did not appear to deter a violent rush from every side of the two gentlemen, with a cry even infuriated by the glittering intentness of De St. Amand's glance, and the almost Spanish beauty of his pale olive features.

"Foreigneers in disguise! Ay, spies from the old King of France!" it was fiercely shouted. "More by token, it's French—they spoke French!"

At a volley of indignant oaths from the Cornet, nevertheless, in most unquestionable vernacular, and at the tranquil front of his companion, the tumult bade fair to turn elsewhere. "If we were so," said the latter, calmly, without an accent to throw doubt on his protest, "we should certainly have avoided the French language, I think. To-night above all. To-night, my good friends, it seems there are too many things in the wind, to allow of such freedoms."

A man thrust forth his rude face, and stared hard at St. Amand: "Ay—but what's the drift of it, I say, master? What's the main news, loike?" said he, earnestly.

St. Amand shook his head. He " knew nothing, and had but come with his friend to hear. They would, doubtless, however, be all willing to drink the health of His Majesty, with confusion to his enemies, wherever found." And with a very liberal gratuity from his ready purse, to which the Cornet graciously added, the crowd moved off hurrahing.

Even as they traversed the open street again, St. Amand did not need to recommend an adherence to the safer idiom. " You see them, Count!" resumed the young officer, fuming still; " a curst shopkeeping, trading, bartering set! No matter—if the regiment do not shift soon, *I* shall. Have had thoughts of selling out, indeed; and in a month or two, who knows, we may meet in Paris. *You* can't stay long about this deuced provincial place ?"

" It is even possible," was the placid reply. " Were Paris still always easy to reach from England—yet Bristol may at any rate detain me a little. Even here, however commercial the tone, I should imagine there are opportunities——But you, probably, Mr. Cobham, know nothing at all of the society ?"

" Faith no, thank heaven !—nothing whatever. Except for my aunt, Lady Die Fanshawe—who introduced us together—why, I never should have set foot in the town at all beyond the Hotwells.

Lady Die is somewhat eccentric, you may notice—
gives rather oddish evening receptions, French
style, intellectual equality, and that. Found 'em,
I must say, promiscuous. Once did meet there,
certainly, with what I understood to be an heiress,
and—and—so went back again a time or two.'
Here the Cornet suddenly flushed up to the hair-
powder, adjusted his lace cravat and cuffs, and, on
the whole, swerved from the topic by looking up
at street windows. "A—a—well—yes, I believe,
in some way connected with foreign trade; but
daughter of a really most extensive merchant—one
of our merchant princes, they call it hereabouts,
hang 'em!"

"Your antipathy to commerce," laughed the
other, gaily, "is excessive! Was the lady, then,
a beauty, as well as an heiress?" His light tone
did not quite agree with the expression of his fine
dark eye, flashing aside for a moment, then readily
wandering off with the Cornet's.

"So 'twas thought; she was rather the rage
about the Wells," admitted Cobham; "is still, I
hear. Confound it, too, as proud along with
the thing as if she'd been an only child! Here
was Lady Die making a pet of her, of course—
does so to this moment—quite a *protégée* of hers;
and rather awkward for me, you know, if I kept
up a habit of visiting there. Odd if my aunt has
not talked to you of the girl already, in fact,

Count. You are pretty sure to meet her, by
Jupiter! so 'tis as well to warn you."

Again the travelled visitor was amused. "Though
I do not come to this Bristol of yours to be
charmed by the Syrens," smiled he, "you excite
an interest very difficult to repress. Yet how,
pray, is the fair one so peculiarly dangerous?
Lovely, rich, accomplished, surely; can the mere
source of her wealth, my dear Mr. Cobham——"

"Pooh! certainly—not that at all, faith," the
latter hastily broke in. "No; you take me up
wrong, St. Amand. The truth was, I had taken
care to make some few particular inquiries as to
the old gentleman—the father. Found all correct
enough about their wealth, you perceive; though,
at the commencement of these paltry squabbles
with the colonies, they *did* seem to have been a
little shaken. Being in the large foreign trade,
as the phrase goes, why, the merest shadow of a
war is apt to play the devil with such houses as
Broadby and Co."

"True, true; I can imagine it," said his
companion. "But take care—Broadby and Company? Yes, I know something of this very
house. They are highly respectable, are they
not—substantial, at least, *now*?"

"Oh, they've got better established than ever,
I find. Not only so, by G——! but old Spencer
has become sole partner," pursued Cobham, with

singular emphasis. "A man known to make, at times, something like a fortune in a day, look ye, by a stroke or two of his pen; rather of good family, too, and, by-the-by, travelled like yourself, Count."

"I am already invited to dine at Mr. Spencer's, Mr. Cobham," remarked the young Comte, pointedly; "and that no later than to-morrow evening. A man of position, highly agreeable, with whom I promise myself, at least, some—yes, some pleasant intercourse. I scarce comprehend your allusions, *mon ami*. Mr. Spencer, it seems, then, is the father of this attractive young lady. Can any doubt attach to the prospects of any daughter of his? He is, as I think you said, now the only representative of the firm designated Broadby and Co., in whose employment he once resided abroad?"

"Yes, yes—nothing clearer, good heavens!" returned the annoyed Cornet. "Everybody knows *that;* everybody told me so in the kindest way imaginable. Old Broadby—a vulgar old money-grubber he was—never in his life out of Bristol, they say, though noway scrupulous as to the African slave-trade, I believe,—*he* retired a long time ago, and Spencer bought out his relations afterwards—a niece, or daughter or something, I can't say which."

"It is delicate, for any purpose, *mon cher* Cornet,"

observed his graceful friend, with some seriousness, " nay, it borders on danger, to make such inquiries in this country. Even *I* had my reasons, I own, for desiring an introduction to this well-known house—and I found, amongst people at all connected with trade themselves, that their caution was difficult to break through, when the most natural questions were put. The mere popular understanding, or fashionable report, is a surer clue—if one but possesses any key to the labyrinth itself. I am glad that our mutual discoveries, yours and mine, agree so nearly. This old Broadby, of whom you spoke, is dead, however—it was an only daughter of his, that married an obscure local manufacturer, a Methodist—another of these plodding residents of the place, who afford such a contrast to Mr. Spencer. But this mystery regarding *him*, then—which has so interfered with your sentiments of admiration for the daughter—which has so defeated your hopes, if I understand you : I trust it can be explained. For my own satisfaction, M. Cobham, may I ask in a general way its—nature ? "

" Oh—well—I thought I had already. Nothing of any consequence after all," said Cobham, still wincing, " when one's not a younger son, look !—damnably in debt besides; and the regiment, I should say, the most expensive in the whole service ! Never for a moment suspected it, upon my honour, till I had gone so far—why, there's no less

than four more of a family, none of 'em visible at
the time—eldest brother at Oxford, younger in the
navy, next sister a great deal in the country somewhere, then another girl not come out yet—all, as
it were, by Jove, hidden away! Egad, an *heiress*,
forsooth!—trade must be good with a witness for
that! As to Spencer's own age, I hear now he has
not turned fifty—married rather young, they say
—may live a good score of years yet!"

The vehement feeling of this speech really precluded aught like mirth in a courteous listener,
such as, beyond all doubt, it addressed. Indeed, it
drew a response of no unconsiderate kind, however
little heeded by Cobham at his striding pace up
street, which seemed to show a deeper sentiment
than he had allowed.

"True—true. This struck me in him," almost
soliloquised his thoughtful companion. "But yet
with that phlegmatic temperament often found in
Britain, after the passions are spent—one of those
blonde complexions that so composedly, so respect-
ably, hide the traces of the past. So pleasant an
English countenance is his, I would have said, my
dear Cobham, in spite of the secret cares of—of the
commerce you thus despise. Apparently, perhaps,
no more than middle-aged, but in fact much past
it, I think—yes, he is *above* fifty—above it by at
least five years, granting so early a return home,
here. Ah! conceive that events may ere long
occur to—to satisfy your views?"

As the Cornet's impetuosity slackened, however, he said with extreme scorn, "Positively the people's affairs have not now the slightest interest for me—none whatever, Count—none, sir."

"My own interest," apologised St. Amand, re-taking the offered arm, " purely regards business. I do not feel your native prejudices against commerce, Mr. Cobham—extensive commerce, that is. Hence, nevertheless, the degree of caution I have admitted. *I*, at all events," added he, more lightly, " shall be in no danger from the temptation to supplant a friend, in the good graces of the daughter. Bah! forget her in Paris, *mon cher*—a mere creature of the mode, doubtless, which you will find already obsolete there. For me, I have not broken away with such an effort from its last charming caprices, from its finished arts which now imitate nature so exquisitely—to fear being moved aside by some awkward copy of Versailles under Louis Quinze !"

"Gad, 'tis as well it don't signify to *me* why you cultivate their acquaintance," said the young man. " You'd have been an unpleasant rival, to say the least of it. As to Paris, though, I fancy you can still play a little in the style that suits you, you know, without being sent to Coventry by the big-wigs ? 'Tis the Court, at Windsor and St. James's, they say, gets stiffer every season against aught like betting or high game—nothing but oratorios and musical festivals, it seems, if we feel

dull at whist, hang it!—or, at the most, like last-
night, a little loo or speculation, with the ladies for
partners."

"Afterwards, however, at your club," rejoined
the Comte, gaily, "it appears to me that some of
your friends revenged themselves a little on both
of us! Myself—except for courtesy—I do not
game. Besides, I should have lost less—perhaps
have gained—had I not entangled myself with a
—yes, excuse me, a partner!"

"I never had luck at cards, d—— 'em!" said
Cobham. "Then, among the rest, we had two of the
very coolest hands round the Hotwells to deal with,
the old parson of Clifton and Lord Eppingbury—as
keen a young rake-helly sprig I remember *him* when
he was Lord Bobby Fortescue, as ever fought his
cock in a tavern pit—always did play best drunk.
But honourable enough, by G——! never had a
breath against *that*—and few men would have liked
even so much as to look it, either, of Lord Robert."
The tranquil meaning of De St. Amand's look, at
least, spoke doubly to this fact; had one inclined to
question it, throughout all his elastic composure
there was nerve probably more than equal to any
task. "No," pursued the Cornet, guiding their final
extrication upward from the noisier streets, "give
me my risk on a horse I know, or even take means
to hear of—*there* I feel at home. I'm told they've
been imitating us in that department, of late, at
Paris; everything English quite the rage, in fact;

and—well—of course there must be room for a
little skill, with that rich fool the Comte de Char-
tres, son of the King's uncle, the Duc d'Orléans,
backing horseflesh!   I dare say, St. Amand,
you'd win your money with as good a grace as you
lose it; but still—why, one needs something to
rouse one now-a-days—I might help even *you*
to a thing or two in Paris? Suppose you try it
too?"

"Ah—I may still be in time to meet you," he
said, kindly enough.   "You and your polite family,
Cobham, have paid me attentions for which I am
grateful—I should have pleasure in the re-union.
Paris is always pleasant; even the cosmopolite, as
I may be allowed to call myself, is tempted there
to feel as a native of such a place—it is rather,
indeed, the miniature of the world he claims.   Yet
I fear I could not repay your civilities there—some
of my French friends, certainly, partook of the
Anglomania you describe, but had resigned it ere
I left them. The great American philosopher,
Franklin, was becoming their enthusiasm, I believe.
Before his return for the colonies he had thrown
horse-racing into the shade—all Paris thronged
towards the saloons where the simple garb and
sturdy frame were visible, eclipsing his more diplomatic colleague, M. Silas Deane, and even the
brilliancy of the heroic Chevalier Jones, who sometimes left his ships to accompany them."

"What! the rebel emissaries — the renegade Scotch pirate, you mean, Count!" Cornet Cobham for the first time turned a sharp look at his new friend, but saw it had been ironically meant.

"Of course the two last are ridiculous," was the reply. "The *first* will be elevated to the Pantheon of futurity, along with the immortal Voltaire, with Montesquieu and his fellows, not to forget your own Locke, Hume, and Smith—when *we* have ceased to think. You forget, I cannot entertain your national prejudices on either side. I am more Spanish, in reality, than French or English; and indifferent, even, to these merely honorary titles you give me — which her ladyship, your aunt, was pleased to——"

"Heavens! And the scoundrels were in fashion, then!" repeated Cobham, breathlessly. "Popular! Gad, this was suspected, too. So, for all their smooth pretences and professions of late, they *may* have declared war! By the way, yonder goes the government telegraph again, at top of the hill —let's know what *they've* actually to say about it, from the harbour or perhaps by news from Town! London post-time is past—should not wonder if all this pother here, Count, really has a cause?"

"Surely. Yet France has long risen above the folly we imagine, Cobham; no, it is but some new shape of our own mad destiny—of that insular

British pride, I mean, which works its own fate. Hear them!—those decorous citizens, those prudent mothers and withered spinsters, those very girls—like yourself, yes, they *wish* for war. Might one not think they and you were indignant at the *peace*, as you arrogantly seem to think it, which I cannot believe Europe will rashly break between this infatuated Island and the rising New World."

The travelled young stranger undoubtedly had formed his theories of civilisation and of political history; at the irresistible excitement that grew and met them again through the populous capital of the west, even he was moved. A riotous mob tossed along Castle-street, towards the thick of the darkened city, where the lamps were already lighting over the subsiding concourse of trade, of labour, or of pleasure; it was wild with the cries, so apt in Bristol, against Catholic and dissenter, against the Whig Opposition of Lord Chatham, against secret agents of Lord Mayor Wilkes or the Americans. Midway, the drum of the recruiting party only ceased to beat while the sergeant bawled his stentorian tidings, more than ever favourable to his purpose: "His Majesty's ambassador just left France, my lads—great news by G——! War, war!—yes, your honour," to the young cavalry officer, whom he now saluted, "so we do hear, sir, in by to-night's post. Certainly, captain, there's more known at the barracks—ship-news, I b'lieve, by signal-post out o' harbour. Sent off by courier for town, this hour past—not likely, sir, they'd have told me. No matter, my lads, war—war!" Upwards, through narrow Mary-le-Port-street, where the quaint high houses overhung to each other, the eager Cornet still hurried his graver friend, whose mood, at least, betrayed a deep annoyance. "Hush, at all events—pray, do not persist in calling me Count!" said he, forcing a little of the previous gaiety. "Recollect the spies, my good friend. De St. Amand, I told you, is but a title of my mother's family, which her recent death in France led me to expect with some degree of certainty. But now—in this case, if one must choose—the truth is, I prefer my own name, Etherege. Etienne Etherege, simply—if you will so oblige me?"

"Certainly — oh certainly," agreed Cobham, raised to his highest spirits at the news astir. "You must join *us*, my dear Etherege."

"For the time," answered he, less gloomily, "fate may almost compel it. Even afterwards, there are possible circumstances—I had almost forgotten them—which——Do you happen to know any officers, here, of your naval service?"

"Well, very few; two or three, or so," allowed the Cornet. "Not the most polished men in the world, but social enough—of good family, you see; and hereabouts, there's a sort of favour for that branch—but you'll be disappointed in 'em. Besides, they join very early in life. Yes; I know one or two."

"Lieutenant Herbert, perhaps? a relative of my own—of Herbert Court, in the adjoining shire. *Commander* Herbert, I believe I should now have said."

But Cobham had not had that honour; only knew the gentleman by report : an officer of merit, he believed, and sure to be soon well employed— by the way, if he mistook not, nephew to old Sir Ralph of Kingswood, who very likely had influence in high quarters. It struck the Cornet with interest then, that "in this case he himself, De St. Amand—Mr. Etherege, that was to say, must be related to the wealthy old baronet too."

"It was so; but not so nearly." The shadows of the steep-built street, and of the early twilight, were on both of them, as they slowly rose above the confusion, toward airier suburbs; more shadowy yet, however, appeared the pressure of unexpected events, or new considerations, on the brows of St. Amand's—or Etherege's—still youthful visage. The spreading intelligence had anticipated their movement in search of it; it was to be gathered now on either side, in this soberer quarter, with a business-like detail, as well as with a settled steadiness, next to demonstration. It was not through the post "from Town," that the main fact had been

made known, though people thronged to hear how
it agreed with the public news, read aloud in some
public tavern, where the *London Gazette* or *Intel-
ligencer* disclosed their scrimped pages on high; it
was brought by the Bristol vessel just come in,
whose name was told, and whose owners were
known. Had not the swift *Mary Jane* got before
her convoy, and been chased and fired at by a pri-
vateer, under rebel colours, but plainly French built?
nay, escaping, had she not spoken, off the very
coast of France, with a smuggling lugger—whose
merry crew had owned the truth, and let out more?
The British ambassador had not left, certainly—no
—they were still always the politer at the Tuileries,
the more he needed to leave. They had not declared war yet—no—but in every French port they
were getting ready, and in every French town; and
Mounseer die Lafayette had gone off to help the
Boston rebels with a shipful of French nobles; and
the Bloody Scotchman ran into French harbours
when pursued; and the truth would hide so little
longer, that they even laughed at it now! Lord
North had spoken in Parliament to that effect—as
the papers showed.

"Damnation!" swore Cornet Cobham, stamp-
ing on the causeway, at the last corner into the
Bath Road. "No wonder the people talk! It
can't be borne longer, by G——! I must hurry to
quarters, though—a lively mess-table we shall have

of it.   But join us, I say, Etherege—yes, as I said,
join us."   The young Cornet's energy gave expression to his common-place features, so supported by
his stature, and sportsman-like robustness, that
Etherege replied with a half-wondering look.
"Thanks; but my dress—it rains, too. No; I
have letters to look for, at my inn ; and may write
others.   My inn, the *New Cannynges Arms*, lies
the other way."

"I meant the regiment," explained Cobham,
somewhat awkwardly—" Ligonier's Light Horse—
the 11th Dragoons.   They said, cavalry couldn't act
in the colonies, you know. Why, I never exactly
understood—but I dare say Cornwallis and Bur-
goyne will soon give a good account of *them;* and
our business will very likely lie in the Low Countries
again.   'Twould be odd, some fine morning,
wouldn't it? to come upon that dull Dutch place
I told you of, where I broke off the tour.   We may
even see Paris together, yet, in a very different
style.   Yes; join us, Etherege.   Commissions will
soon be hard to get; but I'm sure my grandfather,
the old earl, would have pleasure——"

"You flatter me indeed," was the equally warm
reply, though with a decided gesture in the ne-
gative.   "Impossible, Cobham. I have not affected
to hide the contempt for either form of that bigotry,
that popular superstition, which must now be mad-

dening both nations. The sentiment is, in fact, shared by your accomplished aunt, Lady Fanshawe, in common with all the cultivated wit of this age and the last; and you yourself evidently attribute qualities to me on that ground, beyond my merits. I have doubtless travelled more than you; the difference of our age, is, perhaps, greater than it seems, for the blood first warmed under the tropic, runs faster; and were I to say, I have still my creed which I believe in—but your profession, your early associations—no—in the case of war, we have but to differ."

"Faith, yes," said the young officer, more drily. "I have heard of the Quakers doing so; the Friendly Society they're called, or something. If you mean that, why——"

"I can only mean the indifference of a guest among both," said the other, quietly. "There are, indeed, points of honour which may have required this fashionable toy," he just touched the dress-sword he of course wore, "where these points are more fantastic than in England. But *here*—even here, my friend, where my errand might demand the same personal resort—there is at least Justice, the boasted Law of Britain, which I should prefer to claim." The rising passion of his manner still detained the Cornet. "Your war cannot disturb *that*, I trust," persisted Etherege, looking round, his voice husky with its emphasis. "Surely this vulgar panic or fury will not be allowed to affect the due satisfaction on the part of a foreigner."

"No—no—never," answered Cobham, decidedly. "French, or not, no difference whatever on that score; if my services as a friend can help you, you know, command 'em at a moment's warning."

"It is not for myself, but for one who—could not accompany me yet," said Etherege, calmly, with the greater quiet of the suburban place. "A noble Spaniard, whose honour must prescribe the means. Again thanks, Mr. Cobham—but *he* will follow me. Time and caution are requisite—enough of blood, it may be. The sentiment of duty is so little vindictive as to be satisfied, where there are laws that profess to be inflexible." He held out his hand to separate.

"Well, the rain will spoil my shooting-party," concluded Cobham, laughing as they parted. "No matter; full news all to-morrow in the Hotwells pump-room. I forgot—you're to dine t'other way, where you can judge—ha!—well—if the little Spencer be one to swoon at news of war!"

"A marble fair one? Ah!" smiled Etherege, very cordially. "I have seen such—no attractive pastime while awaiting letters from abroad. With war at hand, too, even the fascination of commerce may fail to detain me here. *Au revoir*, however."

He drew his cloak round him, and turned in his

own direction. At that height the wind was troublesome, though sunset under the clouds came flaring far again, from seaward over the deep-banked winding of the Avon : the noise below was settling down, while the street-lamps spread, patrols of watchmen mustered, and pickets of foot-soldiers from the barracks cleared the way, as they gathered drunken comrades home ; not without a warning hint or two of press-gangs from the harbour, who would use no ceremony, if needed. It seemed safe enough now to seek a nearer and more sheltered route to the *New Cannynges Arms* as Etherege did ; his eye even pondered thoughtfully the deep irregular quaintness of the street he took, catching along from the sky a glassy brightness on one side, in brave old Elizabethan fronts that seemed all casement. A stranger could not but note, indeed, how slight the hold taken by passing tumult upon its thriving order, which this way and that way branched to yet busier vistas. From its under-browed shops and booths and stalls, where peri-wigged burghers groped back to light their goods for a while—into chequered tavern doors, whose broad bar-windows glowed and grew jovial ; from the clusters of old gossips stooping their cocked beavers together at each corner, under projecting stories—to the outer stairways, up which lagging damsels hastened with market-basket or water-pitcher—all was but the stir of a coarse civic life, returning to

its channels. Satisfaction at the change might
have been seen in the survey of Etherege; nay,
here and there his vivid face would turn the current of discourse above, between some pair of bare-
armed, close-capped crones, exchanging news from
opposite garrets, or amongst the frilled heads of
matrons set together at a balconied lattice.   An
elevated interest, not unmixed at times with invo-
luntary pity, or sudden ingenuous wonder, marked
his look to shrewder citizens, with one or two of
whom he dropped a courteous word as he asked his
way; and most of all, a flattering whisper rose upon
his steps, from more than one group which his passage drew to sight: groups with true Bristol beauty
in them ; tight young hoydens of rich Somersetshire,
bright-eyed, cherry-cheeked, under their red hoods;
or slim blue eyed Gloucestershire maids, peeping
from behind their sober mothers, with looped un-
powdered hair fringed round their foreheads in little
tags, and tied with a gay bit of ribbon behind the ears,
though kerchiefs of demurest lavender might fold
them from the budded bosom to the dimpled chin.
For Wesleyan evening meetings had strongly influenced the middle classes of Bristol then, and hymn-
books were in hand, to take to the obscure chapel
up some dingy alley, as soon as business should be
well over; humbler people already flocking thither.
Traits so novel to the most practised traveller
were far from being lost on the young stranger from
abroad; his silent thoughts were even vented for

a moment, as if the Cornet were still by, when a
last red reflection fell along the windy sky, and
glanced down to the slanted shade, catching up
these warmer tints of fresh young faces.

"I had not dreamt of *this* in England!" he exclaimed, turning to gaze again. "What bloom!
what nature! Ah—*amigo mio,* Señor Cobham—
if she had chanced to be of the stamp of some of
these—like that little white rosebud, there, who
can blush so, and turn away. *Then,* perhaps, even
Paris——"

The blushing girl did not court the gaze again,
though, as she passed with the rest: the nearest of
the grave-eyed burghers dropped their talk to stare
at the animated speaker, till he was gone. As to
the words so abruptly uttered, they were in Spanish,
and so left no meaning behind.

The last light faded off Bristol's topmost roofs,
leaving their cold-blue slates and dull-red tiles to
glisten out bleakly with the shower; the very flocks
of many-hued pigeons were done with buffeting to
their shelter at home there: it was shadowy below,
the wet thoroughfares into which Etherege hurried
were emptying but too quickly, and shimmered
drearily with reflections of the swinging oil-lamps
that guided his course. He might have been at a
loss for it soon, again coming, as it seemed, upon
signs of the harbour he had left in company with
Cobham: it was but that central quarter, indeed,
where the Froom opens canal-like to the main

stream, amidst piles of warehouses and backs of streets in the town; crossed midway by a jointed swing-bridge, now left fast, over which the distant tower of a known church shot up. The cloudy moon was rising from behind it, as he quickened his steps that way; airily though the dusk stirred there, and promised to clear riverward, he did not care to see how the wet spars of the nearest ships began to gleam, how the sails hung dark and dripping, with a rustle of mooring-ropes in their rings of iron, as they rose tightened from the water, where the welter and groan of docks blew by. Something there was in these things, rather, to rouse a solitary shiver in him, making him clutch his dress-sword, erect though he trod past, and agile; or the cause might lie in that wafted aroma from tropical cargoes, mingling with ruder scents at hand—if not at the long broken yell of some belated crew still hauling in from sea, or some drunken bargeman's half-wakened oath from under the quay; for on Etherege's finger, in the simple guard to a plain mourning-ring he wore, there glistened a half-cut diamond of the largest and rarest sort. Once across, he looked up relieved, to a lamp-lit corner with a name on it, but started all the more at a very natural recognition—"Froom-lane," a place from which he needed no guidance, having sought it before, and passed it since. Even as he turned straight up, another

light came out from the doors of Broadby and Co.'s
counting-house, with guides enough if he had so
required.

An old clerk was leaving the premises for the
night, followed by a porter with keys and a lantern,
who locked the doors while the other waited; near
them stood a young lad in a rough boat-coat,
striking his drenched cap against the wall as he
talked loudly to the clerk. "Well, at any rate,"
he briskly said, "we've got her safe outside the
dock-gates for to-morrow morning. So there's no
doubt now, Mr. Hutton, it was a Frenchman that
gave chase and fired at her—the men told no
lie, either, about the French being bent on war—
we're going to take the start, it seems, and declare it! Does my father know the grand news,
then?"

"Certainly, Master Henry," said the clerk;
"no one more required so to do. As in duty
bound, we sent word up to Beech Grove direct—
but did not see needful to come down in person, sir,
it's true—though a serious matter it is surely. Your
worthy papa will consider so this night, I do fear."
The clerk took the keys, respectfully raised his
high-brimmed beaver, wished good-night, and retired. His young master hastened to the side of the
timber-creek close by, where it proved that a boat
was dipping by the small wharf, with a negro in it,
who sleepily held on.

"Hurrah! here, Diamond, my boy!" the youth shouted. "All's true, and more. More war to be declared. The French have gone and joined Captain Dodge!"

The black man's eyes opened wide indeed, rolling their white wildly around; while his teeth, filed sharp in front, enhanced the savage effect as he leapt at a bound upon the wharf. "Oh! Great Fetish! Cap'n Dosh!" he almost howled, making violent motions of a boat-hook, whether warlike or rather friendly it was hard to tell. "Iss, mas'r Arreeo! Oo—oorr—oorray! But he berry great man, Cap'n Dosh." The boat meanwhile, now let heave away and now pulled back, made, in the dusk, equally strange movements and curvettings.

"Make fast the boat, Dick," said the boy, peremptorily, "and come up and dance the great wardance for the Skipper. Ten to one but you and I will have the odds of him somehow yet, in blue water —a great man, indeed! Wait till you know Commander Herbert—he'll get his frigate now, certain. I bet he takes it, though all the Papist baronets in the world left their money to that cousin of his, that Count! Most likely, from what I hear, an infidel after all—but of course, Diamond, you don't understand me. Don't stare! make fast the boat, I say, and you'll be a topman yet in Captain Herbert's new frigate."

A surprised exclamation broke from the puzzled

Etherege, as he left a pair of chuckling dockmen who had looked on with him, and passed, adding a last question about the way into Brandon-street. "Carramba!" he had ejaculated, in the fluent Spanish which seemed most natural to him, "this is surely *fate*—it is destiny!"

"Who was *that?*" the boy called out, not recognising the cloaked figure, as he himself had probably recalled no personal knowledge on the gentleman's part. "Some voice I've heard before—a Frenchman?"

"Not like it, young master," said the dockmen. "Anyhow, axed wos that 'ere the way to Brandon-street pretty manfullish.—Dutch, as it stroikes *I*," added one.

"Espagnole, Señor Enrico," grinned black Diamond, who had been krooman to Spanish slaves before the unscrupulous American shipmaster seized and kept him.

"Ah, you heard, did you, Dick?" said Harry. "You take better to these lingos, too, somehow. What did he say, then, in plain English?—for it's a voice I somehow didn't like."

Evidently, translation cost the Krooman no little effort, but by dint of slowly grinding his hard seaman's hat about his head, he seemed to circle round upon some synonymous words. "O—he say, ''Dis *fetish*,'" was the rather dark disclosure. "''Dis be Obi for true,' he say. You no savvey *dat*, mass'r

Arrie? Ho! ho! ho! Obi—iss, sar—de berry t'ing—Obi." And Dick Diamond, though falling in behind to his usual station as they walked homeward, showed himself a little disposed to return the compassionate glance of Master Spencer. The Hottentots, peevishly mentioned by that young gentleman, were a distinct tribe of whom Diamond scorned to hear; but he understood well that no mere difference of tongues could strip the mysterious spell from Obi.

CHAPTER VII.

MR. ETHEREGE AT BEECH GROVE.

DESPITE these serious public changes, the appointed dinner-party came off at the merchant's retired suburban residence, with all that due air of unalterable arrangement and of entire domestic relaxation from business cares, which became his conspicuous standing in the city. Complete in the somewhat elaborate self-composure he derived from hereditary good-breeding, as well as from education and travel seldom brought to commercial use in his day, he possessed at home the most suitable of supports, in the placid natural ease of Mrs. Spencer. Beside her, unless the contrast struck at first on a too refining eye, he even showed to advantage; tending to sink the slight prominence of some traits, and to blend others in that manner attributable to long intercourse in the closest bonds.

Soft, fair, full, not saying much nor seeming to
know more, but with a ready dimpling to smile out
her courtesies, she had the undefinable air of what
was then called " quality"—the county air, her
Somersetshire friends were apt to say—the " air
noble," it might almost have appeared to a guest
like him for whom Mr. Spencer had really brought
about the social occasion. Of this latter fact, and of
any special importance in Mr. Etherege beyond
what was shown—beyond that of some who met him
there—she obviously knew little and guessed less.
He was indeed younger than she had expected,
perhaps handsomer, certainly more agreeable by
far; he was not, after all, exactly a foreigner, but
a native of the West India Islands, where British
interests and British power were next thing to
supreme, according to her vague conception—
neither did his fine dark eye and pale olive complexion show the least trace of that blood, so very
unpleasant even to think of—the truth being, that
any such idea had been quite exploded by Harry's
care to report the office rumours touching " the
Count's" English kinship. Certain stubborn English prejudices Mrs. Spencer had doubtless enter-
tained till the last, against all counts or barons
whatsoever, the more particularly if young, handsome, and bringing introductions to British merchants of known means, who had daughters at
home; not all her husband's knowledge of the

world and his characteristic judgment in such
matters, even taken with the very certainty of the
stranger's own wealth and possible prospects, could
prevent her availing herself of the fact that he sat
by her in the place of chief honour, to use her
cautious woman's instinct on the point. Motherly
considerations sharpened the feeling, when she
looked from Jane's acknowledged beauty—set off
that evening in the height of the mode, though
with no lack of taste in hiding unusual care—to
"that *woman*, Lady Diana Fanshawe!" (invited,
certainly, not through any wish of Mrs. Spencer's)
with her crotchet of what she chose to style the
severe classic costume, and her unaccountable rage
to have all sorts of foreigners in her train, and
that airy patchwork talk of hers, all sprinkled
through with Italian and French, which she had a
high-bred way of addressing to select persons alone.
But though her ladyship did not scruple at times
to direct her conversation from some distance to
Mr. Etherege, as if the wit of a remark lay between
them—for Jane on the opposite side to show her
smiling comprehension—and to add, perhaps, a
thought on her own part [which could be quick
enough when she so chose]—still there was a quietness about the manner of the young traveller, a
perfect openness in his notice of Jane's undeniable
attractions, and on the whole an equal readiness to

turn to any other lady, which combined with minor traits to set Mrs. Spencer's mind at rest.

To herself his behaviour was pointed by a scrupulous observance of the attentions due in that place at table; at first so very formally, it might have been, as, without other conversation, to avoid courting any nearer acquaintance; but when she gave up her doubts and won him on to speak with her, there soon succeeded a graver and more genuine considerateness, almost kindly in its response to her own. From the sombre richness of the dress-suit he wore, and the mourning-ring on his hand—secured by the only thing like ornament that marked him, a plain gold guard with its one priceless gem—and still more, as it struck her, from this very gravity underneath his politest smiles, giving occasional gloom to the brilliant eye —it was evident that Mr. Etherege had suffered a family loss not long ago. There was hair in the ring, grey hair—the silky hair of a woman, it had once been; his mother's probably. She did not advert to any such bereavement, nor did he; but of the name Etherege, it was easy to say, gently, that she thought she had heard of it in England somewhere, as being thorough English, and perhaps connected with his own.

"I was not aware of it, madam," he said, no less gently, but briefly; "the resemblance must be accidental, however—on *that* side I have no connexion with this country, except——" at that there seemed to rise a harsh note in his voice, which might have drawn general notice as he stopped abruptly, had there not been a sufficient flow of talk round the busy table before his hostess ventured on the question. She felt from the sudden blenching of his colourless cheek, that it was not embarrassment but a painful emotion; and hastened to pass it off with excuses on her own part. "Nay, it was most natural," he returned, bending acknowledgment to the entire simplicity of her words, and more than ever softening his tone; "for the circumstances must now strip me altogether of any other title, unless—perhaps—yes, Mrs. Spencer, this may not only be my first enjoyment of such a pleasure, but the last also—as I may soon return to France. To do that *now*, one must lose no time, and I have letters so late as last night, pressing me to use the brief opportunity."

"So soon?" she merely asked; for it was quite conceivable how a sudden outbreak of hostilities might have changed his position, rendering it delicate indeed for a stranger situated as he was. "But of course," continued she, "being so bitter against us there, they will want every one to help —they will spare nothing to make enemies to us." Mrs. Spencer was grave in her turn, too, as well as a little pale; but checked herself to add smilingly, what was at once the finest com-

pliment, and most irresistible appeal, from a lady's
lips. "However, my lord, if *you* must be num-
bered among them, I hope it will only be in the
most general sense : you are not asked, I do
trust, to join their army or navy. 'Tis true the
French have not behaved with so gallant a spirit
just now, nor so honourably, but that they may
be glad to enlist these qualities to their help,
wherever free for it. Happily, as yet, *we* have
no particular reason to—to dread the thought;
all are here at home *now*, except our eldest son,
Goscroft, who is at Oxford. But I already suspect my youngest—a mere boy, who sits yonder—
of some wild design which he may find means
to gratify; and—and, in short——" Here there
rose to her face a little uneasy flutter and flush—
perhaps increased by the glimpse of Mr. Etherege's
profile, aquiline and firm, turned for the moment
to a footman's muttered inquiry whether he took
champagne. He had spoken of voyages in her
hearing, and of tropical hurricanes he had seen;
also of an escape in a Bermuda yacht from cor-
sairs he afterwards assisted to capture. Besides,
was he not said to be a cousin of Herbert, the
active young sea-officer, whom, however, she did
not now take the liberty of mentioning. "In short,
it would be the more distressing since we have seen
something of Count Etherege; it would cost *me*

some alarm," she even went so far as to add with
a subtile maternal boldness, " to think he left
England too soon to feel kindly of us—as aught
else than a friend, indeed."

Half conventional though the flattery was, she
had proved his face by no means the mere chiselled
marble it appeared: his low bow did not altogether hide a quick, candid glance of the dark
eye, while in the lowered tones of his answer there
was something almost musically deferential and
tender. "It is nothing but a mother's remembrance that draws me back there, madam. Little
as I had ever known of this feeling, still, perhaps,
when forced to decide, it is enough. Yes—we
shall only be friends there; I have no such offers,
no such ambitions or abilities, as you imply.
The resolution would be difficult indeed—believe
me—which should place any one among the very
few enemies whom Mrs. Spencer and her ingenuous
family could ever have cause to——"

"Thomas!" ordered his host, a little sharply, to
a servant; " carry that dish to Mr. Etherege. To
His Worship the Mayor, also." Mr. Spencer,
through all the general sound and dialogue which
seemed occasionally to engross his management,
had still a thoughtful eye for their guest from
abroad; whose place in a country so aroused to
anger, as well as so novel to a stranger, appeared

to claim peculiar consideration; whose growing cordiality, however, with the lady of the house, was satisfactory to observe.

"I declare I delight for once to think," it had been exclaimed by Lady Die Fanshawe, "of Paris being closed for a little. We poor people about the Hotwells will gain by it. They say Horace Walpole's gout must bring him here, instead of sending him to Ems; and as to your claims on the Versailles Court, my dear M. St. Amand——" Their host's side-directions had been more than once pointed towards such wilful solecisms as her ladyship here persisted in. She favoured him, indeed, with a slight glassy stare of the fashionable kind; but Mr. Spencer was above it. There had been an emphasis in his distinguished young visitor's preference for the plain patronymic, strongly marked at their first interview, which he was decided in supporting, even when the mayor had spoken of "his lordship," and the worthy banker who was present had addressed the young traveller as "Count." "True—true— thank ye, Mr. Spencer," resumed Lady Die; "I mean, *mon cher M. Etherege—à propos* of these affairs, you know, our good English folks care little for 'em; you cannot believe, surely, these silly quarrels between diplomats can signify? No true cosmopolite gives it a thought. We shall do our best here, I vow, this winter, to outshine the town

itself in keeping you quite *disennuyée!*" Mr.
Etherege made some polished response, but without
any decided sparkle of wit. He had gradually
been becoming that evening, as her ladyship whispered to Jane Spencer, more than ever *distrait*
and preoccupied in manner—nay, for *him*, pro-
digiously dull.

"This war, Mr. Spencer, sir," the wealthy
Mayor of Bristol was loudly saying from the
other side, " is most exceedingly unpleasant, to be
sure ; but it's what was to be looked for. Clears
the ground, sir—let us understand who's who, and
where we are—don't it? Some must go to the
wall ere it's done, no doubt ; some, on the contrary,
are a deal too solid to fear it. The country will
stand it, gentlemen, as she's stood it before!"

"Surely, most atrocious on the part of France,
however, Sir Timothy," remarked the milder
banker, head of their host's long-esteemed bank-
ing-house in town, who sat nearer to him. "We
had imagined far otherwise of King Louis XVI.
—always supposed a most amiable, liberal-minded,
intelligent sovereign."

"He'll repent it pretty soon ; he'll be made to
repent it as soon as we've time to turn round !"
hotly continued the old general, who had stirred
the imminent topic. "Our best rising officers seem
to be in India ; but since Wolfe fell in the arms
of glory at Quebec, I deny—I deny that a better

tactician than Lord Cornwallis ever stepped! Bring him home, say I—bring him home, sir! That dull militia-man—what's his name—Washingham—don't need a man of ability to oppose him; just as well beat, depend on't, or lost-to either, by an ordinary brigadier with some irregular local force to back him." The veteran general sat back exhausted, but confident of having spoken from experience; which was modestly corroborated by the only other authority there—an unfortunate exile from ruined Poland, of noble birth and military title, rather allowed than invited to come in the train of Lady Die.

"Infidelity," interposed the sonorous voice of the dignified rector of Emerton and Wrixworth (who was present at Miss Mary Spencer's side by the happy accident of a passing visit to town) —" infidelity having sapped the foundations of the faith in France—such as that faith was—her honour has proved worthless. Can we, then, wonder much, Mr. Spencer, at this foul league with rebellion?"

There was about Mr. Spencer's countenance and manner, as he sat conspicuous, a degree of calmness offering the strongest contrast to the excited tendency of his guests; which he rather laid himself out to soothe. He had once or twice cheeringly alluded to the deep foundations of British power, and to its wide extent, so incompre-

hensible by rivals—to the allowance which must
be made for the latter, too, on the score of old
spites and grudges that came up at sight of her
ceaseless prosperity, however pitiable these. He
had quoted his favourite Horace at least once:
in reference to the various wars in different
quarters of the globe at present carried on by
British arms, or threatening to multiply their
activity—in ancient India, where the " Company "
began to prevail over the great Mogul—in the New
World, where the very vastness of empire was
an encumbrance—now also from French jealousy,
perhaps soon from the envious Dutch, and from
well-known Spanish pique about Gibraltar—in respect of all this he inclined to a somewhat magnilo-
quent confidence in the future. Lady Die herself
was amused by the apt comparison to Roman
grandeur, when he reminded the still anxious
mayor most unanswerably of a circumstance in
classical history, greatly to the restoration of good
humour in the general, and to the rector's high
approval.

"It was affectation, you will say, Sir Timothy—
and I admit it," he said; "but still a grand
affectation, which the event justified. Hannibal
was already fated to ruin when he thundered
before the Roman gates from luxurious Capua;
Carthage was destined to share the doom of his
terrible hostility—sworn, you recollect, out of

intense revenge for a father's wrongs——"
Here even Mrs. Spencer suspended her good
offices at the other end; for it was a kind of
little speech, illuminating the general question that
had doubtless tended to damp the party. Her conspicuous right-hand guest was courteously listening
to a fair neighbour, the general's daughter, who
stopped too—so suddenly, it might be, that the
calm Mr. Etherege even started; his eye taking a
slow turn to his host, with an enquiring flash
in it, as if he questioned some apparent impolite-
ness.

"What was the first Roman act on that occasion?" smiled Mr. Spencer, looking round
unconscious of offence — indeed stimulated by
the respectful pause, as he again turned towards
the mayor. "Why, sir, raised to foresight, it is
possible, by a sagacious augury from these previous
facts on the part of her foe, the stern republic did
not hesitate to send out a legion the other way for
Hither Gaul; and the very ground occupied by
the besiegers was offered for sale that day—ay,
bought too, in her public Forum. Our own
country is not given to such affectations, I rejoice
to add; but it is something remarkable to read
in our public papers, just now, of bills to relieve
Dissenters (however unsuccessful), of charges
against the East India Company in its treatment
of conquered Rajahs, of discussions to regulate
the slave trade, of Captain Cook's new discoveries

toward the austral pole. It is even something, as you and I may venture to say, Mr. Mayor, that with the old British ensign flying from a good convoy—our insurances may rise, indeed—but our most lucrative enterprises can go on securely, nay, in many cases, more profitably than before."

With thorough cordiality the mayor nodded his emphatic assent, amidst a slight but general murmur of approval. Their host signed to his respectable old butler as the wine was duly placed on the shining mahogany; evidently bent on prefacing by a loyal toast the usual health-drinking all round (which at that day had begun, in limited companies, to succeed the old-fashioned naming of favoured belles and beaux respectively, coupled with airy sentiments). " Yes—whether it be revenge for Canada," concluded he, " or what is worse, their fiendish wish to aggravate our natural parental wrongs——"

But Mr. Spencer, happily unnoticed by the enlivened company at large, here hesitated and came to a dead stop very awkwardly, with his eye fascinated toward that of his most honoured guest. Was it that the handsome young traveller meant to pierce into the reality of this composure in his host, or did he mean to sneer at its grounds; or was it rather because good Mr. Fortescue the banker shook his head so inopportunely, dropping one of his timid remarks to Mr. Spencer at the moment, which the latter absolutely delayed to

answer—following Etherege's retracted gaze as he
did, with ill-concealed uneasiness. It seemed but
a fancy, though, for the latter bent again to the
sprightly Miss Bridthorpe with the utmost suavity.
The good banker was not difficult to convince in
a few quiet words; it was owing chiefly to the
moving attendants and shifted wax-lights as the two
conversed, that the shade brought out the lines of
care on the merchant's forehead, or his cheek looked
haggard, as if last night had been sleepless with him.

" Well, well," resumed he aloud, with all hospitable gaiety, " when the wine is left with us,
gentlemen, let's talk it out if you will ! 'Tis no
theme for the dessert, among ladies—as I am glad
to see Lady Diana Fanshawe agreeing. Neither
must an unprejudiced traveller like our young
friend be led to imagine for an instant that we
would *bias*—yes—a—the pine-apples are home-
grown, I think, general—no, Jenkins says from
Jamaica, but good, by our last vessel, a fast sailer.
Are not those grapes, there, my dear, English at all
events? Perhaps Mr. Etherege can be persuaded
to judge between our native forcing, up here at
Beech Grove, and those of Beaujolais or Beaune?
Were *I* to hint a preference from having tasted
both, it might be prejudice still !"

At Mrs. Spencer's gentle instance, Mr. Etherege
took one of the glowing clusters. Having tasted
it, he bowed in reply, with his most ceremonious

smile. "Truly delicious, dear sir!" he said, quickly. "In this, as in other respects, I cannot but confirm your choice. An enviable country, beyond doubt, to other countries—tempting indeed, to any foot once placed on it and claimed by no other soil." And as he turned once more to his attractive neighbour, looks were involuntarily exchanged between host and hostess; which showed the latter for the instant that her husband felt no common pleasure, nor had it been any slight anxiety which his present satisfaction replaced. If their interesting visitor did not yet quite come up to the "Hotwells" report of his brilliant wit, yet a peculiar grace of manner was inseparable from his gravest glances or most accidental attitude; his slightly perceptible accent was not so much foreign, according to the rector's side-remark, as indicative of a scholarly habit amidst the natural disadvantages to be contended with in our plantations abroad; to which view his somewhat obsolete idiom agreed, as if Lord Chesterfield or some other departed model had indeed risen again. But he was far too reanimated, too young, too redolent of whatever was fervid and plenteous in the rich tropics, to suggest the least idea of such dangerous, such fatal and forgotten sentiments as *they* had breathed. By ladies near him, this impression was felt beyond doubt; the old general's daughter, Miss Bridthorpe—though an only child, a real heiress, a country belle—without pretence to wit had sufficient charm to draw out the fact : no more was evident, at the same time, than a repressed proneness in Mr. Etherege to sudden impulse, and a conscious remembrance of enthusiasms he still inclined for ; as she spoke to him in her composed high-bred way, alike of the Alps they had both seen on the grand tour, of the ignorance, the oppression, the serfdom they had both been pained at on the Continent, and of rural Somersetshire which was known only to her and Mrs. Spencer. " Ah ! Again this country of Somerset-sheer, which you paint more than ever alluringly, Miss Bridthorpe !" was the answer, and as he stooped to hand fruit near her plate, the light of his expression was displaced again by a stern shadow. But however stern, however sombre the firm profile might for a moment seem, there still came hovering to the ear that little youthful imperfection of his English speech ; no doubt lessening with practice, but appearing to soften aught Spaniard-like, aught ominous—and in itself, at times, musical. " An interior England, this shire might indeed be imagined," he said. " There, too, it seems, I have a relative—but not a wealthy one, Miss Bridthorpe. No. Those more worth visiting, I was told, live elsewhere—besides, I had already met *them* in London." He laughed slightly then ; the young lady smiling just so much as became her. Miss Bridthorpe was not so young as Jane Spencer, nor by any means so regular a beauty; but her toilet was simpler, her smiles more natural, her voice lower.

"You will visit it, however?" she asked, with polite interest. "Think, Mrs. Spencer! Somersetshire—and Mr. Etherege in too great haste to see it! Even in winter, you know, it is worth while—Christmas is well kept yet, I assure you, down in Somersetshire."

"Yes, we still know that. It could not be better seen than at Herbert Court still, Mr. Etherege," was the matron's warm response. "The Herberts—ah—true, you did not mention them—I only heard my boy Harry talk to his sisters of the relationship. To be sure, as a piece of private counting-house business—which he perhaps ought not to have overheard, still less reported?"

"But it was so far from being confidential, dear madam," said Etherege very blandly, "that Mr. Spencer himself was the first to inform me accurately upon it, as well from common knowledge as from acute inference on his own part. The young gentleman certainly committed no breach of propriety in this, believe me!"

Now, toward the foot of the table, in a perfectly presentable suit, was of course seated Master Harry, offering that mere diminution of the full-grown gentleman which the eighteenth century approved in such cases, and as to his general manner quite

what was called, by his sister Mary, "on his p's
and q's." The sole charge that could have been
made against this, throughout dinner, was his too
marked interest in "the Count"—his comparative
neglect, whether of plain roast beef or made dishes,
of pie, trifle, jelly, or fruit; apparently in order
that he might intently observe any characteristic
trait of Mr. Etherege, or through other sounds
might catch some distinct tone of his voice, from
its softest to its deepest. If his father had once
or twice looked that way with attentive care, or
been led to do so by mingled doubt and satisfaction, Harry had seemed to have double reason; in
fact, so much so, that from his youngest sister,
whose place chanced to be nearly opposite, he had
received more than one significant look of annoyance
as well as reproof and warning. Not that Kate
was in the least danger of being noticed herself by
any one, however occasionally put to it to disguise
a sense of Harry's oddity; much less in any sign
between them did she risk detection from the object of his persevering suspicions, the casual glitter
of whose brilliant eye she was rather glad to escape
altogether, being placed on the same side. She
had assumed the nice arts of fashion, weeks ago,
with its dress, fan, laced handkerchief and vinaigrette, when she had first "come out" under her
grandmother's stately wing, at her uncle's, down
at Wrixworth. On the force of these, and perhaps

owing to discerning gallantry on the part of Major
Vorniwicz, she had been most formally handed
down-stairs by this noble but somewhat forlorn
exile; just when she was keeping back most properly, if demurely, to come down with Harry in
rear of all. She now sat beside the said Polish
patriot, a chivalrous and accomplished man, of irre-
pressible animation, who could speak Latin like
those very Romans Mr. Spencer had talked of,
though scarce intelligibly to Englishmen : gaunt
he was, and possibly too long-bodied and short-
sighted to have availed much in the national
struggle of which he now spoke; but Kate was
trying to understand the broken account in spite of
Harry, who seemed the more stubbornly bent on
those odd demonstrations of his, from having been
left to come down to dinner alone.

Now at last, Mr. Etherege's eye rested openly
on Henry, to his considerable embarrassment, but
not with the least displeasure. He brought the
young gentleman's face to recollection, as having
at first escaped his memory; he had seen it at his
first visit, in the counting-house—true. Nay, on
further thought, this was the same young gentleman he had passed beside a wharf last night : to
which incident he but adverted, very pleasantly,
though more to the mirth of others than to that of
Harry or of his father either. Even his mother had
cast a rather vexed eye in his direction, and said,

" Really, I must own, sir, if Harry goes proclaiming
every secret of his office business in that style——"
She was at a loss for words to express his deserts,
perhaps fearing the marked seafaring destiny that
had appeared to frown for him again, on the
offended parental brow.

"Surely, however, madam," was the soothing
plea of their distinguished guest, "in the case of
news already public, this term is too severe—it
almost condemns the fancied pleasantry of one's
relating such an occurrence. One can conceive
that there may be secrets, as you suggest, which a
great establishment should preserve—which even
the family need not know; but young as Mr.
Harry seems, his air is far from being that of the
bavard—the tattler. Recollect, your son and his
attendant could not hear me till I had passed the
other bystanders, who were at first equally out
of his notice. My cloak, perhaps, prevented the
recognition on his part—he is quick, evidently—
after a single visit, too, which has scarce yet enabled me to repay the compliment!"

"Yes, Henry is very quick indeed," she was
delighted to allow. "He has seen something of
the world very early—has been to New York and
to Jamaica."

"Ah! is it possible—so young?" responded
Mr. Etherege. "Then that exceedingly healthy
tint is accounted for."

" I think myself, too, he is far from being rash or imprudent," she ran on. " Even the other piece of information was drawn from him, I remember, among his sisters—and on the excuse that others had overheard it. He has some boy's admiration, I know, about Mr. Herbert as an officer—from report, too, merely."

" My cousin I have not myself seen, madam," said Etherege, readily letting the topic change. "I had meant to write to him only. Still, if between conflicting reports one may judge—and it were difficult, besides, to resist the Arcadian accounts of so impartial a witness as Miss Bridthorpe——"

The young lady had turned to him as Mrs. Spencer's cares became divided again. " You are so much a traveller, then," said she, gaily, " as to change your mind with the last rumour? Well— but Somersetshire is wide enough to have its bleak parts—which, by the way, are said to be the finest; and for the Wrixworth neighbourhood I cannot speak. Are not all the Herberts very strict Catholics indeed?—all our English Catholics are. Pray," she added, with a smile too sincere to offend, "let me warn you on that point."

" If I could affect any similar creed," was the reply, more than correspondingly serious, "the pretext were easy, like the means. Spanish by the one side—yes, of the ancient blood of—of— excuse me, mademoiselle—and it matters not.

N 2

Even my widowed mother was so devoutly of that faith, both from her English and French origin, as to seek in a convent to forget a tragedy which was little subsequent to my own birth." He had dropped his voice, though hardly required to do so amidst the growing cheerfulness on every side; and he resumed in his lightest tone. "It was in the full odour of sanctity, however, that she died, as *superieure* of the Sacré Cœur near St. Maloes, where I last saw her—very lately—with sufficient remembrance of those priests who interfered, to—to impress their forms on my mind. A Spanish nurse had indeed long accustomed me to them. But every traveller, I think, Miss Bridthorpe, who may have learnt to smile at these—who may have possessed means enough to fortify him against a bribe from them—does not come to this wealthy island, surely, from greed of gold. He might even visit relatives who may need fortune, without the wish to rob them of it." He jested so thoroughly, still so politely though so oddly, through that peculiar idiom of his, that Miss Bridthorpe merrily responded, " Surely—surely, Mr. Etherege : I do think so. I have heard there is money somewhere among the Herberts; but I can answer for Somersetshire hospitality. Pray, put it to trial about Christmas-time."

"The truth was," he explained, "almost deterred at the gloom into which this war appeared to plunge England, I inclined to draw back before entangling myself in unforeseen complications. There is an egotism in the traveller, perhaps, Miss Bridthorpe, which is apt to dread this; England was so unknown to me; one shrinks from forming ties which may so soon be useless—which events may shatter. But looking around this table, can I hesitate longer? How pleasant—how animated— how secure in the confidence of British wealth and power!"

Truly it was so. The master of the house was growing radiant with the exhilaration of a sociality thus shared by all his guests, and in which the principal one took obvious part. Every care had vanished from his countenance, when, seizing the happiest moment ere the ladies must retire, he permitted the worthy mayor to add one further national toast to the late fulfilment of his own loyal duty. The sparkling of Mr. Etherege's increased vivacity helped to throw an *éclat* so perceptible over the departing train of Mrs. Spencer, as to draw a half reproachful sally from Lady Die on her way. "'Tis Phœbus, who only appears to set, child," she whispered, in her loud style, to the piqued beauty of the house. "We but fancy a warmer glow through our clouds, I think; or is it mirrored, rather, my good Vorni- wicz"—to the exiled major, who had sprung to bow them out, "from the liquid deep you have in prospect?" The gallant Pole answered with hand on heart, and an expressive grimace, "Miladi is preferr to shoot like ze Partians, like ze fairest Amazons, I had nearly say; but zis vould have seem to imagine her *immodesté vestitam!* Ah! vile *Luna Dea inter stellas lucet*," he said, in his fluent Latin, " in vain vould ze misvortunate Vorniwicz——" But they were gone; and ere their vacant places allowed closer talk, it had devolved naturally on Mr. Etherege to rise with his few sentences of courtesy to the amiable hostess and her fair friends, over the wine-glass he craved leave to fill in their honour. Among *his* words there was at least no awkwardness and no incongruity; he adopted the native custom with the grace of one to whom it was not altogether strange, and he did not fail to throw in a rapid touch of modest acknowledgment for the hospitality to himself, which had distinguished him, he thought fit to say, far beyond his merits. But whatever these, he hastily concluded, or whatever new doubts a stranger might be exposed to, amidst foreign changes so sudden and unaccountable, he begged once for all to take that opportunity of setting himself right, by the peculiar interest and by the admiring devotion to all the sex, with which he ventured to ask this privilege from his host.

The beaming consent had been already more than implied. The waiting bumpers were drained with true British heartiness, and turned up amidst cheers of applause, as flattering to the speaker as to his toast.   There was emotion in Mr. Spencer's reply—emotion controlled with firmness, indeed, but yet so deepened by the political crisis in question, as to excuse a slight incoherence when he mentioned it—even an abrupt close and husky stammer with which he sat down, also amidst the voice of friendly approbation.   So soon as they drew more snugly together, the very footman retreating after he had stirred the heaped fire— even the quiet old butler gliding out at his master's nod when fresh wine had been placed— the mingled ease and life of conversation was all that the latter could have wished.   The dinner had, after all, been almost a family one—*en famille*—as he had described it in prospect at the counting-house; though, at the same time, quite inconsistent with that notion of a mere casual meeting, already arranged, to which Etherege was to make an accidental addition; still it was plainly not so large as was often to be met round that well-appointed table (nor was it so characterised by a slight approach to pomp as it might have been had the sugar-baker agreed to join it with his coarse estimates of mercantile solidity).   If the careful selection of the rest of the company was rather marked to a keen eye, as having been made at any rate *before* news of war: yet even *after* these, the injudiciousness of the choice had not in every case been verified; while the management in other

respects had been tastefully left to a feminine hand.
The family plate had not been near half used—
not more than half shown. The quiet old butler
had needed only Thomas and a waiting-maid to
serve; while Black Diamond merely helped be-
hind-scenes in the hall, decked out with an
obsolete livery. The coachman, gardener, and
pantry-boy had not been pressed in as awkward
assistants; the dishes, though excellent, had been
few; the delicacies, however recondite, not pro-
fuse; the wine now, above all, suited in quality as
it was to such a *ménage*, involved no pressures of
the kind reported from rude fox-hunting manor-
houses, or from the abodes of a dull, though profligate, nobility.

They had sat some time; so long that the gallant Polish major had slipped away unnoticed
after young Harry, while the old butler made
another of his quiet entrances—and still the diminished company were rather kindling up than
flagging. Mr. Fortescue, the banker, was a man
of some family, of extensive information, of much
political sagacity and historical reading, while far
from the least disposition to obtrude technical allusions or sordid views; except for him, indeed, old
General Bridthorpe's shaken Whiggism might have
waxed hot against the Tory rector, when the latter
was inclined to blame the Opposition for this war,
and yet to build on it a Ministerial triumph. As

it was, aught like discussion was precluded, by the
banker's well known liberality of sentiment, joined
with the mayor's heartiness, which settled everything in frequent toasts; the good humour grew
too jovial to need one hospitable incentive more, or a
single further gaiety, by way of help. Mr. Etherege, in truth, however pointedly restricting himself
to the lighter wine of France, betrayed spirits not
less exuberant, if scarce so elevated, as his host
began to show over generous Oporto. The young
traveller drew his chair yet nearer, and drinking
his bumper to the good mayor's health (coupled en-
thusiastically by Mr. Spencer with that of British
commerce), he nodded most emphatic assent to Sir
Timothy's somewhat hazy reply; in which, very
flattering compliments were yet repaid with interest
to Broadby and Co. Then, no sooner was the merchant free to listen, with a flushed but grateful
look turned towards him, than the guest admitted
an anxiety unfelt before, as regarded those unfavourable effects upon West Indian property, which
the louder speakers were discussing. If the chief
stress of naval operations must indeed pass toward
the "Spanish Main," till the contest hinged between
Barbadoes and Martinique, with their dependent
islets under either flag—then certainly, the question became one he could not affect to slight:
directly, it was true, his fortune had never been involved in the vicissitudes of commerce; he himself

had seldom before given a thought to matters of business, left hitherto with those long-tried agents (of his mother's family, and of his grandfather's) whom Mr. Spencer knew. In Etherege's whole manner, thus drawn aside for the moment, there was a degree of eagerness not to be concealed; he almost confidentially asked for the maturer advice, which it was perhaps delicate to offer so soon.

A transient flutter there might have been on the other part; undoubtedly, at least, there passed a quick side-glance of scrutiny at the inquirer, but it was the latter who had yielded most to the festive influence, and had quite lost the wilful eccentricity, the occasional air of conscious penetration, that marked his somewhat fitful liveliness before ladies. Mr. Spencer was never steadier when dictating his most important correspondence in Froom - lane, than now when passing the decanter as he responded, with disinterested calmness, to his distinguished young friend. He guarded him against procedure on a mere opinion, although that opinion he cheerfully gave. How clear, too, how experienced, how really masterly were his views on the whole question; though he did not now repeat the fact—they were certainly not drawn from second-hand information merely, from geography, or *books* of statistics and travel in those quarters. As to the well-known esteemed agents, Morel, Macfie and Son, Port Castres, St. Lucie—yes—nowhere better managers, or safer to consult upon a sudden sale of property, even from a French island; certainly, he knew them, by correspondence.

"By correspondence? True, and besides, old Morel is now a dotard," muttered the guest, not so incoherently but that the host smiled. There is not now time enough to consult them, Mr. Spencer," added Etherege? "No; after hearing from them by the next packet, with the necessary documents, perhaps you could again spare me an hour in private at your counting-house? It is but some distant property in Cuba which I think of, with the slaves belonging to it—a specimen of the latter will accompany the proofs, I mean. A middle-aged mulatto—no longer a boy, certainly, but whose attachments are faithful, his memory excellent, a good linguist, calculated to be useful as a valet, named Adolphe."

Mr. Spencer doubtless thought of Black Diamond, or secretly deprecated the idea of any more inconvenient presents of that kind; while answering that all proofs were superfluous. The truth being that he had already received, from the agents referred to, a sufficient idea of the young man's position; he had found since, through old Sir Ralph Herbert's solicitors in Town, that the said baronet's younger brother, maternal grandfather of Etherege, long outlawed as a Jacobite and Papist, had in reality accumulated money as a foreign planter under an

altered name; which fortune, as well as his only
daughter's French inheritance in St. Lucie, had
passed to the young man as her sole heir. The latter
had not so much as troubled himself to allude to
this fact; it was all the more strange, therefore, that
with regard to the Spanish property just mentioned,
he dropped his voice to explain that *it* had been his
father's. "It is worth retaining—well worth all else
I have," he said huskily; "it is only Spanish, too,
and Spain is at peace yet—but it is exposed, near
the coast—dangerous, you understand me?" Astonishment at so careless a possession of wealth
might well have overwhelmed Mr. Spencer, yet
he bowed a vague, half scared intelligence. "Yes,
I shall not wait for old Morel; perhaps, not even
for Adolphe with the parchments," rapidly pursued the fortunate young creole, too logical at
every point to be thought mad; indeed, letting out
at last too clear an avidity for speculation, too
obvious a remembrance of the most casual remark
at their first interview the week before. "Since,
as you were good enough to state, sir, the name of
Broadby and Co. will go far as a guarantee on
your Exchange, and——yes—you say the market
cannot yet be affected, as to *all* West Indian secu-
rities—but we must anticipate the effect of any bad
news, or rumours—true—true; then, even should
your English Funds *not* fall——"

"At another time, my dear young friend,"

hastily whispered the merchant, flushing to the
roots of his powdered hair; "to-morrow—whenever it suits you; but *this* does not altogether——"

Etherege glanced keenly round, however, at the
broad-backed mayor, whose growing jollity more
and more coincided with the worthy banker's
harmonious good offices; the politics of the former
were none the less conducive to mirth on that side
of the table from being mixed with special questions of the " timber trade."

" But you do not yet even ask," persevered the
young West Indian, sipping his wine again, and
leaning nearer, " what was the position, the name
of—of my father. I cannot allow this to remain
in doubt, to your possible disadvantage; you may
chance to recollect it—it was *Don Victor de La
Etterega de Castra!*"

The emphatic under tone with which the name
was breathed, the meaning touch of the hand that
was laid at the moment on Mr. Spencer's arm,
could not but draw his gravest attention. He
inwardly repeated the whole title, while a doubtful
remembrance broke on him. "De Castro?" he
said, with a start, which the young man's quiet
pressure tended to check, " I—I think I have
heard of—of it. I was at Jamaica after that
time—considerably afterwards. But—but surely,
Mr. Etherege——"

Even the priceless diamond on young Etherege's hand did not gleam so unquestionably from its rough edge and plain setting, as the roused Spanish pride that warned to caution, from under the seeming languor that would have dropped again over his large rich eye. "He was of the noblest Castilian race, sir," was the almost whispered reply; "unfortunate, certainly—the last who bore the title—reduced to command a mere corvette under the Havannah Governor; but too vigilant, too brave, not to have enemies who maligned him. The guarda-costa service," added Mr. Etherege, in a more ordinary tone, "was even lucrative enough to tempt a traitor to become assassin; but perhaps—yes—it may be that he really shared the fate instigated, no doubt, by a wilier though a safer foe."

"Ah! true—a *guarda costa*, you say. I heard the story spoken of, I confess," allowed Mr. Spencer, wincing slightly. "But this explains whatever puzzled the good Kingston folks in the matter. Certainly—certainly, my esteemed young friend, if I may so be permitted to——" He was still hospitably repassing the wine that way, with a characteristic composure, the more marked as it was abruptly joined to a burning glow of colour, followed by an equally unsuitable paleness. For the good mayor's loud voice was to be heard above the rest, thankfully serious: "It's just as well, at any

rate," concluded he, " none of *us* need be troubled
about sugar."

" Ha, ha! very true indeed!" laughed the general and the rector; while Mr. Fortescue, the
banker, agreed with a quieter smile. " Quite as
well, yes, quite as well, gentlemen," said he; and
his eye involuntarily exchanged glances with their
host, from whose graver talk he had doubtless
avoided at all detaching their young friend. The
latter now passed the decanter on to Mr. Fortescue,
with a gay excuse. " I think even the lightest vin-
tage proves too much for me already," he said.
" Pray, Mr. Spencer, allow me—I need not ask, it
is plain, whether you knew a Portuguese of the
name of Coguel?"

" A—a—Portuguese of—the—name of Coguel?"
repeated the merchant; whether falteringly, or
merely in thought, it was hard to know. He lifted
a ready eye to meet the piercing glance of inquiry
before him. " Coguel. I *do* wish I could help you
in any way," but he shook his head decidedly. "No;
the name is entirely strange to me, I am certain.
My brief residence among the islands was considerably subsequent, as I said, to the incidents in
question." He took out his watch. "But how the
time has flown, I declare, gentlemen! Suppose
we now join the ladies up-stairs?"

They rose accordingly to do so; they were on

their way up when Etherege took the opportunity
to say, with even more than his former *empressement*,
that he would very soon venture to avail himself
of the aid so kindly proffered, on the part of his
host's influential firm. He expressed an excessively
polite fear of having trenched, somewhat, on the
verge of that etiquette of business which was apt
to perplex a stranger, particularly amidst hospitalities so frank, so unrestrained. As to the trivial
inquiry he had chanced to make; it was really
almost too *mal-à-propos*, too much *en passant*, to be
excused; of its precise point, he himself could not
now be certain; it could only refer, he thought, to
some document or other, among those to be waited
for. On reflection, it would be premature to re-
visit the counting-house of Broadby and Co. so
very soon; to engross any of its valuable time as
yet. The interval would even be idly spent near
Bristol—it threatened to be dull, unless one gamed,
betted, or affected to sigh in the train of some
sickly or hypochondriac heiress at the watering-
place. He had thoughts of rather returning to
London for the time, where the blood was at least
stirred by the very rage of wealth, for more wealth;
where it even amounted to a passion, a power, a
destiny that imposed on one.

If the sudden air of the wide staircase and gallery
had thus taken effect, at least the finer bouquet of
Bordeaux or Mâcon was in the speech: dry port and

heavy Madeira were evident, on the other hand, in the very gravity of the good mayor as he steadied himself at the radiant folding-doors, where coffee was handed. Music was astir within; the exiled major singing a vernacular lyric of his unfortunate country, less patriotic than amorous, coldly accompanied by intermittent notes from Miss Spencer's harp, while Lady Die Fanshawe in her tall hanging drapery, with low-dressed powderless hair, and wreath of fancied-classic leaves, held up her bony finger to beckon silence—very like, as the pausing rector whispered, a "Tenth Muse." Mr. Spencer considerately took a turn or two outside with his young and impulsive visitor, under the few choice paintings by old masters, at which the general and Mr. Fortescue looked; and when they entered the spacious withdrawing-rooms together, there was a placid dignity in the merchant's air, which Etherege's subdued vivacity but reflected.

The company up-stairs had received some friendly evening additions; two or three quiet whist-loving people, on easy terms of neighbourhood to Beech Grove, making up a pleasant party in the card-room with the rector's spinster sister (a well bred, but strangely silent, gentlewoman of Bristol, whose presence at dinner could be explained, however, on grounds of politeness); amongst these, a be-jewelled dowager of failing health, though keenly bent upon her game—widow of an elder brother

of Mr. Spencer's, whose fortune had been obtained
in the adventurous East. Manifestly also, so had
been gained the prize now left by him, so pagoda-
like was the towering head-dress in which the bril-
liants trembled at the summit of her powder, so vain
the use of rouge on the sallow cheek below, or even
the stimulus of evident trumps in hand to her bilious
eye. But her slim, pale, jet-eyed young folks had
come with her, joining a few others who had dropped
in; and it was plain from Mrs. Spencer's indulgent
manner that their solicitations had weighed with her,
in spite of caps of state, or enlightened witty talk,
or Lady Diana, or the war itself—to allow an old-
fashioned minuet or two, and Sir Roger de Coverley,
and perhaps a parting country dance. Meanwhile
her daughter Mary had gone to the harpsichord,
to strike the key of one of those quaint old English
glees, or madrigals, to which her father was scarce
less partial than was his dignified son-in-law in
prospect, the Rector of Emerton and Wrixworth.
The youthful quartett of singers stood together,
harmoniously chanting or carolling it, with their
backs to the gentlemen as they came. The rich
bass of Dr. Hickenbooth himself was blended with
the final chorus; even Mr. Etherege listened
curiously, intently, motionless, to the sprightly
strain, with its hollow depth and its clear aërial
echoes; though young Harry's figure made a part
of the choir, and Mr. Spencer's playful hand had

not only marked the time, but was laid familiarly,
at the end, on the shoulder of the fair contralto.
" Your voice has gained vastly, Jane," said her
father, with much paternal satisfaction; " vastly.
Why, child, it positively reminds me, I declare,
of——" She turned a round young cheek, colouring
a little, but dimpling like her mother's to a smile;
more arch though, and brighter; the clear eyes
lightening up without hesitation to her father's, as
he made a start of more than due surprise. " What,
Kitty, only?" laughed he, tapping her cheek with
even an easier fondness.   " Really, I protest I was
unaware that our youngest girl had grown so, still
less——" He looked toward Mr. Etherege, who,
however, after slightly starting too, had moved
away.

" —Still less, I presume, papa, that she had any
voice at all," suggested this youngest but perhaps
most favoured daughter, turning round altogether
with him.   " The truth is, at Wrixworth, we sang
in parts very often, sir."

" What did you *not* do at Wrixworth, I wonder!"
smiled he, and viewed her all over very compla-
cently ere passing on.   " As to growth, no wonder
I mistook; the chit is as tall, I believe, as either of
her sisters."

" That's not so very much to boast of, is it,
Kitty?" whispered her brother.   " I bet you're
taller; even Jane looks it, at least."

Before the first roll of wheels sounded up the avenue, there came the little dancing that had been begged for, in which the chivalrous Polish major himself was not readier to join the younger portion of the company, than Mr. Etherege proved at Mrs. Spencer's instance. To her soft influence, with its kindly little arts of social tact throughout the evening—and yet now, of concession to juvenile visitors and to motherly good-nature—it seemed he would have yielded still more. Amidst the sustained gaieties of the main drawing-room, where successive leave-takings were scarce to be observed, or outer sounds of departure noticed—it might have appeared his will to forget, like Lady Diana and her attendant Pole, that his own carriage had been some time announced. Her ladyship, in fact, had shared its offered use in coming; it was almost her boast that she could only afford to keep "a chair," and though the gallant Vorniwicz would obviously have walked beside it if required, yet its absence left no question now as to their case; but she betrayed no consciousness in the matter, till Mr. Etherege had duly danced with her fair protégée, Jane Spencer, and had showed a rather formal resolution to carry through his duties to the house, by gaining that honour in turn from Mary also. Nay, he was so far from imitating the heedless gallantry of the major—who, twice in quick succession, had consoled himself by asking their younger sister's hand,

that there rose an air of further inevitable obliga-
tion under Etherege's liveliest manner.   And this
impulse, but for her ladyship's rising, and the
major's previous request, would obviously have
prompted the like attention on the new guest's part
to Kate ere they broke up.   Once his momentary
glance had caught hers with a singular attraction,
too grave, too dark through all the courtesy of fea-
ture, to be evaded; not that she dropped her own,
indeed, or feared his, but with a wish to have
searched it to the bottom, or at least to have
frowned if she dared, she rather chose to look
over beyond him very carelessly, as if some wax-
light in the chandelier were wrong, or a trifle on
the chimney-piece struck her.   When Major Vorniwicz's compliment had saved the other all trouble
of paying her any, he might have been thought
to heave a breath of relief, before he turned bowing
another way, with a slight foreign shrug of the
shoulders; and now, in the haste to attend Lady
Die down-stairs, he seemed oddly to have forgot
what her ladyship now had begun to keep in mind,
that there were really *three* Misses Spencer to bid
good-night to.   With Harry, even, he shook hands,
near the door; true, Harry stood in his way, and
had latterly become a little propitiated by a passing
remark or two, grave as well as jocose, which, in
course of these lighter occupations, the gentleman
had made to him.

When parting from Mrs. Spencer, he had
spoken of being compelled to "tear himself from
the allurements of her pleasant circle." In her
turn, she had kindly added to the usual forms an
expression of gladness that he was not to leave the
country, at least, so soon as he had contemplated;
in which case she need not say that it would "always
give them all extreme pleasure to see Mr. Etherege." Mr. Spencer himself had reappeared from
the card-room, where a little early supper was
evidently about to close the evening. The tone of
his good-night was less serious, as not so likely to
be the last. "In the same easy way, my dear sir,
or, indeed, waiving any ceremony — in town at
Froom-lane, at all events, any little service in my
power will be ready for you. From about noon,
till three or four, I am, just now, very seldom
absent." He had himself handed down Lady
Diana, and came up again imperturbably composed,
though with spirits that lasted out the night.

"I quite agree with you, Henry," said his sister,
as they stood together at the end, " in not liking that
French Count; those great pitch-black eyes of his,
they—I scarce know what—like the magnets, you
know—yes, if they *may* not just draw one to them,
they repel you instead." She gave a slight shiver,
standing before the fallen fire in the withdrawing-
room. "Can you help almost fancying he conceals
some dark design?"

"Well—after all," Harry said, "he's not just

exactly the sort of man I took him for ; I can't say
I hate him quite so much.   Design ! pooh ; he has
some business he wants the Firm to help him to, and
I've a shrewd notion, somehow, if Broadby and Co.
had room for what's called a sleeping partner, he'd
have no great objections.   Mind you, even in the
counting-house, there's brains wanted ;   and old
Ffloyd, for all the sharpness he pretends to, was a
fool.   If ever I saw a regularly clever man, it's
Etherege, look—he don't strike me as being cunning with it.   As to money, he's got it, that's clear ;
and besides, you're wrong, it turns out he's neither
Frenchman nor Count.   No ; I don't like him, I
don't admire him——— "

"Admire him !" echoed Kate, implying an
agreement too entire, too settled, and too lofty, to
partake of affectation.   The very thought seemed
to pass beyond a smile, into other and quieter considerations, as she stood eyeing the embers, and
musing ; while Harry for his part was looking at
her curiously from head to foot.   Simply, though
richly dressed in *"a straw-coloured brocaded lustring
sack, trimmed with floss of the same colour,"* which
was but slightly looped up to show a little of *"a
mantua petticoat, blue and silver, with a figured ground,
very rich"*—in her high-heeled buckled shoes, too,
and in her deep open lace-trimmed sleeves, and
muslin tucker—did she herself not really strike
Harry, as by no means an unattractive sister, when
magnets came in question ?   He might be no great

judge, and certainly Jane's elegance of carriage could not be denied, set off by her full bell-hoop and train, nor the dazzling fairness of her skin, and that violet-blueness of her languid eyes, which Lady Die spoke of; then Mary's dark ones, again, and her plump healthy shape, were even preferred by some, (for *she* had altogether the same warm brown complexion as her father, who was still considered one of the handsomest men in Bristol). But on one side of the pier-glass, on the mantelpiece, was an arch nymph of Canova in alabaster, holding up a cluster of crystal drops below a branch of wax-lights; on the other, a Greek Hebe to match : and the one did not appear more elastically slender and straight, nor the other to promise a surer symmetry, than Kate with her forehead pressed rather listlessly against the marble ledge between. She had eyes, to be sure, of a very provoking uncertainty of hue ("English grey," forsooth, the Somersetshire folks chose to call it), lightening up as if to defy all names when opened on you, shadowing down just as annoyingly from hazel; her cheek, too, was even childishly rounded; yet she had as straight a little nose as need be, with a most emphatic spirited nostril—to show, perhaps, that the dimple could wholly vanish on occasion from about her curled mouth. Her very colour—nothing to speak of ordinarily, being but a general babyish carnation over all—really came out

well under the hair-powder, or against the cold
white stone or somehow.

"I must say, though, Miss Kitty Spencer," said
the youth, half mischievously, "everything considered, you need not take up one's word so quickly
—'tis not as to his looks I meant—they're rather
out of the common way, no doubt, but they're
scarce so bad as that comes to, surely! I heard some
lady or other—neither Jane nor Lady Die—com-
paring 'em to some famous old picture of King
Charles the First, that was beheaded. She said if
it had been only younger and sprightlier, with the
face shaved and hair powdered up, and a higher
nose, all it wanted was a shade of olive to make the
likeness striking!"

"Indeed! How royal to be sure!" smiled
Kate, disdainfully, unconvinced. "Most likely Miss
Bridthorpe—who seemed wondrous taken with the
gentleman, considering that she is engaged to be
married."

"I suppose you're disappointed?" persisted
Harry. "At all events," added he, pointedly, "we
seem to have got ourselves vastly improved for the
occasion! I can't just say what it was, Kate—
whether it's the hair, you know?" She raised a
conscious look to see it sideways again in the reflection—that fashionable superstructure of full dress,
which, without yet aspiring to rival Jane's mitre-
like coiffure, crested her for the first time with the

whole dusted glimmer of her light nut-brown
tresses—that still gave out pale golden streaks
through the powder, like the velvet richness of the
auricula, or of the wings of some midsummer moth.
" But I tell you what," he concluded, "if you did
not admire Mr. Etherege, I'm positive he seemed
rather to admire *you!*   So, taking your word for
it, Kate—to say the least of it, it's ungrateful ! "

Still no symptom of aught but utter indifference
on her part, except in a last glance at the mirror
before turning to go.   " On the contrary, he seemed
to think I *needed* colour—which seems plain enough.
But it would not come although you were a
thousand times nearer right, Harry. 'Tis owing to
the late hours after dear old Wrixworth, where we
went to bed early—so good-night ! "

"Stay ! I forgot to ask you—talking of like-
nesses—if he and his cousin Mr. Herbert——"
But though Harry was on his way up too, and could
hear her laugh as he quickened his steps, the door
closed unrelentingly against his questions. He had
to meditate on the warlike future, alone.

CHAPTER VIII.

MR. SPENCER SURPRISED.

DAYS passed, in which the blowy equinoctial weather might alone have accounted for the fact, that the commodious New Cannynges Arms, in Brandon-street, was still honoured by the presence of its most conspicuous inmate; that the sheltered parades and pump-room meetings about the Hot-wells were still graced by his occasional appearance, and that more than one of those light and classical *soirées fraiches,* which were the weekly specialty of Lady Die Fanshawe, received new *éclat* from his polished manner, his travelled intelligence, his piquant though too rarely exerted wit, as well as from his singular but unquestionably handsome person. Other circles were readily opening for him, not exclusive of that which the war-news enlivened in Cornet Cobham's mess-room; he was

in the fair way to be widely heard of in far soberer
spheres, through that mere street-knowledge circu-
lated by his passing face in his coach, and if only
under the designation persisted in by stubborn
popular respect—of " the Count."   Hard weeks of
winter followed, however, whose plodding dulness
throughout Bristol almost effaced this likelihood;
he had posted off to town, and appeared to leave a
wintry torpor of fashion, of wit, of military hope
itself behind.   His apartments at his inn, indeed,
were known to be retained; at Lady Die's he had
evinced no such fitful spirits as at the merchant's
house; nay, he had not so much as cast a doubt on
his renewal of the pleasure ere very long; and not
only was there ground to expect him yet again in
Froom-lane counting-house, given at his second
visit there—but Mr. Fortescue's bank now held for
him what might have been thought, by most men, a
sufficient solid pledge of sincerity.   Yet the Channel, it turned out, was not so closed by the season,
but that a Dover pilot or bold smuggler from
Dieppe might carry a resolute traveller across; the
very war, on the French part, was not yet declared;
Whig members were speechifying still, and Wilksite
newspapers were printing, and diplomatists were
shirking and quibbling because France, save the
mark! was not just ready to fight.   Those promises
might be broken, and those pledges might be
withdrawn—in short, the prejudice against Counts

still clung to the minds of the best friends of Etherege.

Long before this prejudice could have gained the least weight from facts, however, he put it to shame by quietly returning. It was early spring, by that time; the natural exhilaration of the season was even so preceded by his reappearance (after an absence of very moderate duration when looked back upon), that he seemed in some eyes to have brought it in. The Hotwells could boast of him again, among other notabilities whom the east wind drove thither; the *prestige* of Lady Die's *receptions parlantes* was more than restored; while Ligonier's Light Dragoons at last honoured themselves, together with their welcome marching-orders, by liberally entertaining a guest so marked by the sentiments of a cosmopolite, yet whose movements were so unaffected by actual hostilities begun. There was a spring ball at the assembly-rooms, where Etherege did not attract less notice than the gayest and most gallant of the officers who were to depart; with him Miss Bridthorpe danced one of the very few dances in which she joined, on the eve of her marriage to a peer's son; he danced still fewer himself, but there his acquaintance was made, with some trouble on the lady's part, by Mrs. General Beauchamp, of Beauchamp Cliff, the leading chaperon of fashion about Clifton, compared to whom Lady Die herself was but a satellite of some distant

orb—a widow of aristocratic place and property, of
a splendid person to which maturity only added
Juno-like charms, and of a haughtiness as tyranni-
cal, or a favour as wilful, as even was reported of
the imperious goddess.   Then, at the farewell
patronage afforded by the dragoons to the new
theatre of Bristol, for the benefit of Mrs. Jerning-
ham, of the excellent Bath company, Mr. Etherege
could not but attend (during the main performance,
Otway's "Venice Preserved"): finally, at the
private rout in compliment to the officers, at Beauchamp Cliff, and at the very elegant return-ball
which they gave to the ladies of the two county
neighbourhoods (Mrs. Beauchamp of course included), it would have been discourteous had he
not responded at all to the distinguished invitations.
Gaieties so truly British did not appear to be his
special taste; he was so far from courting this
round of notorieties, or honours, that, with the
spring, he had more than once openly expressed
intentions of visiting Somersetshire for a little.
There he had a relative to whom he had written, and
who, indeed, during his absence had done him the
honour to call for him at his inn.   But Etherege's
courtesy was always marked; it was noway in the
least diminished by a more thorough acquaintance with English manners which he showed:
social officers came laughing up the steps of the
new Cannynges Arms with Cobham, or sauntered

past to wait for him, and said the spring was
hardly come yet; they found out it was Herbert of
Herbert Court, who was the cousin he had to visit,
and by the time they began to drink a little claret
up-stairs in his rooms, and play a little piquet or
écarté there of a damp evening, they said that long
before the naval people stirred much in such foggy
weather, the regiment would be gone from Bristol.
He was not a dull host by any means; it was
rather at the theatre and the parties that any gloom
was observed about him, mingled, however, with
vivacity the most fitfully brilliant; and if he seldom
remained long, or was missed on a sudden, yet at
times he had seized his opportunity to gain the ear
of the very fairest and freshest belle, to obtain the
honour of her hand, and pay attentions no less
graceful, it might be, than his dancing was unde-
niably perfect.

Cornet Cobham came up with some lively fellow-
officers one misty evening, and saw a gentleman's
horses and servant under the gate of the inn-court-
way; serviceable roadsters they were, with pistols
in the holsters, and a very obvious naval cloak
thrown over one, as if they had waited no little
while in the damp. The Cornet shrewdly thought
of his friend's sea-serving cousin, and found within
that he had some time been engaged with a visitor.
At that the officers would forthwith have left; but
from the hearth of the smoky coffee-room where

they glanced at the last news, voices were heard
coming down and passing—one Mr. Etherege's own,
the other rougher, even deeper, like a coarse sea-
ordering voice, such as they might soon have enough
of, and that perhaps too long. For they were
ordered straight to Portsmouth; and it seemed
the field of action was not to lie at all in the Low
Countries, but the French were bent on sending
all their force far abroad, where, in the Colonies
themselves, the very Horse-Guards appeared to
think that " Cavalry *must* act ! "

A tall, strong figure, booted, spurred, and bespattered with the road, but not regular enough in
the tread—inclined, in fact, to stoop needlessly under
the door, or keep off that naval hat of his till the
rain reminded him. Etherege, bare-headed too, was
kindly showing him out to the last, even waiting till
he mounted. The windows were close by, as he
gravely turned a rather sunburnt, weather-beaten,
homely kind of face, grasped the hand raised to
his, and said in his deep tones, " Good-night—well
—as it *may* be, cousin Etherege—good-bye till
fairer times. For all I yet know, summer may
find me still at the old place again. I cannot
long stay in town, you know—and at best must
pass this way to Plymouth or Portsmouth. A
country welcome will ever be yours, cousin—ay,
though I were absent as I hope ! "

" My dear Richard," the younger of the cousins

said, more warmly still, " after what you have told
me—after what I already had been given to suppose
—I would fain you had no wish or hope of such a
nature. As soon as you return home, believe me,
I shall not scruple to avail myself of your hospitality, at least long enough to reason with you—to
do more than repeat my arguments, my entreaties.
Weather, nor roads, shall not prevent it either."
He smiled cordially ; the other laughed, waved his
hand, and was gone.

Etherege informed his military friends that it
was his cousin, Mr. Herbert, who had again taken
the trouble to " wait on him," being now on the
way to London. The Cornet admitted that he
had supposed as much—nay, a window being open
in the smoky place below, had unavoidably overheard their casual words together. " So, just as
we leave, it seems," added the Cornet, " and the
balls are over—why, here you do not go to
Somersetshire. Deuced provoking, I must own !
The spring coursing is good, I hear ; and it's a
fox-hunting country, very open thereabouts. Glad
you take it coolly, Etherege—glad 'tis nothing to
us." Their orders were for Portsmouth the next
day ; but all the pleasanter were the parting hours
they spent that evening with Etherege at his inn.

It was undoubtedly somewhat curious—in the
light of Mr. Spencer's friendly offers, and of the
subsequent business matters in which the firm

had assisted Mr. Etherege before his short absence in London, placing its counting-house, its clerks, and its own advice and influence at his service— that, after his return, his visits to Froom-lane were so rare and so merely casual as they became. Taken together with his total omission even to call at Beech Grove, where he had not as yet once presented himself since the occasion of the dinner-party, this circumstance might have been enough to excite the idea of caprice indulged, or of umbrage in some way taken. Vulgar rumours ran, no doubt, that a partnership with Broadby and Co. had been in view by this " opulent young planter," this " wealthy young loyalist colonial," or this " rich young banished Count." Gossip had gone so far as to assert, in other quarters, that he had formed a sudden passion for the beautiful Miss Spencer, for whose hand he had abruptly proposed, and been with suitable promptitude for-bidden the house, though meeting her favour still in general companies. The truth was, that in these companies she now treated him somewhat distantly herself, not without apparent sympathy from her friend, Lady Die. Mrs. General Beau-champ was a *chaperon* too powerful to quarrel with, if too self-willed for co-operation ; and among her various *protégées*, she seemed to have well-concealed designs regarding the distinguished stranger—possibly to hide a deeper infatuation of her own.

Of all which idle hearsay, it was not probable that any portion had reached the ear principally concerned. Mr. Spencer had met it all with the most decided contradiction within his own circle, particularly laying stress upon his indignation at the latter story, so altogether refuted by the whole tenor of his young friend's conduct—indeed, by an evidently practised caution which marked him in reference to the fair sex, despite the gallantries of continental habit. As regarded the business question, it was one on which the gentleman himself had never breathed any direct expression of his wishes. Some of his earlier allusions might, certainly, have been thus construed; his whole behaviour and manner, up to a certain point, *were* thought by neutral parties, sagacious friends of the firm, to have been undoubtedly indicative of a desire of that kind—which, to say the least of it, denoted an excusable ambition. Mr. Etherege's mental parts, the merchant from time to time said, though unformed, were of no ordinary capacity. He was of that bent of genius, to find a special zest in liberal enterprise of an extensive nature, above what the frivolous pursuits of fashion could afford him. His fortune—which was very con siderable, and might, ere long, be vastly increased

—was but a trifle compared with the value of
energies so fresh, young, and vigorous when once
fixed, to any extensive house he might be admitted
to join. Engrossing business, in fact, at present
so occupied Broadby and Co., that but little
attention could be given by them to such contin-
gencies. At intervals, it was true, Mr. Etherege
still showed, by a passing visit at the counting-
house, that he did not wish the acquaintance on
his part, at least, to drop. More than once, so
engrossed had Mr. Spencer individually been, that
the name had been sent in without the possibility
of an interview; nay, calling, at length, one evening, at Beech Grove itself, Mr. Etherege actually
waited so long, with so patient a courtesy, as to
have been all but forgotten in the library, till
late. So truly important were the letters received
and dictated at home that night, in Mr. Spencer's
private study. The merchant found, however,
when ultimately hastening to the room, that his
excuses appeared, in some degree, superfluous.
The fire glowed, the lights were cheerfully complete, but not more cheerful or hospitable than
the domestic party which Mrs. Spencer had
thoughtfully brought around. The gentleman's
own apologies had been easy, for the etiquette of
England was only now becoming clear to him.
The hour and the circumstances forbade all
reference to any other errand, which could be

postponed without inconvenience. He had felt that, during hours of ordinary business at Froom-lane, his slight affair was but a trespass on those of greater moment. To press it *here* would be to lose advantages which, when so offered, far out-weighed it. It could wait; it could even be pleasantly forgotten; though, on invitation so flattering, he could not but come again. And when he came again, which he now preferred to do at Beech Grove, the "slight affair" was still so generally indicative of those unfixed views, or unformed capacities, as to have but little present bearing on the thoughts of his host. Mr. Etherege's visits, however pleasant—his inclina-tions, however enterprising—his speculative inte-rest in commerce, however quick of perception and confidential in tone—were for the time mere mockery by comparison with daily business in Froom-lane.

Early spring had cast an unusual damp upon most houses in Bristol; nor only so, but over very many throughout the three broad kingdoms. At Froom-lane, the effect of unforeseen events, now plain, had been aggravated by the too energetic promptitude towards old Ffloyd. The trouble was passing there, doubtless; but it cost some effort. It was not singular, therefore, that the brow of the "principal" had for many days worn a harder contraction, and his eye an expression of anxiety.

He had been in no mood to linger over the after-dinner table, and converse lightly; but if not obliged to have his carriage ordered again, for an evening visit to the counting-house ere it closed late, would retreat with a clerk, or other business-person, to his own room; whence, till far on in the night, sometimes neither the tea-hour, nor music, nor aught else of evening relaxation that he enjoyed above most men, could so much as venture to draw him. Even young Harry dreaded, lest, ere long, there might be bills of lading to make out, letters to copy, invoices to docket and file, after-hours at home. The private letter-bag was, on such occasions, the sole pretext for Kitty herself, teacup in hand, to glide in coaxingly, and try some little wheedling art of keeping the time in mind—of hinting at fatigued looks and danger to health—or of mentioning that supper was set down-stairs, and *who* formed the frequent whist-party or the casual circle about the harpsichord, that might think his continued absence strange. There was that of latent sternness and reserved distance in his nature, notwithstanding all its cultivation and undoubted liberality of sentiment, with which, thus shown, Mrs. Spencer did not interfere. At no time, during any period of their union, had she been known to come in direct contact with it. Her instincts were acute, but gentle to the excess

of almost cautioning Kate, whose way of pre-
suming upon girlish favour was not the most commendable trait in point.   Kate had a high spirit,
too, perhaps rather much encouraged by her grandmother and uncle at Wrixworth—owing, on their
parts, to a fancy that she took this spirit, along with
her name, from an aunt who died before the girl
was born.   If there had been need, she sometimes
looked as if she could have dared a great deal more.
She said plain things still, and inclined to use freedoms by no means proper to be kept up from nur-
sery days, on the mere ground of early weakliness,
which was long gone, through so much country
liberty.   She sometimes spoke of farming matters,
of hunting topics, with references to horses, dogs,
or gamekeepers' expressions, in a way which her
mother never passed over; though her graver father,
oddly enough, was the one to smile and turn it off.
From her younger brother, too, she had caught an
abrupt, heedless style of phraseology, if not of
technical terms themselves, and was altogether
difficult to keep down since their governess left;
having gone so far as even to hint an impatience
at the fact, that if aught in town were troubling
papa so, and her mamma had need to look unde-
niably anxious, yet the latter did not know the very
least particle about the cause.   To be really angry
—to scold Catherine down—to send her to her

room—was easy enough; to keep the danger of her eyes from flashing round as she went, indignant, straightforward, outspoken to all she might meet, was vain. Mrs. Spencer was the angrier for the truth, perhaps; perhaps her husband was not always the most transparent of men to those who ought to know him best; and perhaps the wife had felt in like manner, long before that, how there were abstruse little corners and delicacies of her own being which *he* had never known, never would know, never had sought to explore. For, whatever he might have been in his earliest youth,—since they two knew each other, there had not been much romance about Dudley Spencer.

Sunshine came out sooner and clearer, however, than might have been expected. Among the first proofs of returning leisure, with its comparative tranquillity, was the signal one of a disposition to nod in his elbow-chair after dinner, over the newspaper—a tendency that had before been growing upon him. He seemed fatigued; and it was with by no means the happiest look in the world, at first, that he perceived his wife carefully shut the dining-room door, after various obscure, rustling, shadowy manœuvres to despatch the rest of the family up-stairs to the withdrawing room; then return silently, in a kind of cautious, half-tiptoe way, to sit formally down opposite him, and spread out her dress, and hem, and begin to say something, yet draw her chair confidentially nearer, till she said, at last, "My dear Dudley, I wish very much to speak with you."

Mr. Spencer lifted up his eyes in a resigned manner, and endeavoured to appear attentive, without changing his attitude.

"Something rather a little important, let me premise," she added, with a degree of matronly dignity, and a self-respectful settling of the lofty head-tire and the hanging lace-pinners, such as sudden visitors could never have observed.

"My dearest Mary, something a little important! Ah! well—and what may it be, pray?" replied the merchant, too little startled to be afraid of any forgotten business care, which had evidently been all disposed of; but yet sitting up in his chair, and setting himself fairly round to the requisition, and checking a yawn. "Well?"

"*Who*, I wish to know, is the Count?" asked Mrs. Spencer.

Her husband for a moment stared. "Oh, Mr. Etherege, you mean, I presume," he said.

"Yes, Mr. Etherege—true; but people persist in calling him so," repeated the lady. "Who is he? is he of good family? is he really rich? where is his property? or do you know anything more about him?"

"Really, my dear," said Mr. Spencer, "you

overwhelm, as well as surprise, me! but I do happen to know everything about Mr. Etherege requisite to his introduction in the best society. He would not otherwise have obtained it, I think. One of the most respected correspondents of our house, in the West Indies, is well acquainted with him, as one of the wealthiest private gentlemen there. His landed property," added the merchant, with a smile, " consists chiefly, I believe, of slaves, sugar-cane, and cane-mills—managed, however, by a factor, with whom it is possible that Broadby and Co. may yet do some lucrative business. So now, my dear, you are as wise as I am, and——"

" Then his title, at least, is not real," persisted Mrs. Spencer, steadfastly. " Some imitation, or hoax, or imposition, or something—I was sure of it."

" My dear Mary," repeated her husband, in increased surprise, " what can all this mean ? I really should be glad to know. Mr. Etherege's title, such as it is—for his candour is one of his most pleasing qualities—is a French one, to which he laid claim through his mother, a niece, at the same time, of old Sir Ralph Herbert's—her father having married a wealthy French creole of high family. As money can purchase a patent of nobility in France, he is sure of it, should he choose to wear the thing. Though anything French is at this moment so abhorrent to every honest man—so base, so dangerous to have to do with—that I—I—I question if—if——" His face flushed as he spoke; a frown was on his forehead, and he almost ground his teeth together in the anger excited by recent French diplomacy and effrontery. "But a truce to this—why do you put these odd inquiries, my dear?"

"Is it really possible, Dudley," rejoined his wife, gravely, "you have never suspected the Count's meaning in these visits?"

Mr. Spencer was rather startled, and threw as penetrating a glance across the dining-room hearth as if the subject of the conversation had sat there, instead of his wife. "What on this earth *do* you intend?" he said, in an emphatic tone; "I must really beg you to be at once explicit, Mary."

"Why, to be sure," was the hurried answer, "the attentions may not have been so marked as to strike everybody; but a mother's eye cannot be deceived, Dudley. Besides, I had a pretty broad hint from Lady Diana Fanshawe, t'other day. There is another lady, whom I scarcely know, but of undoubted position and reputation—a Mrs. Beauchamp, of Beauchamp Cliff—who, it seems, had taken opportunities to throw the gentleman, as much as she could, in my girl's way. Vastly kind, 'tis true, in Mrs. Beauchamp; but I wish I had sooner known of it."

A smile had been diffusing itself over the merchant's surprised countenance, and he looked exceedingly well-pleased, though apparently incredulous, as he said, " Then you really believe, my dear Mary, that Mr. Etherege is smitten with the charms of one of your fair daughters? Upon my word, madam, you look high. But have you grounds for this?" His wife's air of extreme importance and gravity would have been sufficient answer, even without the reproachful glance of reply, or the utterance of his name in astonished emphasis. " Well," he pursued, "such an idea certainly had not occurred to me. As for these late visits of the gentleman's, or all that gaiety and rout-going with Lady Die—who, by the way, is rather a silly, vain woman—why, I have been too busy to think of such matters. Still, I need hardly wonder, on the whole, for Jane has really some very considerable pretensions to beauty, and to a man like Etherege—a West Ind——"

" You mistake a little, though, my love," interrupted Mrs. Spencer, smiling. " 'Tis not Jane at all."

Mr. Spencer became grave. "That alters the case, however," he said. " An engagement, although of a tacit nature—even though not fully satisfactory, either, to all the parties interested— is binding while it lasts. You are aware, in Mary's case, also, I was not early enough consulted; but

still, when the living at Chelmer-cum-Toovey *does*
fall in to him, my word is passed to Dr. Hickenbooth. At best, too, depend on't, although the girl
has what's pleasant about her—and to some of your
modish young sparks of the day her portion itself
would be beauty enough, I warrant me—yet, really,
now, Mary—really, with all your partiality—whatever a worthy bookworm like the excellent rector of
St. Jude's may think, as a widower with a boy to
take care of—still, between ourselves, you know,
as people of the world—why—pooh! I should be
cautious—exceedingly cautious—in allowing the
slightest alteration of—of sentiment. For a mere
likelihood, observe, too—a shadow, as it were."

The merchant had a wise air of rather severe
morality as he spoke; but Mrs. Spencer, after
taking his meaning with some surprise, only smiled
the more wisely still. "No, indeed, Dudley," she
said, very seriously. "I hope not. Dr. Hickenbooth is far too worthy a man for me to wish
another in his stead; nor, if I did, do I sufficiently
affect this Count—this Etherege, in *that* aspect. I
confess I have been a little led away, myself—he
is most agreeable as a visitor, there is but too insidious a pleasantness and attractive candour about
him, 'twas *this* which chiefly made me notice
things! And really it has cost me a great deal of
concern to observe his manner—his looks—with
those fiery black eyes of his, and all that high-

flown foreign way of talking! People with such
eyes are always so sudden and violent, and you
don't know what may happen; and, more than
all, I suspect the silly child thoughtlessly leads
him on!"

" Who—what *can* you mean!" was the impatient
rejoinder. " You cannot possibly be speaking of—
of Kitty?"

" 'Tis Catherine I am talking of, of course," said
Mrs. Spencer. " Since her last visit to Wrixworth
—when she staid so long—I really don't know *what*
ails the girl! Sometimes one fancies it mere liveliness of spirits—at another time 'tis more her idle
turn one has to chide, or some little tiff with
Harry; but as for these addresses on the Count's
part, there cannot be a doubt."

Mr. Spencer eyed his wife in no ordinary amaze.
" Why, 'tis a mere school-girl, the merest child!"
he exclaimed. " Absurd! Psha!"

" You forget, Kate is near seventeen," said the
mother, quietly. Mr. Spencer mused. " But such
coquetry as she proves herself capable of," his wife
continued, " is past comprehension; 'tis absolute
wickedness! The girl declares to her sisters she
knows the Count affects *her* most—and that he has
as much as signified his passion—while she laughs
at Jane's disappointment, as she styles it! Whether
her heart be concerned, I know not; but she shows
a manner, now winning, and now disdainful, with

so much of her sportive disposition, and such inconceivable gay sallies of wit, as visibly have had their effect. You know how she could always contrive to get every one to spoil her and allow her whims, from a child. Besides, there is her voice— and I'm sure 'tis impossible to say where or how she can have learnt it—but she would stand by Mary's harpsichord and sing, if allowed, to Henry's tenor and Mr. Etherege's bass, like any Italian opera-woman! The mischief is but begun —though I fear some strange outbreak of Jane— and, at all events, my dearest Dudley, 'tis better to stop such matters early."

"The wilful little chit!" ejaculated Mr. Spencer, though he smiled. "I could not have imagined it, indeed!"

"The best thing, do you not think," pursued his wife, confidentially, "will be to despatch her down to Wrixworth again, out of the way?"

"Pooh, pooh! why treat the affair with such seriousness!" was the response; and Mr. Spencer, pouring out for himself another glass of wine, seemed unusually complacent as he sipped it. "Were Etherege a lover, he would have nothing to do but go down near Wrixworth, to his own relation's house, after her! That might be well enough, you know, my dear, at a later stage of the affair; but as I scarcely suppose things can have gone so far, as yet—why, it would just defeat your end! Your simplicity, my dear Mary, is scarce a match for this evil world! Or worse, the gentleman would see through the little artifice, of course, stay where he was, and grow cool!"

"To be sure—and that is exactly what I hope," Mrs. Spencer said; the more smartly for the light way in which her solicitude had been met. "It would be very disagreeable, I should think, to have to decline his addresses afterwards—perhaps even at the risk of there being some kind of preference on her part, to check! And really there is no saying—foreigners are so insinuating, at least to young creatures at Kate's age!"

It seemed now Mr. Spencer's turn, however, to be surprised and grave. "Surely, my dear Mary," he said, "you cannot be in earnest when you suppose me declining, for any one of my daughters, the honourable open addresses of a man like Mr. Etherege. On the contrary, he is one whom I am disposed to regard, so far as I have made his acquaintance, with no common esteem. Well-bred, elegant, travelled, liberal, and a man of fortune— it would give me pleasure, on maturer knowledge, to receive him in such a capacity."

It was not only disappointment, with a shade of consternation, that appeared on Mrs. Spencer's features; she drew herself together with a kind of shrinking or loathing in her motion and look.

"But a foreigner!" she said, gazing fixedly at her husband. "Think of that, Dudley—and particularly, somehow, for Kate! Pah! 'Tis absolutely unnatural! I cannot tell you why, but when I think of it I have had a growing horror of that man—pleasant, handsome, and without ill-design as he seems. With Jane, now, 'twould have seemed a great deal more fitting; besides, there's the war, you know, and though most foreigners are infidels, why, I almost fancy what is called renegado were worse if possible!"

"Mary," said her husband, a little severely, "this is too preposterous. So far as the word 'foreigner' has any meaning at all, it so happens that Mr. Etherege is none. As for his sentiments, they are on all points those of the polished man of the world. I confess, were I to choose from among my acquaintance at present, 'twere hard to select the man I could more gladly entrust with the welfare of one of my children—to see whom properly established, let us recollect, is among the heaviest cares to dispose of ere retiring from active life!"

He sighed, reposed his head upon his hand, and, as he gazed thoughtfully towards the fire, looked rather venerably dignified, by the help of the white hair-powder of the day. Mrs. Spencer, when she looked across at him, forgot their topic for the moment, in concern of a more intimate kind, and she drew closer, leaning over, laying her hand on his arm, and saying, "You have talked of that for the last few years, Dudley! When will it be?"

He shook his head. "It is this war makes you so anxious," she said, looking into his face. "Why not leave *now*? We have enough, surely."

"Not quite. No; 'tis these partnerships. Partnerships, Mary," and Mr. Spencer turned round with a playful allusion, "seem a necessary—hem! —a necessary advantage. But as one partner at a time is enough, why, I have now begun paying out the share of Mr. Ffloyd, who has retired wholly— wholly into his sugar-baking line. As you may imagine at a time like the present, this does not take place without an effort and anxiety. A provoking thing has just occurred."

In his wife's interrogative look, there was the interest and willing sympathy, and soothing quiet, of the true partner.

"There was a place, a real country place, suitable in every respect, on which I had set my mind for some time, without any very distinct hope of getting it. 'Twas scarce so much on my own account—as——well, at all events, you know the place, Herbert Court."

"Herbert Court! Yes; know it? what a question, Dudley," and they instinctively exchanged glances; a fulness of memories and of associations of their earliest acquaintance, could not but come at that name.

" 'Tis a long time since that fine evening you and I walked there, Mary," he said, sitting up to stir the fire; " but I recollect quite well, even then, as we looked in at the gates, wishing it were mine, and wondering what it might bring in the market." Mrs. Spencer said nothing, but she looked down, and a faint colour mounted in her cheek, and doubtless she could not help remembering how little such thoughts as these had entered into her mind, or had seemed then to fill Dudley's. " 'Tis mortgaged up to the park pales, you know," he went on, "and 'twas natural to imagine the young man might be glad to get rid of it for his own share of the fair price, though his solicitor's reply to mine was, since Mr. Herbert's return, that no such intention existed. Conceive my annoyance, but the other day, at receiving information, that, as he was about to return to active service abroad, the wreck of the estate would be parted with, should the various mortgagees agree. At this moment, 'tis impossible for me to make any offer— so that at best, my dear, you must wait a year or two before you can expect exactly to be Mrs. Spencer of Herbert Court—ha ! "

Mrs. Spencer had seemed startled by the thought, as if it were something sacrilegious. " Part with

Herbert Court!" she exclaimed, almost breathless.
"Did he really intend it? The noble old place!
Dear me, something most unfortunate must have
happened."

"Nothing of the kind," said the merchant,
standing up before the fireplace in easy English
fashion, with skirts upheld. "He has simply, I
understand, been appointed to the command of a
frigate; a great step for one so recently a lieutenant,
but, natural enough, considering the interest of
Lord Edward de Vere, whose recent election he
was so instrumental in bringing about. What has
a naval officer on service to do with an old house,
and an encumbered property?"

"As for living there," said Mrs. Spencer, "I am
quite sure, my dear Dudley, I could not have done
it; so perhaps you will take less to heart this—this
disappointment you speak of. Just think how
melancholy it would be—I recollect the family so
well when I was a girl: Mr. Herbert, the present
young man's father, with his long, grave face, and
his singular height, and his lovely, delicate
wife; and the younger boy in his dark hat and
feather, looking so old-fashioned and proud, by his
tutor's side—the abbé, as they called the chaplain
—for you know they were Catholics. Next time
I went, after my marriage, what a change! they
were both dead, their eldest hope crushed before—

the other poor boy at sea, and nobody there but an old housekeeper, and the old abbé with the same odd scoop beaver, and his thin golden hair parted, and his fingers spread out by the side of his long coat, like loose gloves. They say there is a ghost in the house—and the peacocks scream so on the old terrace sometimes, that people fancy something has happened. I'm sure I could ill bear to go near it now."

" Pho! my dear," was the self-possessed rejoinder, "that is merely because you never *have* gone near it; the place is dreary, no doubt, because going to ruin; but in summer, if improved, and furnished with a proper establishment, 'twere admittedly a perfect gem of our old domestic architecture. The style is Elizabethan. What a place, now, for Etherege and — and — yes, unlikelier things have happened—and Kate!"

His wife started and stared again; the thought seemed additionally strange to her in that connexion; still it was difficult to resist; there was a plausibility, and possibility, and detailed interest, about the notion, which by degrees drew a smile from her, in response to the extreme complacency it diffused over her husband's features. "Yes, I do think, Dudley," she remarked, at length—"I rather think you mistake as to young Herbert's prospects—that is, the present proprietor—for he can't be so very young *now;* if I recollect rightly, he will succeed to the title of that uncle of his in the north of England, who must be an old man by this time, and they say he has become wealthy."

"Why, yes," was the composed answer; "poor as I am told the baronet's property was, they discovered coal in it, some years ago. At the same time, however, I learn that Sir Ralph Herbert is one of the most rigid Papists in the kingdom, and rather than leave anything he can help to a Protestant, would make a will in favour of the Scotch infidel David Hume himself, who may be quite possibly a Jesuit in deep disguise. Whereas, a nephew who ventures to assert his English liberty of conscience against his interest must be—the very deuce."

"But all *our* Herberts were well-known Catholics," hastily interposed Mrs. Spencer.

"My dear," returned the merchant, with a deliberate suavity, which was characteristic of him, when most sensible of his superior ground above other people; "just observe this simple fact: no naval officer can now obtain his Majesty's commission without having first taken the oath of abjuration, and fully declared himself, not merely a Protestant, but a layman. Not only so careful is our excellent constitution against treachery, but so essentially opposed is the maritime profession itself to the Romish Creed, that ever since our admirals ceased to be sea-sick when they embarked, and our hardy tars to go to prayers in a storm, I question whether anything like a real Papist has appeared at sea, unless to go to the bottom. *We*, now—that is to say, 'Broadby and Co.'"—here the merchant thoroughly enjoyed a stock joke—"we have the felicity, I believe, of employing a number of pagan shipmasters, the particular faith of whose various crews I am unable even to imagine; but this I know, that if I were to hear of their entertaining any deference towards his Holiness at Rome, so as to implore a miracle instead of doing their duty, I should decline their services for the future. Ha! ha! ha! But really—why—here are we talking of these people, this Herbert, in whom I take no special interest—as if fate depended on't. To the point, my dear, then; observe, I do not for a moment think of constraining the girl's wishes in any way, as *you*, Mary, to my excessive surprise, seemed inclined to do; but on no account—on no account whatever, would I have discouragement offered to a man like——"

The parlour door opened as he spoke, and some one came hastily in; it was Kate herself, holding an open letter, and looking unusually serious. "Mamma," she said, advancing, "I have just had this letter from uncle Charles, to inform us that gran'ma is again rather ailing. He thinks it would do her good were we to nurse her a little—with my

usual excess of spirits to divert her, you know.   So
I should wish, please, to have the coach early to-
morrow, half way to Wrixworth; they will send
the chaise to meet it, at Deepbridge turnpike; and
Harry will go with me, I dare say.   Can you spare
Harry, papa?"

Mrs. Spencer and her husband exchanged glances,
but to concert anything was impossible.   The look
of each said plainly, she must be let have her way.
Mr. Spencer said he would see.   Why, yes Harry's
value was not so great but that he might be parted
with.   At bidding her good-night that evening, he
could not resist saying playfully, as he chucked
her under the chin, "Aha, Kitty!   Soho, indeed, Miss Puss, you grow, do you?   Who would
have fancied—but I must not say a word, I suppose?"

An entire ignorance of his mystic meaning was
so clear in the quick, direct, interrogative glance of
Kate, that he spoke plainer.   "Meanwhile, I say,
then—what is our poor Count to do, Mademoiselle
Gipsy?"

There was something singularly perplexing in
her look—half arch, half scornful.

"We must not whisper a word of Wrixworth, I
suppose?" he asked.   Kate turned her head from
the door, and looked inquiringly, gravely, at her
father.   "*Why?*" she said, without the least suffusion of a blush on her composed face, tinted as i

was with life all over, like the inner enamel of an
Indian shell—on either side a little warmer.   "Oh,
well, but at all events, sir, I leave my place to
Jane."

Mr. Spencer shook an indulgent finger at her, and
thought for the first time,with a benign smile, how
really beautiful she was growing; her figure had shot
up of late, her shaded grey eyes shone darker, and
she had a strangely conscious glow and attitude as
she passed gaily from the room.

CHAPTER IX.

HERBERT COURT.

On the old balustraded stone terrace that ran half round Herbert Court, there were two gentlemen talking together, as they slowly turned towards the front of the house : where a particularly well-mounted groom, with a superb hunter in hand, was walking his charge leisurely about, lest the spring breeze might chill them after a smart heat; while a rustic lad with a spade stood uselessly by, and followed the process each way with deferential looks; though a buxom servant-wench, all sunshine and smiles at an open upper-casement, seemed the object of much more gracious consideration on the rider's part. There were half-a-dozen coupled beagles about, and a brace of greyhounds; the master of this retinue being easily distinguishable, in one of the two more conspicuous interlocutors in the foreground. He wore white leather hunting-breeches, riding-boots all dusty and bespattered, a tightly-cut green coat and a skull-shaped black velvet cap with a shade to it; he had a clear, keen, colourless, restless, staring eye, and a prominent aquiline nose, that gave his face a hard, passionless, animal-like effect, sometimes almost fierce. He spoke with a kind of supercilious slur in his voice, too, as if the language were troublesome; and he often mispronounced the words, after a fashion which was rather singular at that day. But he looked young; there was some indescribable trait of what was fine about his features, and a certain generous turn that had been given them, with a regardless air of perfect ease, and a loud freedom of tone, especially when he laughed—all of which made his manner pleasant. He was the former captain of the *Diana* frigate, Lord Edward de Vere, now member for Somersetshire, in which he had a country-seat not far remote from Herbert Court: being a duke's third brother, and having recently sustained a family loss, he had become Lord Beaufoy.

The other, coming bare-headed from within the house with his visitor—tall, powerful, stooping a little, with a face deeply embrowned and bronzed by climates and weathers, and somewhat marked, too, by the small-pox [so common in the days when he could have been a boy], yet still with frank blue eyes in contrast to this, and open, cordial, manly look, and crisp light-brown, careless hair, that gave

out a tint through the powder—it was Herbert
himself.   He seemed much older than he probably
was; far from his being handsome, there was little
at first sight in his favour, save the commanding
height and vigour, which lost somewhat by the sea-
stoop and undisguisable sea-gait.

They had talked of the French fleet that was
said to be ready for sea, with the rumour as to
Spain and Holland joining the enemy.   Then
Lord Beaufoy spoke of the frigate to the command of which Herbert's new commission appointed him, and was indignant at its not being a
line-of-battle ship; while, at the same time, he
mingled with it occasional interjections or cuts of
the horsewhip to his dogs. "By ——, Herbert,"
he said, vehemently, "this Admirawlty must be
blown up. Must make my first speech against 'em,
in—hang it! no, though—that won't do!   I forget
I support Government now.   Well—cawse it, it's
too bad!—how many yaars have ye been a liftenant now?"

"Nine, I think," replied his host, smiling rather
sadly; "but a commander, I ought to recollect,
only *one*."

"Atrocious!—atrocious!" exclaimed Lord Beaufoy. "—— it, Herbert—no wonder ya know so
much. Was only hawf a yaar a liftenant myself,
if I recollect rightly, and never, doorin' that time,
could have been a day on the water. Never could

bear water in my life, else I should say I should
have liked the navy. By —— ! I liked the *Diana*,
you know, Herbert—especially after *you* came to
her. Somehow, ya always understood my orders;
D—— it! the ship seemed never to sail before,
coppar'd though she was; and hang me! I abso-
lootly hated that fella, Turner, or Horner, or
somethin', that I had in the ship befaw! I say,
Herbert, I don't mean to flatter ye; but ye were
by faw the best *first* I evar had; and by —— ! I
should have liked if we could have fought the
Diana against a French ship of her size. Here,
Ponto—you hussy, you! Shan't stay long in
Parliament, I suspect—too doosed talkative for my
taste—all party, you know; and one don't agree
with either of 'em. The fact is, Herbert, I liked
the service; shouldn't wonder, some day, if the
Admirawlty gave me my flag—ha! ha! ha!—these
fellas *are* such d—— obsequious fools, you know,
when a man has any interest! So by —— ! I'll
hoist it at once, and you shall be my flag-captain!
Cawse me! you're the only man I know that I'd
trust with the thing—a fleet, I mean."

Mr. Herbert smiled again, and shook his head.
"I shall be very glad, my lord," he said, "if I
can do my duty satisfactorily in the *Astræa*. She
is a very fine new ship—a forty-four; and but for
your lordship's kind services, I should not have
had the slightest chance of her, I am aware. A

sloop-of-war at the very best would have been my charge; and really, I can scarcely express——"

"Pooh, pooh, Herbert!" interrupted the young nobleman, hastily—"reely, reely! In fact, didn't even know the ship's name—*Astræa*, eh? Is she coppar'd, I say, Herbert?—shouldn't wonder if she weren't even built; they're such fooles, these Admirawlty fellaws; but be sure she's coppar'd, like the *Diana*."

Most new ships were about to be so, Mr. Herbert said, as the system had been found quite successful.

"By-the-by, Herbert," asked his lordship, confidentially, as they turned again on the terrace, "I never used to inquire much into these things, you know, at sea; in fact, never *was* a great hand at the ropes; because, you see, navigation and tactics, and so on, were more my forte—but where *was* the coppahr? Do they stick it astarn, or under the keel, or where, eh? Hang it! never exactly liked to ask; but I suppose it had somethin' to do with her sailin' trim, or steerage, or somethin'."

It was with difficulty that the quondam lieutenant preserved a grave face while explaining to his former captain that the copper in question was a substitute, on vessels' bottoms, for the defective wooden sheathing on which worms, barnacles, rot, and weeds, produced such detriment of every kind.

"Ah, so!—I perceive!" was the reply; and

thereupon Lord Beaufoy, with a sagacious air, meditated a little.

He looked round at the quaint old mansion beside them, where the spring sunshine—blowing past, as it were—mottled the old deep-red wall with flying lights, and widened on it to the clasping ivy-leaves round a buttress, and glittered in some many-framed broad casement, till it vanished. He glanced down at the fine old high-hedged garden, from which the terrace rose at the back; where the dark hornbeam and glistening crisp-edged holly were green about the budding bushes, and round the newly-turned black mould of sloped strawberry-banks, or formal flower-beds edged with box; and where the pleached trellises and branch-spread southern wall of brick were visible through the want of leaves: with the bare orchard hard-by that sheltered it all from the east; the hollow of the park behind, rising up into massive timber; and the skirt of firs upon the other side, which hid the offices from view. It was early in the day; the forenoon was full of white, windy light, gushing out at times in hazy amber rays from under clouds, while the dry March dust blew abroad, and the sounds of farm-work were everywhere near, with crows following the harrow. To catch the scent of fresh earth that was in the air, and the fume of rubbish-burning, or the very smell of stable-stuff tossed over in the fields, was

pleasant indeed. About two miles over the woods
that way could be seen the smoke of Wrixworth
village; beyond, the faint glitter of the river
Axe; far distant, like a visionary shape, the
spires of Wells Cathedral. Close at hand, a
sunny steam rose from the stirred garden-soil;
the green winter-mouldiness about the branches of
trees shone out; the breeze bore off the harsh
clamour of the rookery beside the front avenue,
and the monotonous love-cooings of the rows of
pigeons on the porch-roofs, with incessant chirp-
ings of sparrows in the load of ivy and woodbine
there, leaving only a warm, moist, shaded stillness
by the library windows; from whence, by a glass-
door that still stood open, the two gentlemen had
at first come. This room was long and spacious,
and with its log-fire glowing on the wide hearth-
place, its darkly-polished floor, and broad, mul-
lioned casements of Queen Bess's time, crossed by
the light from one end that was well-nigh all
window, it showed cheerfully transparent. The
vellum of old books, red labelled, and the few
more modern shelves of these in calf, with gilt
letterings, served to enrich its interior; and even
some antiquated family portraits, in ruffs and
peaked beards, or with deep-curled wigs, and large,
smooth visages, contributed an ornamental effect
from outside: but it was the inmate, with his
occupation, that gave its chief peculiarity to the

apartment. He was seen distinctly, as the day-light went through and through; a thin old man, in a loose, long-skirted coat of a clerical colour, and a dark velvet skull-cap, looking busily from book to book among a number before him on the library-table. Till he raised his head, he might have been thought some modern alchemist or old magician; but his mild, bare face, with the spectacles, and the scanty remnants of light-coloured hair parted toward either side, could confirm no such fancy. The thin locks had a golden tinge in the sun, so that he looked at that distance partly boyish, partly like what angels are represented in old pictures. A huge dog of the Newfoundland breed, lying amidst the floor, lifted its head from its paws at any motion, to watch with a wise air; and when the old man rose, took off his spectacles, and went to the great casement at the end, it sat up on its hind legs to look, as if with interest. In the recess of the projecting bay-casement was a deal table, so covered with stray articles, tools, and odd furniture, as to re-semble a work-bench; a birdcage hung near, with some ingenious mechanism for its prisoner's occupation; beside it was a clock of some strange construction; opposite, the perfect model of a full-rigged ship-of-war—a three-decker; chemical apparatus, retorts, Leyden jars, crucibles, wheel-work, were in confused possession of the space.

Nor was it doubtful to whose industry they all testified, when the occupant of the library put a watchmaker's eye-glass into one eye, seized some implement from the table, and stooped over a vice that was fastened by the edge. The worn velvet of his skull-cap glistened with a dusky streak of light to the glare of noon beyond, in which, on the balustrade of the terrace outside, a pair of peacocks, for which Herbert Court was rather noted, sat sunning themselves quietly, with crested heads against the south, and flaunting gorgeousness of train let down aslant—blue, green, and glossy emerald with shifting purples, and the gathered richness of moon-spotted fringes—like living fabrics from the Orient, or things from an Arabian tale.

Lord Beaufoy eyed it all carelessly, and looked from Mr. Herbert round to the terrace-steps again, with an expression of countenance as if he checked a whistle. "They've put Rear-Admiral Keppel over the Channel Fleet, I hear," he said, as he flicked off a very early butterfly from the wall with his whip; "and Sir Hugh Palliser, next in command—a Whig and a Tory! Very fine and liberal in a Tory Government! But hang it, why——Here, Juno; Ponto, you devil! By the lord, these two dogs'll strangle themselves round that balustrade!—Why, it's weak. Can't please all parties, you know. I hope they've given you a good *first*, though, Herbert."

"I have not seen my first-lieutenant yet," was the answer; "but I know something of him—an active, steady officer, older than myself, I am ashamed to say, who will understand his duty, I have no doubt. However, I shall at once go down to Portsmouth, and see the ship fitted out under my own eye."

"Take my advice, and see you've got a good *first*," persisted his lordship. "It's a great point, Herbert. Why, if you don't fyind him to yar taste, kick up a noise—nothin' like a noise; these Admirawlty fools can't stand it, they're so infernally weak just now—doosed weak, privately speaking, I assure you. I say, Herbert, though," and Lord Beaufoy looked scrutinisingly round again; "my dear fellow, you—you must be—I mean, excuse me, I suppose you are particularly partial to the sarvice, are you?"

A deeper colour was visible in his host's sunburnt complexion; but Lord Beaufoy did not look at him. "Why, hardly," Mr. Herbert said. "No, my lord; if I ever had any boyish desires about fame, or adventure, or any such idle notion, they are gone a good while ago, I think. Even the war scarce stirs me; I had seen enough of it before. I went to sea in a thoughtless moment, while a younger brother; and pride kept me there. 'Twas soon necessity."

Lord Beaufoy winced, and coloured redder far than Mr. Herbert. "By ——," he said, confusedly; "of course, I forgot—yes. But hang it, you ought to stay at home. Herbert, a man like you should go into Parliament. You must have some prime shootin', too, about."

"Excellent, my lord," said his companion. "Over the whole estate, I have at least that right; and the game is so very plentiful, as to be seriously complained of by the farmers. Your lordship would do me a favour, as I shall not be here to see it kept down, by shooting over the ground, with any friends whom the season brings hereabout. Somersetshire sport is famous."

Lord Beaufoy muttered something hastily about seeing the land-bailiff about it—a lease of the thing—money always useful, in fact—found so himself, hang it! And again he vented execrations on the navy, ships, seamen, the sea, and salt provisions. The learned Dr. Johnson could not now be more emphatic in detestation of them.

"'Tis habit with me," said his host, gravely; "duty, I trust, I may say, and loyalty. Besides, I am a restless man, my lord. Strange as it may seem at this moment, the very thought of spending my days here—of seeing this summer come in— bright, hot, green, endless—I shudder at it. I had rather—ah, well, pardon me." Mr. Herbert passed his hand vacantly across his forehead, and Lord Beaufoy stared at him a little. "'Tis odd," the former continued; "but I dare say my old friend and tutor within, there—the Abbé Horne—takes a livelier concern in this war than I do. As for the art, I am sure he understands it a hundred times better."

"Oh," said his lordship, turning again to eye the library windows. "Hang it, though!—what the doose *is* his reverence about *now*, eh?"

"'Tis a model of a new field-piece, I believe, to fire without a touch-hole, so as never to be spiked by the enemy," Herbert answered. "'Tis but one, however, out of a hundred of his projects and inventions. Priest and scholar as he is, and he devoutest, I think, of men, his great earthly delight is in science. He corresponds with various learned men, and has been named by some to the present vacancy in the French Academy."

"Very fine old man," said his lordship, using his eye-glass admiringly—"very fine. But corse me, a gun, you know, Herbert, eh?—for a priest, too! Quite sure he is not a Jesuit?"

"The abbé *is* a Jesuit, my lord," said the master of Herbert Court, tranquilly, "and so simple a being—so ignorant of the world, and incapable of harming even a worm or a fly—that I know he has kept a sad blank in that part of his cabinet for natural history. Still his knowledge of fortification, gunnery, or tactics; his acuteness in military plans, or even naval ones; above all, his ingenuity in inventing engines for destruction, with the manner of their use—has the more surprised me."

" By ——" ejaculated the young nobleman, " a perfect treasure! Take him with ye, man ; make him chaplain to the *Astræa.* Let's see—a frigate don't carry chaplains, perhaps. I'll get my brother Chester to give the Admirawlty a hint, d—— it ; why, 'twould do the sarvice a mighty deal o' good —a man of science, look ye. Hang me, Herbert, my dear fellow, he'd have opportunities of practice he cannot have in this d—— place ; he'd put you up to capturing a seventy-four. You'd get knighted at *least.* They're such doosed fools, the Admirawlty men ; they'll do anything of the sort."

"My dear lord," said Mr. Herbert, restraining a smile, " you forget the abbé's religion. He is a Catholic, like the family he has been so faithful to; ay, even though the last of them has not proved so himself. Happily for his gentle mind, *that* is as yet unknown to him. But a Catholic, my lord, in this free country—especially a priest—has still reason to rejoice if he escapes the penalty of high treason for celebrating the holy mass; or if he can retain landed property, not to speak for a moment of acquiring it." A gloom came over Mr.

Herbert's countenance, as they turned together from the windows, and he was silent.

"True, true," exclaimed Lord Beaufoy, with a desponding and desperate look in every direction but that of his friend. "Hang it, yes; we're a set of bigots, tyrants—low scoundrels, in fact. Curse me, it's not fair. I'd turn Catholic to-morrow— but there's the seat for the county, you know; couldn't take the oaths—'twould fall vacant at once; and, by George, I want to *speak!* But, I say, didn't I hear something lately about a bill of relief, or somethin' that the Whigs are bringin' in just now? By ——, Herbert, though I support Government, I'll go up and vote for it—do you think——"

"The ministry have already agreed, I think, my lord," replied his host, "to accept the measure. 'Tis said, however, that the Presbyterians in Scotland are vehemently indignant, although it does not extend to that country; and that, in case of the bill passing, mobs are ready to rise in the manufacturing towns here, over England. Even reason itself could not convince a man so far, I think, as to lead him *just now* to desert the religion of his fathers."

"By Jove! no," said Lord Beaufoy, emphatically. "The fellow would be a dem poltroon, sir; and by all that's holy, I'd tell him so. Confound all such prejudice; hang it, what is it, after all? nothin' but sooperstition. Mr. Herbert, I didn't know till this moment you were a Catholic; but, 'pon my word, I honour you for't."

Mr. Herbert drew himself to his full height, and almost stared in his turn at Lord Beaufoy; till his lordship's utter unconsciousness was too evident to be doubted. "Pardon me, my dear Lord Beaufoy," he said, stopping still, and very seriously; "but your lordship slightly mistakes me. I am, of course, no Catholic, else I could not hold his Majesty's commission; for the Test Act is not likely to be repealed at present, I suspect—which prescribes that every British officer, in either service, who does not take the sacrament according to the usage of the Church of England within a certain time, shall not only incur the heaviest penalties, but become an absolute outlaw in the gravest respects."

Lord Beaufoy bit his lip, and, stifling some fearful oath, looked about for some of his dogs to bestow a cut of the whip upon; in default of which he again turned to pace the terrace with his host. "Most infernal," he said. "No wonder the sarvice goes to the doose—eh!"

"Why, I entered it young," responded his companion, "and in the navy, while a midshipman—'tis little matter what faith one's family may entertain. At home, here, ere accepting my first commission, I had the strongest scruples—indeed, the very thought of it would have hastened a

widowed parent to the grave; and I had the deepest reverence, as well as affection, for my old tutor.
I consulted him, ready to throw up the profession
when it perhaps promised most brightly, and then
there were no temptations whatever *here*. The abbé
himself had a singular interest in the sea; in discovery, astronomical observation, foreign rarities or
products; though he had never made any voyage,
save across to Calais in his youth, and back, later
in life. He had taught me geometry and navigation too, with an extreme zest, during the intervals
of my stay at home. It was he himself who, on consideration of the difficulty, pronounced it a casuis-
tical point, which he would take into his own hands
—a reserve in conscience was allowable, he said—
the end justified the means; and he was my confessor, besides. I took my commission, my lord,
and found in the end that the abbé, with all his
geometry, did not know the world. One cannot
go round it, and beat about it, carrying one's church
with one, or one's confessor, or one's trust in Holy
Mary and the saints."

"Hang it, no, of corse not, Herbert," said his
lordship, nodding approval. "The old gentleman
should have advised you to enter the French navy.
They're all Catholics there, I'm told."

"It seems to me, my lord," rejoined Mr. Herbert,
"that there is something in an Englishman—but
especially in a seaman—by nature opposed to that

faith.   One sees much—he too often does much—
which he cannot reconcile with it; no doubt I have
met with that at sea, my lord, as well as sometimes felt it, that has been like to shame one into
religion; nay, it is a calling in which you cannot
but stand resolved at times on a better life; but
'tis too soon forgot."

Lord Beaufoy made a gesture of assent, looking
much more solemn than his former first-lieutenant.

"The truth is, my lord," the latter continued,
looking down thoughtfully, as they mechanically
retraced the terrace in quarter-deck fashion, "'tis
a dangerous thing, at best, to change one's religion
—to leave that wherein one was bred, however
unthinkingly.   It raises bitter qualms at a time—
often, you know not if you have got any in its
place.   'Twould touch any one, on the other hand,
to know how the abbé, though a Jesuit as I said,
doubts to this day, without knowing the effect of
his counsel, whether he did rightly in delivering it.
His conscience the more seems to prick him, as the
time grows longer—lest in steering aside from the
true course, as it were, he may have caused some
evil we none of us know.   The good soul; how
little does he suspect the actual truth !   The effect
is, my lord, that when the abbé reads the morning
and evening Latin to the housekeeper, the servants, and the one or two stray adherents he has
at his Sunday chapel, too, and at mass—I must, in

mere mockery, attend, if at home. 'Twould kill
the old man to discover that the master of the
house—through *him*, too—had become a heretic,
perhaps worse. I must even still confess to him
on occasion; and well meant though it is—while
on his favourite topics he would confide everything
to me, still keeping up somewhat of the tutor, as
his acute intellect easily enables him—all this
troubles one very deeply, my lord. Were there
no other cause—were peace renewed to-morrow—
still, methinks, this house—this old, empty, half-
decayed home of mine—could not hold me in
quiet. While summer sequesters it deeper in the
woods, with its dull little household, and the abbé
patiently brooding over his books and models,
either I must be on my way to something active—
something that quickens the blood, and stirs the
mind; or there will be some——Ah! talk of
shadows, spectres—there are horrors that haunt
one most at noon-day."

Mr. Herbert's deep voice trembled; he seemed
flushed and excited; and, as he quickened his pace
or stopped, Lord Beaufoy instinctively kept time
with him. "Pooh, pooh, my good fellow—my
dear Herbert," said his lordship, in a soothing tone,
as he laid a hand on his friend's arm, "I'm afraid
you *have* got a leetle sooparstitious, eh? Come,
come, hang it, you know, man—it won't do. A
first-class man—first-class officer like *you*, too."

Herbert looked round vaguely; but there was something in the well-meant kindness of Lord Beaufoy, that made his host warmly grasp the hand which touched him. "Hist!" whispered Lord Beaufoy, suddenly, "here he comes—your abbé, Herbert. Not a word, ye know. S't! Here, Viper, sir—Ponto, you slut ye, *down*."

CHAPTER X

THE OLD STORY.

THE Abbé Horne emerged from the glass-door upon the back terrace, putting on his clerical scoop-hat, and holding at the same time a trowel and a watering-pan; while the great dog, gravely following, carried a basket of roots and seeds. Nor would the gentlemen have been perceived, as the abbé was making straight for the steps down into the garden; but Lord Beaufoy, in his restless way, affecting an unconscious, indifferent, careless air, and calling with a chirp to the Newfoundland, drew the old man's notice perforce. The abbé bowed with a courtly grace, that savoured, however, rather of old Versailles than modern England.

"H'm—hem! What a splendid fellow of a dog, sir!" said Lord Beaufoy, hastily. "By G——

that's to say—hang it, I mean the Virgin Mary—
I envy your reverence! What—Neptune is his
name? and a very good name too! Here, Neptune
—here, boy!"

Neptune's tail slightly waved, but he did not
approach.

The abbé bowed again, though with great
gravity of expression. He looked straight up into
the snowy whiteness and fitful radiance of the
windy March sky. "What genial weather, gentlemen!" he said, with a pleased look, and turned
to Mr. Herbert. "The violets must be out, I
think, Richard," he added, "and the early
cowslips, and saxifrage. I should have put in
these bulbs sooner, but the seeds will be in good
time. We ought not to expect without working,
ought we, Richard?"

"No, my father, no!" replied Mr. Herbert,
looking away.

"And we need not. *Laborare est orare*, we
know!" continued the abbé, smiling mildly towards both. "What a real miracle, after all, is
this world, this air, this growth, these buds and
dry clods, opening into newness of life! It leads
an old man like myself almost into the sense of
youth again, though rather it should awe him by
the sacred mystery of Easter to come—of a sure
resurrection!" He crossed himself, and for a
moment the expression of his eyes was not visible.

"I bid you good-day again, my lord; 'tis such weather, I should think, as the hunter loves!" As the abbé passed on, he approached Herbert, and added, lowering his voice, "You will be glad to know, my son, that our new field-piece is likely to succeed. I am on the point of the discovery; but it tries the eyes—I vary it a little by the garden."

There had been remote sounds of the hunting-horn now and then from the woods, and they now broke out distincter, nearer, with a halloo and a tantivy, and the querulous yelp of the hounds. Lord Beaufoy started. "Yoicks! hark-away!" he cried, waving his cap suddenly, and hurrying towards the front. "You, there! Where's my horse, d—— it? These dogs are only in the way now—take them, *you* Tom. Well now, Herbert, I wish you'd have joined us; they've found the scent again, the last of the season, too! Yoicks! Tally-ho! It can't be helped though—shall see ye, of course, before you sail—so——" He waved his hand, and was off at full speed.

Mr. Herbert stood till they were out of sight, then turned into the house. Shortly after, he came out again with his hat on, and passed round into the park, and began to wander idly away. Suddenly he quickened his pace, and struck into a by-path that led through the woods, where the galloping sound of his dog Neptune's feet and the

panting of his breath were soon close behind him.
" Ha, Neptune !" said Herbert, turning and
stooping to stroke the dog. " You seem to know
my mind better than I do ! 'Tis the old path—ay,
you and I are two equally silly fools!" But
Neptune wagged his tail, and looked up very wisely
indeed. So they went on until the sunlit smoke
of Wrixworth village burst upon them from among
its bare orchards, with the breezy rippling of the
small river, and the changeful glitter of the church
weathercock. Beneath them was the ugly old
squat-shaped Hall, all yellow-washed and black-
windowed, with its rich meadows, snug paddocks,
and fat cattle newly turned out, and the busy
labours in a map-like variety of fields ; beyond it
again, a mournful fragment of the ancient Priory
glimpsed from the distant water-side, steeped in
mellow sunshine, softly reflected under its green
base of sward, with azure space above it and below.
There Herbert stood leaning against the stile, and
gazed for perhaps half an hour ; the dog stood
also, then looked to Herbert, and sat down on his
hind legs and contemplated the scene again, till he
at last lay down composedly. But his capricious
master, after heaving a profound sigh or two, one
of them well-nigh amounting to a groan, forthwith
began, as it were, to make a distant circuit of the
place.

They were passing quickly under a high hedge-

topped bank, where the early primroses already
peeped out, and the brassy-yellow dandelion-flower
and starry wind-weed, and pink-blossomed, large-
leafed coltsfoot flared along, like things that bore
their own sunshine; and Herbert was about to
spring up over it to the open common that spread
homeward, when he heard voices there. On the
other side, in fact, were a party from the Hall,
just collected at that spot to see the hunt go past,
as the sounds from the moory upland seemed to
promise. He knew them at once by their mourning dresses for old Mrs. Duttridge, who had been
three weeks dead. The elderly Miss Duttridge
and her niece, Miss Mary Spencer, in black riding-
habits, with black beaver hats and veils, sat on
their ponies, one of which, showing restlessness as
the cry of the dogs came nearer, was held by a
black man, with a black ribbon round his straw hat.
Behind, stood Master Henry Spencer, very eager,
and somewhat noisy in his sympathy with the
hunt; while his sister Catherine, in deep mourning, but in plain walking-dress, stood silent near
him. Her back was towards the hedge, but he
who was looking at her could not err in the matter;
though it was singular to see her so motionless, so
quiet, and apparently grave. It was, indeed, the
first time he had caught a glimpse of her since her
grandmother's death; for, considering the Abbé

Horne, he could scarce have ventured to go much to Wrixworth church.

Herbert drew back without a sound—a breath. No rustle of the hedge had betrayed him, and he crouched himself a little to go down the path again, the way he had come, to avoid them. Could it be borne that he should be thought actually to seek them out, or to devise ways of apparent accident for it!

All at once he heard an exclamation. He had, indeed, forgotten Neptune. Neptune, scrambling through a gap, and bounding up, had thrust his cold nose into the young lady's hand as she stood, and held his head up for her to pat, while his tail waved grandly. From her brother there was a shout of, "Hallo, Neptune! where have *you* come from, eh? Why, Kate," he added, "Mr. Herbert must be about himself!" The youth turned, and jumped upon the bank to look over. Herbert came sauntering forward with a calm manner. He nodded to Henry, and, though annoyed, could not help a smile. "I was sure you were coming, sir, of course," said the lad, in a deferential way, "as soon as I saw Neptune."

So Mr. Herbert came round by the turnstile upon the common, with a serious bow. He met a general utterance of pleased recognition from the ladies; though it was unavoidable to English people, after the late event at the Hall, that a degree of gravity and a rather awkward pause should follow the hand-taking, health-ascertaining, and weather-settling. But just then some farm-folks in a neighbouring field were seen running towards the dingle beyond, while some boys from the common rushed shouting to the same point; at which Harry Spencer darted down the slope, waving his cap; while, as the noise of the pack burst forth in full cry, the ponies and their riders also, with the attendant negro, and even Neptune, so partook of the excitement as to start off toge-ther in a body round the brow of the hill.

The pair who were thus suddenly and unex-pectedly left behind, walking forward by the path at a quick rate, did not at first exchange words. All Herbert's pride rose in his mind, and frowned sternly upon the discovery he had been lately making there, of that insidious, senseless, useless passion of his—which he had resolved to run no risk of betraying; for it was not only the wealth of the family that interposed such a bar, nor the recent well-known fact that old Mrs. Duttridge had left the bulk of her fortune to her youngest granddaughter; but had nothing of the kind existed, she was a mere girl, and he almost twice her age. The truth was, that from the moment when he had perceived the enchantment he was under, her budding beauty had seemed to rise still more immeasurably above his reach each time he saw it again. Not very many weeks ago, indeed, when the last autumn shooting-season first introduced him at the Hall, and at the bustling election-time that had led to frequent intercourse there, she had been to him but a gay-eyed, sprightly figure among others, with something of ¦the favourite's caprice, and the girlish glee of one fresh from school and town. Her obvious interest in the field-sports had helped to throw him off his guard. In the old English madrigal singing which he had joined at, she had corrected his "time" as openly as she did her uncle's; before the election she had been . an eagerer Tory by far than any of them, laying plans on behoof of Lord Beaufoy, sewing favours of blue ribbon for his lordship, and canvassing among farmers' wives, or even amidst the cross-grained Whigs and stubborn freeholders themselves. So that if they had all been made quite well acquainted in this manner—till Neptune was a half-spoiled dog, and no one wondered to see Miss Duttridge and her niece thus accompanied on their return from the village, or the squire and his niece coming slowly from their ride with the same escort—Herbert had tranquilly plumed himself all the while on the impossibility of any danger. No doubt, seeing so little of society, he found their circle pleasant; they were neighbours, and had a homely ease and genuineness about them. But as

for Miss Kate Spencer, nobody had ever said anything about her face, or her voice, or any peculiar
attraction hovering round what she said and did;
nor had these struck him at the outset with the
least alarm; while he had thought that even *he*
could every day more carefully distinguish, slight
as was his knowledge of the *land*-world, or his experience of the sex, how remote that girlish liveliness and sisterly intimacy were from all but
friendship.

Thus, by the most prudent and imperceptible
degrees, had Herbert lost himself, and with the
sudden consciousness had resolved, as he thought,
never to betray it by look, word, or sign ; while he
surrendered his whole heart to the strange luxury—
more strange to him than to most men of his age.
Till at the dread of some hasty glance or rash expression, he had drawn back, and kept as much as
was possible away from Wrixworth. He had endeavoured still, with a great deal of self-command,
to keep up the due courtesies, and be civil and
calm, yet not cold; meantime applying, very
sensibly, for his appointment to active service
again. She herself, indeed, he fancied, had by
degrees grown more reserved and distant; nay, all
the opportunities that had been open, could he
have sought them, seemed in some undefinable
way at an end with the party of guests at the Hall,
and the election week. Yet *once*—in the porch-

door, when the squire was pressing his stay to
dinner—had his brain turned giddy between indignation and a strange delight, when the group of
ladies seemed urging Kate with smiles to try her
power; but she had put on a disdainful air, and
almost tossed her head, looking indifferent as some
face at a fine ball, or at a play, or in a picture.
How constantly gay, too, had she been afterwards,
the few times he had seen her; so young, so but-
terfly-like, in fact, and full of spirits, and at times
absolutely frivolous, that he had tried to underrate
her, with a bitterness which by that ever-growing
beauty of hers was made desperate. Then, without
his hearing of it—without the chance of a good-bye
—her sudden return home to Bristol had taken place.
So that, when her absence came out as it were by
accident in the Hall parlour, at his next random
visit, there came a chill like death for that moment
about his heart; nor was it difficult to perceive
that the squire's heartiness had then lost somewhat
of its previous warmth, while the maiden aunt was
visibly stiff amidst her hospitalities, and even the
deaf, venerable old lady in her high-backed chair,
who had shown a partiality to his name and house,
had looked less benevolently interested in what he
said than usual. This was all over, and he had been
gaining a degree of calm, in the expectation to be
soon gone; but now at the sight of her face, the
sound of the voices, the touch of hands, with the

mourning dress and the unaccustomed gravity, all
these things rushing back, seemed as if they would
have choked him. He walked on, mastering himself sternly, and meaning to speak next moment of
the spring weather again, of the fine sport, the Somersetshire pack, the pleasure and excitement even
to on-lookers—anything—but it was vain; the
pretence would have made his voice sound, he felt,
like some unnatural or uncouth noise in a jest.
All this awkwardness is doubly awkward, when a
man comes to the first full knowledge of it at
thirty, or a little past that age—aware, too, that he
looks/feels and/still older—not sure, either, where
the passion may lead.

It was the young lady who broke the silence
herself, as they hastened on; perhaps forced to it,
but, if gravely enough, by no means in a fluttered
or uneasy way. "Since last seeing him—Mr. Herbert—they had suffered a severe loss at the Hall,"
she said, and her tone was so unfalteringly distinct
and self-possessed, yet serious, while she slightly
turned towards him, that it at once made Herbert
comparatively calm.

He answered scarce less composedly, and still
more gravely. "Yes, it *must* have been so. Mrs.
Duttridge," he had found, "had slightly known
his own mother, and had regretted not knowing
her more, although circumstances had of course
kept them necessarily apart. He had too seldom

enjoyed the privilege of seeing Mrs. Duttridge; of talking with her; but, in so far as he had done so, it had deeply gratified him. True, the event had revived recollections in his mind that were painful indeed."

There was something still softer than its wont in the voice which responded; it seemed desirous to soothe. "Her dear grandmother had more than once spoken of Mrs. Herbert. She had never ceased, to the last, to think and speak of those she knew well, even very early friends; and among them had been—that is, she had more than once happened to mention Mrs. Herbert and her two boys. It had been difficult to keep her in mind, indeed, how *he*—Mr. Herbert—was really the same with the younger of these. But she always spoke of him so very kindly." "Grandmamma's opinion, Mr. Herbert, I assure you," she said, turning with more animation towards him, "is worth gaining; she is so wise—so good a judge of people's characters, so very superior, indeed, to most other——"

But her steady voice suddenly faltered, and she stopped at the sharp recollection of a loss that had evidently been too gradual, too much according to the course of nature, to be always realised as it was thought to deserve. He saw her eyes fill with tears, and she turned her head away again. Though in the utter silence of the moment he had still seen her, while the breezy air was blowing in her veil and hair, and all the open light of the

south swimming up and beating against her face,
so that her colour glowed out fair and warm in it
from the mourning silk and crape, and a shadow
of her dark hat and veil fell round half her hair—
making the gold threads elsewhere in it shine but
the distincter through its up-drawn, off-turned mesh,
whose brownness the white powder softened yet
enriched, like morning hoar-frost on the abbé's
sunniest bank of spring thyme, of marjoram and
balm. To Herbert her countenance had never yet
seemed so exquisite; perhaps because he had not
before seen it in such a mood. She was the mere
girl no longer, he felt, as she had been three
months ago; but in motion, accent, thought, as in
dress—young although she was—a woman. Her
slight tears agonised him; he forgot what it was
they had talked of, though he would have given
the world to have said something suitable, if not
consolatory. But, amidst it all, how completely
distant from his mind then, in the pure unsuitable-
ness of the thing, and in its absolute uselessness,
became the least approach to hope or passion,
eager wishes or tremulous ardour, or the poignant,
longing uncertainty of a lover. It was not despair
he felt; rather an intense wonder and delight at
being thus favoured to walk there, none other
accompanying them; with which he went on,
shutting his thoughts against the question of how
soon it must end.

"She *was* so, at least," said his companion more

firmly, correcting herself after a slight pause, which to Herbert may have seemed some whole celestial cycle, or measureless chaotic blank, full of blended light and darkness, mingling ecstacy and pain. The words recalled his thoughts, and he hastened to say such things as he could, or had heard, of the tranquil end of the pious—with the precious worth and charity of venerable ladies, and their sage and benign examples. So they talked on more and more intimately, till, as Herbert, drawing from the Abbé Horne and his own old associations, slid unawares into some account of a Romish martyr, or Papal saint, involving virtues and works that seemed superhuman, or merits which were ambiguous, if not questionable—he was checked all at once by the growing expression of archness on his hearer's face. Catherine Spencer fairly smiled at his perplexed look, as if her former sprightliness of temper overcame her; there was a half-ironical point in what she said, with a mischievous sparkle of the eye, which would have been annoying but for the sweetness of the tone.

" We are such Protestants, you see, Mr. Herbert, at Wrixworth."

Mr. Herbert stammered, and murmured something in vague explanation; the more confusedly, [on the Abbé Horne's account,] as he remembered how everybody thereabouts must suppose him of the same faith as his family had been. Nor was

it a thing he was proud of, or very well knew how
to justify, if *he* had ceased to be so. What, indeed,
had he to put in its place?

"'Tis perhaps bigoted," rejoined the young
lady, quickly; "for we all think the fifth of
November a very great day indeed. My uncle
would fain, too, have me read 'Fox's Book of
Martyrs;' though I am sure he knows very little
about it himself—such mere cruel, mistaken zeal,
that has long repented, or would so now-a-days,
would it not? And all his vehemence were gone
on the instant, I *do* think, Mr. Herbert, were he to
see a priest or a monk, at least were he to speak with
them, or even with the Pope himself."

When Herbert glanced downward at her composed, smiling face, thus young and unconscious
of his hidden emotion; and when he heard the
unhesitating music of those accents, feeling at the
same time that collected manner, as she rapidly
kept pace with him—he was deeply thankful at
never having been led to precipitate himself, in
some rash moment, down the passionate abyss—to
transfer himself in an instant from the acquaintance, the friend, to the lover, with that wild
probability hovering above which seems possible
even to the securest or most cautious suit; of the
surprised glance, the inanimately cold expression,
and rigid withdrawal, and set civility of reply.
How much better as it was—the admitted friend,

almost the brother! For once or twice, as he spoke on, she looked up with that smiling, half-respectful, half-inquiring confidence, which younger sisters show; nor was it with other feelings than of high guidance and protection, though the blood *must* rush more violently toward the heart, that at the stile he gave his hand to aid her over. Yet, Heavens! just once again, the arch expression flitting through that smile! And the bright after-glance could not be caught, but was turned to the sky, and the distant hill, and to the trees at hand. If she still smiled or laughed, looked serious or looked gay, he could not see. Did that lustrous, airy, twinkling little consciousness, mock him, or tempt with its shy light to some infatuation? In what a silence they were walking on, too, and how slow! It were worth worlds, could any magic bring it to pass, only to see round into that face, and meet those eyes, and hear but a syllable of the remotest hope from those rosy lips. The wide, fluttering, dusty noon-day, was dreamlike around; the March sounds, the spring rustlings, the confused place and time. Ha! why, Neptune! Yes, Neptune, poor dog! bounding, basking, springing from his peremptory master to the more favouring patronage by his side. Where were they? Where was the hunt—the party—the common itself, or that dell near Wrixworth?

Herbert stopped, and looked round him, much

confused, nor knowing, at first sight, where they were. They had hurried off into wood and park, and wandered afterwards, so that an hour must have passed at least. Miss Catherine Spencer stood surprised too, and looked somewhat dismayed to hear that they were now somewhere about three miles and a half from Wrixworth; till, at Mr. Herbert's earnest excuses, she spoke of it laughingly, with boasts of her hardy country-breeding. So they had turned to go back, when Harry Spencer appeared on the bank above, shouting, glowing with exercise, and flourishing a stick he had just cut. Harry had followed Neptune, thinking Neptune was only on his way back to Herbert Court, where he (Harry) had promised some tough ash-wood some day to the abbé, whom he knew by this time very well. He had forgot all about Kate, and said the rest were very likely gone home, though he wasn't sure.

"What! ain't you going back by Herbert Court, Kitty?" asked he, in a lower voice, as he stood by her. "You look tired, I'm sure; and, at any rate, you'd be all the better of a rest, you know. Mrs. Brinds, the housekeeper, keeps first-rate bread, besides all sorts of home-made sweetmeats; and I know her quite well; in fact, I really can't go home with you, I'm afraid, without I see the abbé. Why, from where we are, it's the nearest way."

Kate Spencer coloured for the first time, with a

vexed look at her brother. But it was impossible to help laughing; and Mr. Herbert laughed also, when he knew the point in question from Harry. Since first seeing his eager young admirer, and late co-professional in an humbler sphere, the *Astræa's* captain-elect had, indeed, treated the former with a natural favour, even showing some degree of interest in his unlucky experiences, if not of real disapproval towards the unsuitable commanders who had darkened his early prospects at sea. The boy, in turn, with all his quick forwardness, venturing now no further than to display a profound and distant deference for the holder of the King's full commission. Decayed old Herbert Court was nothing in his eyes to the new *Astræa* of forty-four guns, that lay, as all the world knew, fitting out at Portsmouth. As for his previous ambition of a post under Mr. Herbert, it was plainly too wild to stand the test of such a circumstance. He only betrayed his feelings by some annoyed glances at Kate's matter-of-fact air, with the mighty cool assurance of the easy way in which she took her honours.

But at Mr. Herbert's serious pressure of the point in hand, with some more than wonted courtliness of manner as he proffered the hospitalities of his old house, the girl blushed again, and laughed and hesitated, looking from Harry to the path, from the path to Harry. " Shall I see the Abbé

Horne," she said. Mr. Herbert evidently wondered at the query. "Harry is so often talking
about him," she pursued, "that we are all curious."

"Nothing, I assure you, Miss Spencer," was the
frank reply, "will please the abbé more."

"If he do not try to convert us," Kate merrily
said, and turned, smiling, up the slope.

CHAPTER XI.

AWAY.

I⊤ was the first time within the memory of man or woman that any lady from Wrixworth Hall had been under the roof of Herbert Court; and whether religious prejudices weighed with Mrs. Brinds, the housekeeper, or whether she considered the Duttridge family inferior in station to the Herberts, and desired in some measure to sustain their dignity—while, at the same time, rather taken by surprise—she had at first a good deal of stiff primness in her aspect, and persisted in having her visitors ushered formally to the dining-hall, where dark wainscot, and antiquated furniture, and want of use, were enough to make most people dreary. She, herself, had much of the old-fashioned gentlewoman, and it was chiefly towards Mr. Herbert that her great deference was shown.

When he was gone, therefore, to seek the Abbé
Horne about the garden, her hospitalities grew
easier, warming with the faint refusals of Master
Henry in regard to a second glass of her old
currant wine, and opening out to his sister, so soon
as he also had disappeared, in somewhat partial
excuses for his restlessness, his loud voice, and
blunt manner.

" Young gentlemen *would* be young gentlemen.
She remembered even his Honour himself, as
mannerly and quiet as he now was, having a hoop
and trundling it along the terrace, and once break-
ing a window-pane with his ball ; which it was the
more surprising, because, at that time, excepting
his poor, weakly elder brother, he had no play-
fellows ; nor could he have, seeing there was no
young people of his station near by. But that
must have been years and years before Miss
Spencer was born."

The hale, homely features of the old dame had
the texture and tint of a well-kept withered apple,
and a cheerful, busy, managing air, besides;
though, in her close-plaited cap with a high back,
and her black kerchief and gown of grey-shining
silk, she looked something between a widowed
Quakeress and a lay-sister in a convent, sitting
straight up in her chair at a ceremonious distance,
and smoothing down her silk, and benignly gossip-
ing in a cracked voice to the merchant's youngest

daughter; while Dolly, the niece, with blooming
cheeks and a high apron, stood simpering and looking down beside the salver of cake she had brought,
with furtive glances now and then at the shoe, the
dress, or hat, of an heiress no older than herself.
Kate Spencer, resting in a tall-backed chair that
raised its crest above her, did not seem by any
means over-fatigued, however; leading Mrs.
Brinds on by all sorts of questions, to talk of
the rooms, the furniture, everything, up to her
favourite pea-fowl, till they were forthwith at the
height of acquaintance; yet still fondling Neptune, whom she had detained by force, and looking
all round with lively eyes, and talking too. Outside, in the air, was the full radiance of the sun,
like summer come before the leaves. Through
one opened portion of a casement could be seen the
brightness of the stone balustrade bathed in it;
the dusky sunbeam, through another, clove the
shadow and fell in, steel-coloured, and gleaming
like some angelic sword, throwing broken checkers
on the oaken floor, while it smote with a pitiless
glare by the way upon the faded old mud-coloured
window-tapestry, going on in a swarm of motes to
the quilted table-cover of green silk, all scaled
like the pine-apple or tortoise, where the quaint
silver salver was, and the blue china plate of
dried conserves, with the decanter of home-made
cordial. Kate Spencer basked in it, as Neptune

did. She put her hand in it, with a childish light dancing in her eyes, perhaps because it was so quaintly pleasant and summer-like, bringing to mind how the budding elm-branches opposite would soon screen off the heat; then she checked a mischievous smile, as she praised the curtains, but feared the sun would " fade them" in time.

"*Curtains!*—dear bless her! they were the oldest tapestry. Saving her presence, money could not buy such a thing; the sun did 'em but little harm. They had been a hundred years at least in the house up-stairs, and were said to have been sewed by some old ancestress of the Herberts, with her maids about her, when the lord of the castle was away at the Holy Sepulchre for some great crime."

Mrs. Brinds crossed herself, and bowed. Then she rose; and, lifting the skirt of the tapestry, showed in embroidered relief upon it, though blanched and discoloured, where female patience of old had at least equalled the exploits of the crusader in representing the whole wild struggle of some violent deed, life-size, with all the weapons, and in attitudes of an awkwardness perhaps more unpleasant than the reality; though it had, by good luck, been cut in half, with a provident view to the two casements; which, on a snowy winter's night, no doubt, with firelight, and curtains drawn, and slight draughts of air, would present the somewhat ghastly scene in its liveliest completeness.

To the bright-eyed guest, however, it cost but a moment's shiver. She had even begun to ask, with the more girlish waywardness, if it were all true about a haunted chamber; greatly to the evident disturbance of the housekeeper, who crossed herself again, looking grave, and shaking her head, when the abbé's entrance, with Henry, stopped her.

The Abbé Horne bowed deeply, and smiled gently, begging Mrs. Brinds to remain seated, and taking a chair by the fair visitor to talk to her; which he did with much of the elaborate polish, and somewhat of the epigrammatic point, the witty sparkle, or insincere allegorical pastoral style of the old court of Versailles towards ladies, with even a degree of its fancied knowledge of life and the world, that might have seemed doubly preposterous on a spring day down in Somersetshire, more than thirty years after the meridian glory of Louis-le-Grand. But the kindness of the old man, and his own grave, simple character, were conspicuous through all, so that it only added a charm to what had already a pleasant strangeness. Amidst it, as Kate Spencer sat leaning back, she cast her eyes on one among the old portraits high up against the wainscot with a sudden sense of discomfort. It was more vividly life-like than the rest, showing merely a middle-aged ordinary man, in a demure dark dress, and plain cravat and band, displaying a parchment with both hands; but the pale forehead, full and bald, made the dark eyes beneath it shine out keener in their intentness, as if the face really looked forth; while the bluish plum-bloom-like tint of a close-shaven jaw, as in strongly saturnine complexions, was depicted skilfully. The more she eyed it, the more did it compel the girl's notice by a kind of vague fascination, till she at last said, " What a disagreeable face? Who was it, pray, Mr. Abbé ? "

The old chaplain turned to see, and put on his spectacles; while Henry Spencer stared up, too, saying it was very like somebody he had seen—in fact whom he must have known quite well; but he couldn't just remember.

" Ah !" said the Abbé Horne, growing grave at once, " that was Sir Thomas Shadd, a collateral ancestor, merely, of the family; the most restless intellect, and among the most brilliant of his time; a lawyer, a man of science, a courtier, statesman, diplomatist, plotter, successful traitor and apostate ; the world smiled on him to the end; yet was that fickleness, that unprincipled ambition, his ruin."

" How, Father Horne ? " asked the boy. " What happened to him ? "

" It could only be explained, even by lawyers,"

replied the abbé, "on the ground of insanity. He had cut off a profligate heir, and illegally bequeathed his fortune to the annual demonstration of a refined and moral atheism. His wealth was, indeed, successfully claimed and quickly spent by the profligate; yet it seems doubtful whether the insanity differed in kind from that which his whole life exemplified. The merit of the picture as a work of art, I believe, mademoiselle, is the chief reason for its being retained here, where it has been little seen of late; but such memorials, I think, though painful, possess a——"

"Oh, I'll tell you who it is, Kate!" interrupted her brother, eagerly, with a triumphant slap of his hand against his thigh, "it's my old skipper, I think—old Itefell Dodge! At any rate, there's something about the mouth, or something—I wonder now, if Diamond were here, if he'd——"

"Resemblances may lead us away, my dear young gentleman," resumed the abbé, putting his hand, with a smile, on Harry's shoulder, so as to save his sister further vexation at his rudeness, for he stopped and looked down very awkwardly, shifting from one foot to the other. "Were vulgar superstition more sagacious, Miss Spencer," resumed the chaplain, while the housekeeper continued reverently to stoop forward in her chair catching all that dropped from his lips, with sundry nods, devout adjurations, and pious cross-ings of herself—"would it not rather imagine this person's memory to trouble the earth, than conceive some unknown, aimless spectre in this peaceful house, to haunt a sleeping-chamber? 'Tis abroad at this moment, doubtless—the same rash, heartless, cold, and insatiable spirit—yet, thank Heaven! though that man's blood may have mingled with the Herberts', it has not infected them! Sorrow may have been theirs, but no shame, I trust."

"Dear, dear, your reverence, no!" exclaimed Mrs. Brinds, throwing up her hands, "never, never in the world! Holy saints preserve us!"

"We grow rich, too, Mrs. Brinds," said the ecclesiastic, playfully, "that is a great thing! You must know, Mademoiselle Kate, that obsolete as we may seem here—perhaps dilapidated somewhat, in spite of good Mrs. Brinds' sedulous care— we may yet revive some of our faded splendour, of which the poor peacocks yonder are but a faint emblem and relic. There are coal mines found of late in the North, on a very bleak estate, which make Mr. Herbert's uncle a rich man, and will some day make himself a richer one."

"My dear father," said a grave voice near them, "hush, pray, hush! You forget the undoubted conditions." And as both the abbé and the others turned, they saw Mr. Herbert coming in again, with an air of seriousness that seemed the result of something in the interval he had spent apart.

The Abbé Horne showed the confused look of a child detected in a fault, or of some too boastful person overheard. He rose, and said hastily, as he moved towards Mr. Herbert, assuming great calmness, " True, true, Richard—true. I have always thought Sir Ralph's avowed stipulation injudicious; nay, prejudicial in effect, since it must constrain the will even of the best disposed. Surely our Church can afford to trust her sons; and, as one of the fathers hath it, ' Dearer to the Lord is the free gift than any treasure—*dilectius Domino quam ulla gaza est munus gratuitum !* ' The new law of England allows of it, indeed; but to require that the very heir to the baronetcy itself should take the mass in public, or forfeit the property in favour of the next of kin, a female, the superior of a foreign convent, or her lawful heirs— in our Church's behoof, in short—'tis zeal, zeal, my dear boy, but ill-judged, methinks ! I have lately written as much to my friend Father Joseph, Sir Ralph's confessor, who—who, you know, informs me of everything, perhaps too freely. Father Joseph, I fear, is inclined to be incautious; he has little knowledge of the world, and must naturally have been a very simple man, I think. What if the post-office people at Brookbridge were to apply their reputed curiosity ! True, the

letters are in Latin, and Father Joseph often adds
the cypher; yet what talk would there be of bigotry,
designs, Jesuit plots!"

As he spoke, he and Mr. Herbert stood near the
other end of the room from where the young lady
sat; but the gathered gloom on Mr. Herbert's
brow had been visible to her in a moment, like a
shadow brought into the place, and seemed almost
to amount to sternness as he looked down, listening
to the old chaplain; while it was with an air of
utter vacancy that he glanced up at him, appearing to gaze round abstracted, yet to nod, and say
something in assent, till a sudden surprised expression broke out in his eyes, and he fixedly surveyed the abbé for a moment or two, then turned
his face from him with a throe of manifest pain
upon it. Even as he came forward with his courteous look, the firm effort to smile was perceptible.

Kate Spencer glanced up involuntarily to the
portrait again, and back toward the master of the
house. No two visages could well be more different, and yet some vague association in her mind
might have prompted the grave glance of comparison, or perhaps of contrast. Indeed, her quick-
eyed brother had all the while been evidently
weighing the question of the picture with singular
intentness of meditation; he caught her look, and
followed it. Next moment, however, he turned
all at once on his heel, thrusting both hands into

his genteel breeches-pockets, as if they had been the old canvas trousers, and walking quickly up to Kate, with a whistle, and with a smile of general disdain and compassion for the dulness of all their speculations on the matter, his own included. "Pooh, Kitty, what have we all been dreaming of?" he said, loudly. "Why, it's that creole, or foreigner, or whatever he is, that it's like! The Count, you know. Just take another look!"

His sister turned abruptly, rising up, and seeming to survey the portrait with the utmost attention.

"It's not so good-looking, I suppose you'll say," added Harry, in his thoughtless, random way, "for he was such a beau of yours at home; and Jane and Mary both call him the handsomest man they know. For my part, the more they talk, it always sets me the more against him again. Now, if it weren't the bald forehead, Kate—and if there were hair-powder, with a higher sort of a nose, and a touch of creole about the skin—I just ask if it isn't the Count's very image?"

Kate answered in a very distinct, steady voice, without turning, however: "Yes, it really is so, I declare! I think you are right, Henry, and I wonder I did not see it before. Oh, yes, there *is* a plain likeness to the Comte de St. Amand." But even one standing behind, on the other side of the table, might see that in the silence there spread a rose-red suffusion on the girl's cheek, flushing the fair glimpse of her neck, till, through the very fold of the upturned veil, the ear-tip from beneath one powdered tress glowed scarlet.

"De St. Amand, Mademoiselle Kate?" repeated the Abbé Horne, and turned again to Herbert. "Surely I have heard the title before!"

"It was the title, you recollect, father," said Mr. Herbert, quietly, "derived by my cousin Etherege's mother—Sir Ralph's niece, my cousin-german—in her own maternal right. On all that concerns the memory of either of his parents my cousin shows the most resolute disposition to lay stress; but he seems as little influenced by motives of ambition as he is by mercenary views."

"I remember—true," said the old abbé, sitting down near the table, and eyeing the portrait again. "This likeness, then—do *you*, too, observe it? A strong resemblance to your cousin Etienne, it seems? Not as yet having seen the young man, you know, Richard, I feel a natural interest in the question."

"Since the remark has been made, I have noticed its correctness," was the deliberate answer. "Yes; the old family connexion *does* come out— even singularly obvious, as one looks for it. 'Tis a portrait I never much heeded before, in truth. Both he and I, however, it must be acknowledged, partake alike of the blood of Sir Thomas Shadd, who—in whom Miss Spencer and her brother appear to have been so much interested."

"A proof, at all events," continued Father Horne, resting his chin on his hand, and gazing down thoughtfully—"a quite sufficient proof, if that were needed; though scarce an agreeable one. His mother, the Spanish adventurer's widow, could hardly have forsaken the world on better cause—ahem! *tuâ veniâ, Sanctissima!* Grant to us all—charity!" He glanced up, though with acute secular intelligence in his eyes, to add, "Madame the Abbess—or Superior—may doubtless have devised away her rights and titles to her son, before assuming the veil. The law of France, not the canon law, will rule in that case; but the one and the other must go together, one would think—I mean, both as to his title and his estate from *her?*"

"My dear abbé," rejoined Mr. Herbert, quickly, "I have told you my cousin is already a man of wealth, and that mainly through his mother; I think it will be no fault of *his*, however, if your hopes fail. He was open with me, to a fault; he neither needs nor desires additions to his fortune."

"On all points of law, home or foreign," concluded the old chaplain, rising, "Father Joseph of Kingswood is a complete authority: I need but consult him by a note or two. 'Tis necessary in this world to be on our guard against our very friends

—the most ingenuous of them. Father Joseph
himself has the Church at heart, perhaps, a little
too closely; yet be at ease, Richard; you may sail
more secure in this respect, than even on the question as to my actual improvement on the compass-
box, or whether the new swinging-barometer cor-
rectly prognosticates a tropical——"

He paused, with a sudden notice of the utter in-
attention paid to his words; the whole of these
subjects appeared to have lost their importance,
however vital, in the mere concern of "Richard"
at leaving his young visitors to the housekeeper
alone — and the good abbé had betrayed too
evident a perception for the charming face he saw,
not to be pleasantly startled at last by its marked
effect on Mr. Herbert. His eye watched anxiously
when the young Miss Spencer looked towards her
brother, with manifest desire to go. When she
had taken leave of Mrs. Brinds, they all passed out
together on the terrace, to gain the nearest foot-
way towards Wrixworth Hall. The Abbé Horne
summoned all his court-manner of the *ancien régime*,
to accompany them; but stopped soon, at the first
turnstile, on the plea not only of his age, but of
the rarity also of his appearance abroad; though it
was amidst the liveliest discourse between him and
the young lady. "Besides, Miss Spencer," he said,
a little out of breath, though with a smiling bow,
"not even the influence of beauty can always—

enable us to keep pace—we find—with youth." This regret and her own flattered consciousness, together, made the girl's varying look a bright one; she rejoined with a mingled sprightliness and deference that became her very gracefully, repelling the implied charge against herself, by playful blame of the abbé's own conversation, so gay, so polished, and so charmingly entertaining; and but for the sincere, half-filial air, it might have been thought she coquetted with the old ecclesiastic.

"But Mademoiselle Kate," the latter hoped, at parting, "will not quite desert the old priest at Herbert Court, when Mr. Herbert has left him there alone. Your passing visits, *ma petite*, to show your friends the rooms, the pictures, the view up-stairs, would please me almost as much as they would flatter Mrs. Brinds. The little chapel is worth seeing, too; the library contains a few choice modern works —and still more, in summer, the flower-garden, of which I am so vain. You, Mademoiselle Kate, are like sunshine coming into the old house; I seem to have seen some such one, I think,—only long ago—at Versailles, or Marly, for a moment at a window, it strikes me, blushing and smiling to some one in the cavalcade, and shrinking back from above velvet hangings and sumptuous cloths of gold and embroideries, as we were all riding, with trumpeters before us, through the street."

And when the abbé had said this, closing his

eyes towards the end, as if he saw the face before him, Kate had indeed blushed and laughed, making some confused promise for her next visit from Bristol to the country, and hastening on with Harry and Mr. Herbert. The latter, saying little, and seeming grave, persisted still in seeing them as far as the Hall gates. An indescribable change had come over the little conversation there was. Harry alone, with the dog Neptune, was *not* mutually laconic, formally polite, distant in manner. Harry sustained the chief part, and made odd enough remarks; it was chiefly to Harry that his sister spoke, and when they came to the gates and Mr. Herbert stopped, holding out his hand and bidding good afternoon without going farther, she seemed perfectly unconcerned by this circumstance. In vain did Harry give a private push to her elbow, that she might ask Mr. Herbert to come up to the Hall, or say she was sure her uncle would expect him and take his denial ill. It was Mr. Herbert who lingered a little, turning round and suddenly saying, in a husky voice, that he ought to have said *good-bye*—as he had just had letters which would oblige him to leave much earlier than he expected; he might not again, in fact, have this—this pleasure.

Harry Spencer stared, and made a sudden exclamation. "Why, I heard the *Astræa* wasn't to be ready for a month, sir," he blurted out, looking much dismayed, and then somewhat ashamed at his freedom. Mr. Herbert turned to him with a smile: "The powers-that-be are in haste, Mr. Harry," he said, in a good-natured way. "The ship must now be at sea in a fortnight, and I shall be on the spot in a day or two, to secure her readiness."

"Then, Father Horne hasn't kept his promise," said Harry, in evident distress. "He was to—to speak to you, sir, about it—but Kate knows she engaged to break it to my father, in case you agreed, sir, that is."

Mr. Herbert looked perplexed from the boy to his sister, and back again. "Pray, what is it you exactly wish, my boy?" he asked, with great kindness in his manner. "If anything *I* can do, Master Henry, it has only to be named."

So, at Harry's appealing look, Kate Spencer, with an air of some vexation, was compelled to make the matter known. "The truth was, having already been at sea, and tired of it, Henry was so silly as now to wish to go again; he seemed quite crazed about war, and against foreigners; so he wished to go in a ship of war, but particularly,"—she glanced again to Harry—"yes, particularly with Mr. Herbert; under Mr. Herbert."

"Yes, sir," eagerly said Harry himself, "I used to hear of you at Port Royal, sir, when you were in the *Diana*. I had got in such low rubbish of craft—such a deal depends on that, sir, and one's officers. I could bring a capital hand along with me, too, sir; a thorough able seaman he is, and I don't mind what I am, or what I do—I've cleaned binnacle-lamps and cabin candlesticks in my time —I'll enter at first as a powder-boy if you like, sir, so as I can only get into *your* ship, the *Astræa*."

Mr. Herbert had folded his arms, and stood looking narrowly at the boy. From head to foot he viewed him, and suddenly smiled, taking hold of Harry's arm. "I see, my boy," he said, "there's the true sailor's stuff in you—leave it to me—you and I shall sail together."

"If Kate writes off one of her letters at once to my father, it's all right," said Harry, overflowing with joy. "Kitty can coax him to anything, when nobody else can."

It was arranged that Henry was to hear from Mr. Herbert from Portsmouth; so they parted. As the sister and brother went up the approach, Harry could scarce at all restrain his spirits; he thanked Kate twenty times: she had just *better* get it carried through, though, he said,—else he should run off; in a fortnight he and Diamond would be smelling blue water, as sure as fate. "Did you ever see a man like Commander Herbert —*Captain* Herbert, I mean?" was his triumphant inquiry. "I wonder at you, Kitty, taking the honour so coolly.   Why, as splendid a man as he is *here*, you can't have any notion, though, what he'll be afloat."

She only laughed at Harry, with his idea of Mr. Herbert's being thought "splendid;" and ran up-stairs to dress for dinner.

A day or two after, Mr. Herbert was gone from Herbert Court.

CHAPTER XII.

DULL TIMES AFLOAT.

FRANCE, so far on as the spring of 1778, did not yet make any formal declaration of war against Great Britain; since not even the ingenuity of a baffled rival, smarting from the losses of the previous contest, could discover any pretext for seizing the lucky moment to begin a new one. She only made a treaty with the revolted colonies, formally acknowledging their independence—and sent a polite diplomatic message, of the most elaborate refinement in insult, to acquaint the Court of St. James's with the fact; which she was "firmly persuaded" would elicit "new proofs of his Britannic Majesty's constant and sincere disposition for peace," and "the good harmony of which, His Majesty would no doubt equally avoid to disturb."

While everybody had meantime been perfectly

aware of the expedition of the young Marquis de Lafayette, under the form of a pretended escape, to assist the colonies; and of the continual presence of the busy little Mr. Silas Deane in Paris, with his unscrupulous ways—of the robust, large-headed, thick-legged Dr. Franklin also, and the red-faced, pimply Mr. Thomas Paine, originally of Suffolk, and the melodramatic yet valiant Chevalier Paul Jones from Scotland: nor had naval preparations at Brest been unresponded to by similar launchings and fittings-out, on a greater scale, at Portsmouth and Plymouth. It had all come out quite naturally, just as might have been expected; the war grew popular; the Opposition, which old Chatham yet led, sank into a still more patriotically-disinterested minority; the Ministry, for all its weight of dulness, rose hourly into the dangerous importance of being considered a loyal, consistent, far-seeing, thoroughly British set of men, who knew what they were about: and the *Country*—that strange compound of stolid agriculture and quick-witted handicraft, riotous town-mobs and rural field-preachings, of loud squires, bold highwaymen, fine wits, gay men-about-town, jovial parsons, thrifty housewives, French *petits-maîtres*, actresses, honest fathers-of-families, earnest Wesleyan preachers, bright-witted Irishmen, sombre or sneering Scotchmen, roaring sailors, Jews, pickpockets, recruiting-sergeants, bargemen

by canals, and unknown shepherds up the hills, and
many a householder unheard of, with red-cowled
fishermen at work by the splashing coast—the
Country was thought to be united.

With all its fields and woods and uplands,
steeple, windmill, and sparrow-frequented thatch,
and from the utmost rocky limits of the Orcades,
or the Irish turf-cabins that blended with the soil,
in again to the tumult about great St. Paul's, and
the two steady sentinels at the Horse-Guards, and
the humming precincts of old Whitehall;—Great
Britain went the more determinedly to war, since
Europe had lent gratuitous aid to the rebels. A
bitterness of hostility was really unveiled against
her, on the part of the politest nations, which had
scarce been suspected; it was difficult to imagine a
reason, save her prosperity: and if there had been
no other good result, people now bade fair to re-
consider their grand cosmopolitan ideas seriously,
with those heroic, classic, fifth-act virtues for
which stupid English diffidence was indebted to
cultivated French assurance,—and to try whether
loyalty, pride in one's country, and the fear of God,
had not some use. So, to distant India, where a
new empire was being conquered by British arms
against secret French aid, and to all home-coming
ships, or with Captain Cook going out to be killed
at Owhyhee, [though France philosophically ex-
cepted *him* and his expedition from all martial law,]

there went out the open tidings. Things seemed to move quicker and sound louder everywhere through the land; life itself had a fuller pulse, its meaning appeared redoubled, its zest was greater, yet men were more ready to peril it on a cast.

Would indeed that a proper picture could here be given of that country—for which Fielding, Richardson, Smollett or Goldsmith, have ceased to hold the mirror up—where William Cowper had but of late retreated, to nurse his endless despair beside that rough parson John Newton (ex-captain in the slave-trade), happily by Mrs. Unwin's hearth, with hares to tame and rural sights at hand. The sturdiness of honest old Samuel Johnson is failing fast; the chirping *dilettante* tattle of Horace Walpole is troubled, and begins to croak of the end of all things, when Madame du Deffand with the *salons* shall be accessible no more, if only because "England is sinking." It is the strange time when dulness and deadness go forth to in-effectual war with one another, like spectres—when the cold hour comes before the dawn, and "against stupidity the gods themselves refuse to strive." Profligate young Mirabeau himself does not yet scent the Parisian morning air, but looks for clients from the provinces. The plough upon the Ayrshire mountain-side is already followed, indeed, by its glorious Peasant, but not "in glory and not in joy"—for he, too, turns his gloomy thoughts West-

ward, and thinks, at nineteen, of flying to the
Colonies. Action—action—blindly as might be,
but still action—is the common engrossing purpose,
amidst whose haste a Whitfield might now have
thundered unheeded, a Chatham himself must in-
veigh in vain, a Milton would have followed
Chatterton's fate, even a Junius need not write.
"Great George our King" is throned once for all
in his people's heart, where the homely memory of
his unalterable firmness, and of his will above the
will of statesmanship, is to outlast mere royal
tragedies to come, to shed a tenderer light about
his own sublime calamity, to turn the very sneers
of Walpoles yet unborn. No more citizenship-of-
the-world, no more elegant sentiment, no more
Vicar of Wakefield, nor Inkle and Yarico, nor
Paul and Virginia (so recently the rage about
Versailles!). Soldiers, Generals, Admirals, only—
though alas! where were they? No heroes to
speak of on either side—nothing but mediocrity
at best; and the land-battles are backwood skir-
mishes, where tomahawks alone are distinguished,
and the sea-fights for years are but mutual display
of naval tactics, to be recorded by "Clerk of
Eldin," save where Paul Jones came in. Sir
George Brydges Rodney was abroad in France,
hiding from his creditors; where the Duc de Biron,
at the instance of M. de Sartines, the King's
Minister of Marine, happily failed to bribe him

with a Chief Admiral's flag, bearing the *fleur-de-lys:* but Rodney was not sent for as yet, neither had the Scotch tactician fallen hitherto upon the slightest trace of a chance to anticipate the grand secret.   The Abbé Horne, at Herbert Court, among others of his multifarious studies, included this one; nay, out of the number of his many correspondents in various lands, would undoubtedly have heard of so like-minded a contemporary as the ingenious Edinburgh lawyer, had he yet hit upon a discovery thus startlingly inconsistent with the dulness of the age.

Dull occurrences must therefore be recorded as to the opening of the campaign.   Even at sea, where some relief might be expected from the general monotony, there is at first a similar aspect of events requiring notice, though by no means to be dwelt upon; hackneyed incidents occurring to rather common-place characters, whose slight pro-gress nevertheless affects the course of others.   A week brought Henry Spencer's much-looked-for letter, informing him of his appointment as a first-class volunteer among the midshipmen of the *Astræa* frigate; not, certainly, in the autograph of Captain Herbert, but of the ship's clerk.   Still, for all that, overwhelming the youth with so strong a sense of prompt kindness and most un-merited consideration, as at once to urge his sister Kate, who had returned home with him, to broach his wishes, and plead them earnestly to their father. On the strength of her good offices, as well as of the captain's word pledged, Harry had got his clothes already ordered. Mr. Spencer's astonished mind, amidst the cares of business, yielded the less reluctantly to the boy's desire, in that Kate's caprices seemed now to be more privileged than before, almost deferred to, since they grew fewer but graver, and since she had become of her own right, though in a small way, an heiress. The consent was given, however, with this peremptory *salvo* on the father's part, that, come what might—peace or war, disgust or ardour —he need never alter his choice again—must look forward to his profession for his fortune in life, and content himself with the moderate fixed allowance he might thenceforth begin to draw, at regular periods, for the reasonable necessities of his earlier career.

So Henry was driven off, one fine April morning, from Beech Grove, amidst much of the usual circumstances of such revolutions—domestic excitement and family emotion, mother's tears and paternal self-control; all a little modified by the fact that it had happened, even in his case, before. With his luggage and Black Diamond once more behind (the departure of the latter being least felt by the head of the house and firm), he took coach for Portsmouth very stoically; neither the vicissi-

tudes of the journey, the bustle and redoubled din
of the warlike seaport, nor those on board the
frigate itself, when he joined it at Spithead, afterwards shaking him much from this experienced
frame of mind. He fell into his proper place
with most commendable readiness, seeming to
have worn a uniform, dirk, and flat-cocked " fore-
and-aft " hat for months previous. As for Dick
Diamond, unprovided with all credentials, save
canvas-trousers, duck-frock, and seaman's bag,
his figure, his manners, his still easier aptitude,
procured him a welcome yet more undoubted.
They melted apart into the common rush of that
orderly confusion, swarming at its work till the
ship sailed. Their coming was known no further;
the captain was not even on board yet. The
general buzz, and stir, and plashing echo of sea-
going war, absorbed them till the fleet and they
were out of sight of land together.

They were part of a strong squadron which left
Spithead in May, 1778, under a commodore's
broad pendant, to convoy the India and China
fleet through the thickening dangers of the Channel, down the Bay of Biscay and the wide Atlantic. Some transports and troop-ships were in
the convoy; bearing, among other supplies for
Lord Cornwallis in the west, the regiment of
Ligonier's Light Horse, with which Cornet Cobham was. But they were taken up, ere long, by a

portion of Admiral Byron's line-of-battle, on its
way for the West Indies; and the *Astræa* never
was near enough to the troop-ships to show if the
Cornet were really there; nor could the Cornet
have caught another glimpse of his pleasant
friend's cousin, or have guessed that the fair Jane
Spencer had a brother under that gentleman's
command—if, indeed, the young dragoon would
now have cared to do so. Proverbially dull work
is that of convoys; the more so, if well performed,
and too strong for danger. Touching at the
usual islands, they in due time reached the Dutch
settlement at the Cape of Good Hope; where no
occurrence varied the routine, save the covert
proneness of the Dutch to insolence, checked until
the squadron and its charge were gone upon their
course. The frigate had been left there to return
northward alone, with general cruising orders;
when the Dutch governor himself grew apt to
presume, but was summarily turned from that
mood, for the time, by Captain Herbert's quiet
firmness, ere they two parted. Then she safely
rounded the Cape again, ere the wild September
weather had well begun; and, always with a
somewhat provoking accuracy (to some on board),
struck the south-east trade-wind that slants to the
equator, crossed the calms by skilful use of their
squally fits, reached her appointed cruising-station
off the Bahama banks without trouble or disaster.

She had parted from her convoy-work, in fact, like a deer-hound slipped from the leash beside mastiffs and poodles; but hitherto it had been a most uneventful voyage. In those days, even during peace, there were few scattered vessels, few independent navigators trying new courses, few bold "running-ships." Every morning now, the *Astræa*, as a cruiser, looked at a bare horizon; each night, if a gull's wing or a spouting-fish might deceive the best, the case was but little varied. One cordial patron of her natural discontent, it might have been justly hoped by those who felt it deepest, was available in the zealous first-lieutenant whom the *Astræa* boasted. A tolerably pleasant officer was Mr. Holmes in common—an active, quick-eyed little man with a long nose, well known to have a wife and family, and whom the faintest hope of a prize, in any shape, at what cost of pains soever, had seldom failed to render agreeable before. But conflicting motives worked upon his temper now. There was about the captain a seemingly utter unconsciousness that the commodore had been mistaken in assigning this station to such a frigate; that neither prizes, salvages, nor enemies, were here at this season, and that he might fairly take a little latitude or longitude to himself. The weather became, in this light, authoritative to Mr. Holmes. He would have anticipated the effect of currents;

he would have forestalled the failure of easterly breezes; he denoted, above all, a strange tendency to have given in respectfully to "the tail" of a Jamaica hurricane; and to have cruised, notwithstanding this, more southerly. But there was plainly too strong a hand behind him, for which he at the same time evinced an ever-growing deference of the most irresistible kind. The captain was grave; he was no great speaker; he was little seen, except at the set times, in ceremonial naval state. And as to his resolutions, they were of that sort which is above argument; but yet his rare smile diffused a pleasure along the mustered divisions of the ship's company: so far from dulness as regarded *him*, therefore, it was thought that he had secret orders of great importance, or at least sealed ones to be broken after a certain time, which gave his step at times a sudden briskness to-and-fro on the weather-side of the quarter-deck, or now and then of a night drew him firmly up where he stood, looking out into the weather-streak of the sky.

Thus was strict discipline somewhat lightened, and life at least supported, in the solitary *Astræa;* while from time to time only falling in with the stragglers of some Jamaica convoy, whom it was her business to drive in together to their proper track, or exchanging numbers with some impatient frigate bound more especially to that task; at best

overtaking a doubtful sail that turned out "neutral"
in the end, or boarding one of suspicious swiftness,
merely to find a rather shame-faced " slaver,"
who still humanely drove his lawful trade. She
was herself as fast a ship as she was new and
roomy; her copper had proved an entire success,
her compasses correct to a marvel, her improved
swinging-barometer still more admirable in its
prediction of sudden gales: blow high, blow low,
it was really something extraordinary how the
first-lieutenant could make her keep her place
when held to it; how delicately, too, the company
of young-gentlemen, with their quadrants or sex-
tants, daily and nightly, were brought up to find
it out. As to the rest of this painful trial, First-
Lieutenant Holmes was of all men the most fitted
to meet it when he chose; the queen-bee, the
prime-minister of ants, the viceroy of beavers, was
not more ingenious or inevitable in finding things
to do for the deadest calm, when the very watch
on deck might look idly over the side. Many of
them so looked, in those days, with most vivid recollections of the buccaneers, of the blacker flag at the
back of Cuba, or of the rural highway with the
pleasant country burglaries and easy civic pocket-
pickings; joined to writhing spites at the press-gang,
the crimps, the Jews, the jail on land, the cat-o'-nine-
tails afloat. Some veteran tars of Benbow's school
were in the *Astræa*—more of prime ones from the

later glories of Sir Edward Hawke (well-named),
and smart young hands who might have whaled to
the north, or made peaceful discoveries with
Captain Cook or Bligh. The large new frigate
had attracted these, by the help of Captain
Herbert's name as both officer and gentleman:
but there were twice as many doubtful fellows
who, but for chance and force, might have preferred Paul Jones; with not a few guardship-
sweepings and random captures of dock-lanes,
that might chance to hold him for their chief
enemy; among which, most undoubtedly, lurked
divers of those peculiar unchanged villains, never
yet wanting at sea, with the heads as well as the
hearts, of bolder ruffianism than Paul's own. It
happened, somehow, that when even Mr. Holmes's
scrutinising eye could be faced from the crowd by
such as these, one sweeping glance from that of
the captain seemed to pick them out and cast
them down, though without further sign. There
was no frequent severity, no martinet-fretting nor
tartar-like rigour, in the frigate; but deliberate
and most inflexible certainty at need. And whenever Mr. Holmes's fertility in employment appeared at a loss, it did not so much as require that
old cables should be untwisted, oakum teased, or
the rust beaten off anchors: without a hint, as if
brought by divination from his innermost stern-
cabin, the captain came, and had unaccountable new

occupations for all on deck; soundings to get, of
which officers themselves scarce comprehended the
use; altitudes to take; experiments to try; odd
conclusions to certify from the most trifling current or most ordinary weather; setting boats to
work, and careful look-out-men aloft, in a manner
to excite the very watch below. To crown all
which, he here kept up a singular exercise for the
crew, that at first had been taken for a mad whim
of his own. Each day, when the drums beat to
quarters, if the weather was still light, particularly
with a tropical swell upon the water, the guns
were shotted as if an enemy were really in sight;
and firing-practice was made at an empty hogs-
head, dropped astern or taken a-head. At different
distances, from all sorts of positions, they had to
take single sights at it, or give it what was called
"a concentrated broadside;" and as the cask
dipped and rose, bobbing eccentrically on the wide
glassy-blue swell, the *Astræa* rolling too, curvetting
round, prancing opposite, all the time blazing and
thundering away at it—First-Lieutenant Holmes
himself was too hard put to it with her steering-
trim, to have the grin upon his side. No one
grinned or frowned at it ere long; there were
prizes given to the guns that hit the mark; and
Captain Herbert, standing on the poop, watch-in-
hand, timing the whole, took the first clumsy trials
with a remarkable patience, that nothing else
dared put to the test. The surgeon, and other

" idlers," looked on seriously. The marines were
drawn up, too stiff to have their joke; even when
the black cask would suddenly seem to have run
round to the opposite horizon, as the ship lost
steerage; or when the dark back-fin of the "ship's
shark," that had cruised respectfully apart, would
make a rush-in at an interval of the firing, as if
to see how little damage had been done.

Otherwise, it might have been thought the
captain was but a navigating, bookish, mild sort
of a man, fain to have surveyed a coast, joined
company with Cook, or gone in search of
Mounseer La Perouse. His secret orders might
have come to be thought all smoke. There might
have been no war in the world, for all Harry
Spencer saw; as the frigate at times flew rolling
before the cloudy trades, with studding-sails hung
on one side only, to keep her pace moderate; or
when, in chase of some stranger who was sure to be
all regular, she made long sliding cleaves through
blue water, mounting the while, and rose—too stiff
to the breeze for any merchantman to escape her;
ever buoyant, high, stately over the spray, with wet
black bows, spouting hawse-hole, dripping breast-
hooks, and *Astræa's* snowy figure beckoning on. In
the hollow that sank past, the golden gleam of
her copper was reflected brokenly, with transparent
emerald glosses floating over it, foam-freckled;
ever the same recurring motion, as one great

bright billow gave up its burden to another, and its lesser waves surged against the side or recoiled; with flights of flying-fish, and frolicking droves of porpoises, and the small sea-birds that run or hover in the track behind. Harry Spencer, at all events, could not confess to himself that it was the least dull; the counting-house was worse by far; Master White, of the *Dorothy*, was more despicable than ever; and Skipper Dodge, of the schooner, still more odious than before. He had not come to look for prize-money; he was learning the profession he had aspired to, and saw it clearly to be his choice. He was one of those who were quick enough to see, on the captain's distant visage, reflections of the certainty that what was learnt would yet be put to sufficient proof.

Confessedly to himself, however, he was troubled by something rather less than he had expected on Captain Herbert's part. Down in Somersetshire, how good-natured, how accessible, how cordial had Mr. Herbert been! In his kind services from Portsmouth, how prompt, considerate, and almost eager! Not that the lad had been unaware from the first what a wide interval must separate them on board the ship; he had taken special care not to let out there, *whence* his interest in high quarters had come, or that he knew the captain in the least before; even in the case of Dick Diamond, now so effective a hand in the fore-top, and so

popular round the galley on the main-deck below,
he had observed a still stricter caution, not so much
as openly appearing to know Dick from other men.
He forgot that Dick had not in turn been pledged
to secresy, and might be inclined to gossip in proportion as his English improved. Harry *had* che-
rished a hope, though, to gain his captain's distinct
notice, to earn his full approval, and to do something that would show himself not altogether un-
worthy of the apparent liking at first sight, which
he could not help thinking had been vouchsafed to
him. It was not so much to reach honour in the
service, or to rise and be known in it, that he
burned as yet; but to have won a single gracious
glance of that clear eye, which had certainly recognised him among others, and once or twice at
the outset had marked him with interest, as he
raised his hat to the quarter-deck, or brought some
message to a lieutenant. And he had imagined
there might be opportunities to prove the conscious
quickness, to test the acquired dexterity, or the
practised courage of both head and limb, and gradually to evince the eager zeal and deep reliance
which Captain Herbert, of all men ever seen, was
rousing in him yet. Till the real chance should
come to make it all of use, when the stuff that
people were made of must appear, when the question
would be, who would stand coolest or follow closest
—Harry would have been content with a smile, a

word now and then; perhaps to be made signal-midshipman, even young-gentleman of the barge hanging over the starboard-quarter. That barge occasionally was dropped in this light weather to take the captain, with the surgeon it might be, or his clerk, or the master, where steady observations could be got from a low-water reef; or where—doubtless on the part of the good Abbé Horne at home—some object curious to science might be found in mid-ocean itself. For, did not Harry know the abbé very well, and Neptune, and Mrs. Brinds; did he not know that there were many such curiosities at old Herbert Court, kept with more care than its own dusty and faded grandeurs; nay, could he not have told that the few books in the upper stern-cabins of the *Astræa*, however uncommonly numerous to the very cleverest lieutenant's view, were but a handful compared with the old library of the Herberts, whose crest they bore and whose spirit they might help to hand down? The old Herberts, when their country required them, had ever joined the boldest action with their studious kind of habits. The very abbé, though such a scholar, was wonderfully practical; in fact, some of his inventions were next thing to bloody!

But so far from getting any such difference made between him and others, it seemed to young Spencer that the captain was from the first more

distant to him than to the rest of the cockpit mess ;
if there had not actually of late been still less cordiality in the notice given him, when it could not
be withheld. The first-lieutenant, in spite of a
half-hidden favour for the lad's zeal, had sometimes rather sharply called it "forwardness;" he
"mast-headed" him once, for a rash act aloft
out of his proper watch; the truth being, that
Mr. Holmes was usually most disagreeable to
those he might be thought to regard with a partial
eye, and he not only kept Harry back when over-
active, but, catching him the least deficient, rated
him all the more roundly. Mr. Holmes was apt
to swear profane oaths on such occasions, a thing
by no means strange at sea in those days, even
from an officer of that rank ; and one night doing
it thus on the lee-side of the quarter-deck, when
the captain stood nearly opposite, no public notice
was, of course, taken by the latter ; his stern frown
was more obviously directed toward young Spencer,
whose faults he appeared of late to observe with a
special seriousness. On the other hand, he had
always shown particular displeasure, from the first,
against all unofficer-like and ungentlemanly language on deck; and now, when Mr. Holmes dis-
missed his culprit, the captain drew him casually
apart, where they walked and talked a little as
usual. From thenceforward, indeed, the youth
remarked that the first-lieutenant never swore at

him again, in fact was rather kindlier in his patronage ; still, fearing to be " forward," and in other respects not a little checked, he began to feel as if dull
thoughts must be yielded to, and made the best of.

True, there was a pleasant new naval fashion
in the *Astræa*, that two midshipmen of the watch
dined in turn at the captain's table, along with
those of the gun-room officers who might be
invited; so that about once a week Harry was
there, was spoken to, perhaps answered a question
in a formal way about Bristol and Beech Grove.
It was nothing more than a part of the evident
system on board, judiciously aiming, in common
with but a few rising commanders of the day, to
spread a general spirit of courtesy as far as the
cockpit itself, and diffuse a softness further round
on those manners which Smollett had painted. As
to the steering of the captain's barge when needed,
this was always done by little Blakely, the youngest
middy of all—a small urchin, with great black
eyes and a soul above his size or strength, whom
Harry Spencer could not but like. Then, the
charge of the flags and signalling had been all
along committed to the senior young gentleman,
Mr. Coventry, a tall fellow but far from bright-
witted, understood to be a very rich baronet's
natural son; with whom, however, Harry was
becoming friendly. The cockpit mess was other-

wise made (by powers beyond the captain's suspicion) what Coventry styled, in less delicate
words, "Pandemonium afloat." For good reasons,
indeed, it did not matter much to Coventry; while
for Harry's part, he "grinned and bore it" with
the ease of one who had known Skipper Itefell
Dodge of Nantucket.

It was autumn already—though not in the pe-
rennial midsummer of those tropical waters—when
at last, running nearer in to the Jamaica Channel,
they spoke a sloop-of-war on that station, and
heard that the Government despatches had come
in, with mail-bags from home. The corvette was
going in for her own letters, and soon returned,
bringing those for the *Astræa*.

At dinner that day, Harry chancing to be of the
cabin party, Captain Herbert quietly asked him,
" And how are all your relatives, Mr. Spencer—in
old Somersetshire and at Bristol? Quite well, I
hope; indeed, by a postscript from your friend,
the Abbé Horne—who, by the way, inquires after
you very kindly—it would appear that the fine
summer has brought several members of your
family down to Wrixworth. Something of more
than wonted cheerfulness, in fact, seems to have
been imparted to the good father's flower-garden
and book-shelves, by occasional visits from Wrixworth Hall."

"They are all quite well, sir, thank you," replied the lad, with all due depth of respect as a midshipman. "My sister Mary writes from home, where they seem all to be at the time; though there is not much in her letter. I trust, Captain Herbert, the abbé himself enjoys good health, and Neptune also, sir?"

The captain's tone was friendly, there was even an approach to a smile about his lips, but his eye and attitude more than ever kept up the requisite distance; he did not so much as notice the concluding question by which Harry rounded off this modest return of civilities.

"Pray, Mr. Blakely," said the captain, raising his voice to address his youngest midshipman, who on that occasion happened to be the other guest from the cockpit, "help yourself to a glass of wine." The small "reefer" did so; his delicate little face brightening to the full smile turned upon him, as he bowed very politely: but, for all that, he was looking paler than usual, and had a depressed air altogether; owing to which, it became still more obvious that there was a bump under the hair near one of his temples, with a slight discoloration toward the eye. At his entrance to the cabin with the rest, too, little Blakely had in vain tried to conceal a limp in his gait—the consequence, he had said, of an accidental sprain when going below, that morning. " Why, my boy," was the remark now added, "your head is hurt, too—was *that* another effect of the fall you speak of ? "

" Yes, sir," said little Blakely, with a downcast steadiness, which did not prevent his throwing an uneasy confidential glance at his bolder and much bigger messmate. " It don't signify, though ; really, sir, it looks worse than it feels." The surgeon was at table, and kindly hastened to corroborate the whole statement from a professional inspection during the day; the first-lieutenant being severe enough as to all boyish quarrels or mischievous practical jokes in the ship, (the latter of which were still rather too gay and light-hearted a thing for naval cadets in the early days of King George III.).

Mr. Holmes dining with the gun-room that day, he was not there to receive the meaning look which partly fell on young Spencer—with some inquiring sternness besides, at that intercepted glance of his small companion's. Harry, indeed, met the commanding eye without fear, so far as his own part in the matter was concerned ; but knew too well what Blakely meant, and what the youngster wished rather to bear quietly, like the little Spartan he was. A vague suspicion was all that the captain extracted. He might have expected more from the lad, who sat near enough to have spoken

his mind; and there was an annoyed expression
left on the captain's brow, which seemed to in-
clude Harry himself in its charge. Yet what good
was he to do if he tried! The secrets of their
prison-house, below, were too much made up of
details to be explained. 'Twas questionable whether
the very Admiralty itself could have altered them
—Harry shared their weight with Little Blakely,
and bore them still more quietly. He must have
made a real martyr of himself to do otherwise—
not that he dreaded *that* for any good purpose.
One had only to outgrow such miseries, and no-
make amends by wreaking them in turn : and then
again, on deck, on duty, in blowing work, or above
all with active service coming on, how did all seem
to vanish out of thought; how little—as even poor
young Blakely had said—did it " signify !"

"All our letters should now be ready, gentlemen,"
said the Captain, just as the lieutenant of the watch
made his movement to rise, which was more to the
midshipmen than a signal from a hostess to the
ladies. " The letter-bag will be sent off to the
Iris by daybreak, in one of the cutters. Ah, you
have yours with you, I see, Mr. Blakely; yes, I
will take safe charge of it." The little lad had
halted in passing out, half drawing forth a full-
sized black-edged letter to his mother, ready backed
with a great schoolboy address, and solemnly

sealed in black, with some solid coin of the realm for stamp—for he was only some late clergyman's son, in the North. As the Captain took it, he eyed the seal and held it carefully, while he looked up to Harry in turn. "I see," he said; "you may wish to finish yours, Mr. Spencer. If you will bring it to me at night, after 'evening divisions' are piped down, I shall have pleasure in enclosing a few words of my own, which otherwise would have been written to your friend the Abbé. It may gratify your father to know more directly, how you are like to succeed in your profession."

Harry flushed deeply at this; although there was something in it to bring a glow to his eye too, he yet hung his head; not having found anything as yet worth writing home about, since the first short hurried scrawl sent off by way of course from the chops of the Channel, with a joining Indiaman's pilot-boat. "I have nothing ready at all, Captain Herbert," answered he. "Not being very quick at my pen, sir, I think 'twill be better to wait next chance; my sister really writes nothing to answer; she says Kitty was prevented, but will write next, and may have much more to tell. I hope, sir, so may I!"

"True—that is true," was the quick rejoinder—to some inward consideration, perhaps, more than to Harry. "Father Horne, at all events, will not be so indifferent to your welfare, young gentleman, as it might seem you think your friends will—that is to say," he corrected himself, "at Wrixworth Hall it is sure to be *heard*, meanwhile, how you do." With that, the Captain turned somewhat coldly away: while young Spencer passed back to his deck duties, with the kind of injured feeling which rises at unaccountable reproof, only where we cherish a high affection.

END OF VOL. I.

C. WHITING, BEAUFORT HOUSE, STRAND.